As It Was in the Beginning

As It Was in the Beginning

Gertrude Trevelyan

Introduction by Kim Adrian
Afterword by Stanislava Dikova

RECOVERED BOOKS
BOILER HOUSE PRESS

Contents

Introduction
by Kim Adrian

Gertrude Trevelyan wrote eight novels in her short lifetime (1903-1941). *As It Was in the Beginning*, her third, was originally published by Martin Secker (London) in 1934, but by mid-century it had, like its author, disappeared from the literary scene. Boiler House Press' republication of the work in 2024 thus constitutes a kind of informal request made of the reading public: *Give this one another shot?* But giving a book a shot means, of course, reading it. And reading a book is always an investment, on so many levels. Which is no doubt why you're reading this introduction — trying to decide whether or not this particular book is worthy of such an investment. Dear reader, fellow bibliophile, I cannot answer this question for you. Not neatly, anyway. Not unequivocally. Because while *As It Was in the Beginning* is many admirable things — ambitious, structurally elegant, at times linguistically magical — it is also a thoroughly maddening, hair-tearingly repetitive, and hermetic work of literature. And yet, although I finished reading it months ago (with some impatience), I remain deeply haunted by it.

Trevelyan was roughly contemporary with Virginia Woolf, Jean Toomer, and Djuana Barnes, and, like these fellow Modernists, she was interested in formal experimentation. That experimentation, in *As It Was in the Beginning*, results in a drastic restriction of both form and scope. The story is told entirely through the then-popular stream-of-consciousness form: a ceaseless flow of thoughts and memories from one Lady Millicent Chesborough as she lies dying of a mysterious illness in a genteel nursing home.

When a novel pushes the limits of storytelling in this way — with an exceedingly tight focus on a single perspective — the emotional depth and social breadth of the narrative necessarily depends upon the depth and breadth of the consciousness at its center. But in *As It Was in the Beginning*, we have, at center, a hardcore navel-gazer, as well as a bit of a grouser. Yes, Lady Chesborough is a whiner, an old-school Karen forever complaining about the temperature of her tea, the height of her pillows, and the slowness of those shadowy figures ("idiot," "pink-cheeked booby," "hatchet-faced automaton") who attend her basic physical needs. It's almost as if Trevelyan were daring her readers to bolt, not only by constricting the narrative to the claustrophobic confines of a single human consciousness, but by assigning that consciousness to — sin of all sins — an "unlikeable" woman.

Of course, Lady Chesborough has an excuse for being churlish: she's dying. Yet she's been something of a pill most of her life, because Lady Chesborough's main problem, her tragic flaw, runs deep, as tragic flaws will do. This flaw can be traced to puberty, which she resisted with every fiber of her growing, budding, plumping, bleeding, feminine being. That resistance ("I'm not [a grown-up woman]. I won't be … I'm not a grown-up young lady … I don't want to be a young lady. I won't. I won't, I won't, I won't") was a wise if futile impulse. Because even though her womanhood ultimately unfolds in an atmosphere of wealth and privilege, it nevertheless manages to hem her in on every plush, velveteen side; so much so that when reviewing her life from her deathbed, she can't seem to locate the flimsiest sense of a self anywhere outside of her romantic attachments to men.

There are three of these men, and we learn about them in reverse chronological order. Ingeniously, Trevelyan structures the novel as a kind of spiral or nautilus in which memories of Lady Chesborough's most recent past function as the widest, outermost portion of the shell, so that the two or three years just prior to her illness constitute about half the narrative. At the center of these memories is a mendacious gold-digger named Phil, ten years Lady Chesborough's junior. The trials, travails, and occasional sexy spots of brightness in this clearly imbalanced relationship cause her ego to rally and flag by turns. She wonders whether she should get another facelift so that Phil won't have to pretend he's not nauseated by her gray and wrinkled skin, and whether she should buy him another car (something nicer than the Bentley she's already given him). Probably! Because she's nuts about Phil. Why? Because "He's cruel. He's brutal. I love him" and because "I don't want to be Millicent any more … only part of [Phil]. And not even that … I don't want to be at all."

Trevelyan's spiral then begins to tighten as drug-addled, half-hallucinated, brink-of-sleep memories spin out of her protagonist at a faster and faster clip. We learn about Lady Chesborough's childless, occasionally sweet, but on the whole cordial marriage to a man named Harold, whom she wed not of her own accord, but because of a gentlemen's agreement hammered out between her father and future husband. (At the wedding itself, she is "the victim," "something correct in white satin, labelled The Bride.") A little later, we meet her first romantic attachment, Michael, during that critical witching hour of her life, puberty. In one scene, she and Michael watch a group of men working a wooden press that turns apples into cider. Millicent proclaims the operation "horrid," and wonders why the men can't leave the apples as they were. "It's like me," she tells Michael. It's like "what they do to me: trying to make me into a grown-up young lady." From this point onward, the dying woman's ever-receding memories run through her increasingly unhinged mind at a dizzying rate as she rushes toward her own death: she's a girl, a child, a toddler, an infant staring up at the ceiling from her crib...

And peppered throughout the entire, ever-narrowing gyre of this narrative are hundreds of curious existential asides ("I'm not anything ... I'm hollow," "I always felt I was something very small cowering inside a figure labelled The Squire's Wife," "I've never been afraid of being nothing: only of having to be something"). In the end, these tossed-off remarks stand as a stark testament to one woman's struggle to operate as an autonomous human being under all of those implicit and explicit patriarchal structures and strictures that reduced her, even as an upper-class citizen of 1930's England, to a person "who wasn't really a person."

It's exactly this — Trevelyan's quietly enraged feminism, cloaked in the neurotic, narcissistic ego of a dying woman's smudged and self-less memories — that's stayed with me all this time. *As It Was in the Beginning* now sits, in my mind, in conversation with several other "maddening" novels — like Clarice Lispector's *The Passion According to G.H.* and Elfriede Jelinek's *The Piano Teacher* and Ingeborg Bachmann's *Malina*. None of which are easy reads. All of which are uncompromising in their rigorous and stubbornly singular investigations of the slippery, often painful juncture between the self and its points of contact with society, sexuality, gender, language, and existence itself.

The question now goes to you. Shall Gertrude Trevelyan's long-forgotten novel be granted new life? Shall it generate new and unexpected ideas? Shall it, with your encouragement, elicit fresh responses, and in this way re-enter the great, ongoing conversation we call literature? There's only one way to find out...

As It Was in
the Beginning

by Gertrude Trevelyan

"Too much light. C-c-can't you draw down that blind?"

Light, pressing down. The white, light sheets; top of the mirror, across on the dressing-table, tipped back, sending light on to the white ceiling. Small fire struggling against the sunshine, and Sonia's legs crossed: Sonia in the wicker-chair between the bed and fire-place, with one high-heeled foot a-tap at the fender.

Too white, everything: all this white furniture and white screen and the white counterpane. Nothing friendly about it. They might as well shut you up in a cell. A white cell, quite clean and sterilized of course. Too clean, insultingly clean. As if one were something dirty that had to be disguised by external, obtrusive cleanliness, just because one was ill.

"Oh th-thank you."

And an upward shove against the creased, yielding pillows. Upward push and shove with the right shoulder, and the left following, dull and disinterested: dragged up, and the arm dragged after it. Hand flopping up, heavily, over the white, folded sheet.

13

Better, the softening of outlines behind the drawn blind. Intimate, unsterilized things coming back out of the glare: magazines and fruit on the small table beside the bed; brushes and bottles against the diminished white of the dressing-table: the few things they gave you time to pick up and bring from your room. What's happening to my room? Ought to be locked. Don't suppose Sonia thought of locking it. Chambermaids must be poking round, turning over my things. Oh well.

Even Sonia dimmed, momentarily.

That's one thing.

Sonia, brisk and efficient in her bright sympathy. Sitting up straight in the wicker easy-chair, with her little hat at a ridiculous angle.

Suppose they're wearing them like that now. When you can't get out, get over to the High Street.... One gets out of touch. Oh well, only a week or so, isn't it. Day or so, I mean. Time goes so slowly here. But quite time I was about again. Kensington High Street, now: that's alive, at least. Somewhere to go. And no fear of meeting people there. The last place you'd meet Phil! Never come so far. Don't suppose he's been further west than Knightsbridge since....

What do you want to sit there for? So bright and tiring. Go away. I don't want you here. Why should you come like this, popping up from nowhere, making trouble?

Rather look out of the window. Oh, well, they've drawn the blind. Nothing to see, in any case. Laurel bushes. Suppose they can't manage anything else in these small London gardens. Wisteria and jasmine and thick, sweet-smelling syringa. But that was in the old days. Harold took a lot of trouble with the garden and grounds. And the Gloire-de-Dijon under the study window. Funny, haven't thought of that garden for years.

"Know you? Of course I know you. Why sh-sh-shouldn't I know you?"

Do you know me Aunt Millicent, indeed. As if I shouldn't know you. Needn't call me Aunt, either. Sitting up so bright and perky. Pert, we should have called it, when I was young. Little girls should be seen and not heard. A lot to be said for the old ways: the way things were done when I was a girl.

Oh, well, I'm not that anymore.

Can't be young at fifty, can you? People think not. No. No, that's it. Ought to have known it, I suppose. Philip knew it, of course; that's why....

Who'd want to be young again, in any case? Bad enough when you are. Young: sitting up brisk and chirpy like that. 'Aunt Millicent,' indeed. Needn't call *me* Aunt. *I'm* not your aunt. Harold's niece. Harold always did favour her, even then, when she was a little thing. Having her there to stay, playing in the garden. Pert little thing, even then. *I* don't want to be your aunt. Haven't seen much of you, all these years.

What's she saying? Can't be bothered to listen.

Sonia's legs uncrossed and recrossed; glint of fire-light on a patent-leather toe.

Yes, after all, you might have been to see me, since Harold died. Might have wondered how I was getting on. But no, take your money and go, like all the rest of them. Why he left you anything is beyond me. Always had been a pert little thing. But Harold liked it, of course. Besides, it was his duty: provide for his sister's children. Not that they needed it. But Harold always did his duty.

Yes, that was what was the matter with Harold.

Did his duty to the family. What about me, though? Oh well, I had plenty, I suppose. Shouldn't have wanted to stay down there in the country. Shouldn't have wanted to stay on at Chesborough, even if the place hadn't had to be let. If we'd had a child it might have been different. Rather live in town; less trouble in a hotel. And I had enough for that. Though if I'd had more perhaps Phil....

"W-w-what's that?"

What's she saying?

"Yes. No. I don't know."

What she want? Don't know. Doesn't matter.

Oh yes, Harold did his duty by his widow, no doubt. Harold would. Always saw people like that, in some definite relation to himself: widow, dependents. Not as people, not like Phil. And if we'd had a child it would have been the same thing: Harold's son. Well, I'm glad. Yes, I am, I'm glad. Though I don't know why I should feel vindictive, after all these years.

All the same, it wouldn't have hurt her to come and see how I was getting on. It might have been lonely, mightn't it, in the hotel? For all you knew, there mightn't have been anybody to care whether I lived or died. And there wasn't, either, for a long time.

Not that they were bad, those years before Phil came. Not really. Quiet, there, in my room. Nobody to bother one. And if you wanted to see people, plenty of them about in the streets. And no bother: nobody to recognize. Well, what more can you want? And then have your own room to go back to, and shut the door, and be yourself.

"Oh, you're going, are you? Yes, I suppose they are coming to do me up for the night. Oh yes: thank you for coming to see me."

She wouldn't see it, Sonia wouldn't. Sonia never saw anything. Never did see how I disliked her when she was a child, coming there, forced on me. And how I hated her just because... Well, why did I? I'm sure I don't know. Disagreeable child, I suppose. Never sees anything, now, but her own pert ideas of what she ought to see. People are ill, and you visit them, and they're grateful. Aunt Millicent, then, 'an invalid', instead of 'my aunt in Bayswater.' Not even that. Don't suppose she thought about me at all. If she did: 'an aunt I've got'; 'my aunt by marriage.' Like Harold.

Letters?

No, nothing of course. Only light. The white tray-cloth and white tea-pot. The fat, dumpy one, Sister knows I like that. And the white cup. The green rim, this morning. The light hurts. There's no hurry, after all. Take time. It'll get cold, but it doesn't matter.

They'll have to draw those curtains before I sit up. Shall I ring? Too much bother. Let it wait. I don't want breakfast. Nurse will be in, in a minute. Why should I have breakfast? There isn't anything.

As if there would be anything. It isn't likely. Not many people left to write to me nowadays. Must expect that, at my age.

Well, I'm not old. Really, one would think I was seventy, the way....

Peculiar, the way people have gone. Oughtn't to have married a man older than myself.

Though what should I have done if Harold had lived? When I met Phil?

Oh well, I shouldn't have met Phil. Of course not. I should still be down there at Chesborough. Behind the silver urn; instead of a dumpy, china tea-pot. Lot of good that would have done me. And the taps burnt your fingers unless you took your handkerchief, and how Harold did dislike that. Harold was like that: fussy about little things. Harold would have hated the dumpy tea-pot. Is it an egg this morning? I didn't look.

Oh, and I didn't look at the back of the tray, against the sugar-bowl. Sometimes they prop them up there.

Oh.

Oh, oh yes.

Yes, well, I'm not going to reach for them just yet. They can wait. They can't really be anything. Bills, probably, though I thought there was nothing outstanding. But the top one is: a long envelope, and forwarded from the hotel. So they are forwarding. I suppose if Phil rang up they'd tell him I was here?

As if he would.

And I won't look at the other one, just yet.

No, I suppose it can't be. So likely he'd write after all this time, isn't it. Well, you never know. If he'd just been away for a time, just been for a cruise....

I suppose there really is something wrong with my heart.

Nonsense. Ridiculous, after all this time. If you really think, Philip, that your writing on an envelope is going to bring me trotting, after the way you've behaved....

Well, better see, I suppose.

Oh, it's an egg, is it. Cold, of course. They ought to have those warmers, like we had at Chesborough. Harold was so particular about having things hot. I wish they'd prop up the pillows when they bring the breakfast.

Push and shove upwards against the yielding pillow; hand dragging over the sheet.

Long envelope: Kensington postmark: so I thought. And that leaves.... No, I'm not going to look. Though it wasn't, was it? But I don't care. I'm not going to rush on it. You needn't think I am.

Yes, of course, I knew this was only a bill. Though I can't think.... Oh, well, just a circular. They've no business to put them in envelopes like this. Ridiculous. And now we come....

Yes, of course, just as I thought. So likely it would have been anything else.

It's from somebody, though, isn't it? Not an advertisement? An educated hand. I don't know it, though. How odd: now who can it be?

Oh, yes. Yes, of course. That new upper plate I had. Now if I'd known I was coming here I might have saved myself the trouble. Yes. Oh yes. Dentists do keep educated secretaries, don't they? People who write an educated hand. Graduates, I shouldn't wonder. The kind of thing Philip might do, if he weren't a great lazy oaf. Plenty of people better than he do it. Ha! Well they might easily be that. How I do hate you, Philip. No. No, I mustn't think about that. Mustn't think. No, besides, I don't. As if I'd waste my time…. So much to do with it, haven't I? No, well, I don't pay you such a compliment as that, my dear. Oh no, you needn't think it. Queer, a really educated hand, and a good envelope: thick paper. Well, naturally, it would be. Yes. Oh yes, of course, I knew all the time it was that.

"C-come in.

Yes, I've f-f-finished. No, I don't want it. No, I don't like eggs, I've told you so before. Why don't you have those patent w-warmers we used to have? Oh, very well, don't bring me an egg again then, I've told you I don't like them.

Yes, that's better. The pillows aren't high enough; tighten the straps a bit. I wish you'd do it before breakfast.

Yes, it's quite sunny, isn't it. Quite br-bright for October. You want to wash me now? Very well."

Thank goodness she's gone. Such a fuss. As if it mattered, the sheet being smooth under your arms. For all the people who are going to see it…. Quite smooth and antiseptic: nothing human about it.

And a good thing, too. Get rid of humans for a bit. Alone with the white sheets and the polished floor and the fire crackling jerkily in the sunken grate and the sun beating against the yellow blinds, and the dull white furniture. All quite clean. Everybody finished up and gone.

Yes, that's the way things happen with a life. People do their duty by you — or they don't. Oh, not always, not by any means — and finish with you, and go out with a bright nod, leaving everything around you quite clean and empty.

Except Philip. One thing about Philip: he never did his duty. Not like Harold. One thing you couldn't accuse Philip of. There wasn't much cleanliness and polish about things when *he'd* gone: you could say that for him.

"Phil, Phil. Phil, I love you."

No I don't. I don't mean that. That doesn't mean anything, it's just mechanical. I hate you, Philip.

Well, what's the good of being bitter. You couldn't expect him to waste his youth on an old woman like me: old enough to be his mother. No, not quite. No, of course not. Oh, well, yes, I suppose so. Still, he didn't think of me like that, did he? Not until the end. That is.... No, of course he didn't.

No, he's not that kind. I oughtn't to think like that about him.

I wish I hadn't let him have the car, though.

Well, why not?

Because I should have been sure, then.

Well, I am sure. You know perfectly well that when we first met he couldn't have known I had money.

Even though it was an expensive hotel, that place at Brighton.

Well, that's not saying anything. He was staying there too, wasn't he? Besides, I'm not rich.

No, but he thought I was.

But I was only staying there for a change, just for a holiday. If you can't have a holiday, now and then. I hadn't had a holiday for the best part of twenty years. Besides, it wasn't so much that, as that I thought if I went to stay at that place where I used to go with Harold I should be glad to get back. My room seemed snug, after that garish place at Brighton. I hate those big places. I like my room. I like being shut away from people, like that.

Yes, I suppose it *is* funny I took a fancy to Phil, like that. But you can't always get on without people. Besides, Phil's different. He isn't 'people.'

I mean, he wasn't. I knew it the minute he came into the lounge that day.

Well, he still isn't, I suppose. Even though I wouldn't see him if he came here and begged me to.

Blank, white half of a door beyond the white, blank screen.

Door-knob, unmoving, expressionless, and the little, white enamel tongue pushed up, over the key. If he came in and went across and sat. White wicker-chair with its curved seat turned to the fire, and the corner of a curtain caught up on its rounded back.

No you don't, my boy. No you don't. No, I won't see you. I won't have anything to do with you. No, Philip, it's no use; no good looking like that. I know your coaxing ways. But it's not a bit of good. You've done much the best thing. Oh, quite the wisest course you could have taken, and now you'd better stick to it. You haven't much staying-power, my dear; you never had. That was always the trouble with you, wasn't it. Or you wouldn't have left the post your father had found for you and been hanging round at that hotel at Brighton, looking for an old fool like me. No, I'm not going to reproach you. I'm past all that, you know. A long, long time ago. Quite calm and dispassionate. I think it's quite a long time since I even hated you. Because I did, you know, Phil. I did. Oh, forgive me, my dear.

No, I don't mean that.

No. No, I mean, I'm not going to reproach you. That's all a long, long way away. What I mean is, that day you came into the lounge....

I'd always hated that lounge: that conservatory place, with the palms and the little tables. I don't know why I hate palms so much. They were blue enamel, the tables, with a sheet of glass over the enamel and wicker-work round the edge. And there was a kind of shelf under the table, so that you couldn't put your feet under it comfortably. Otherwise I shouldn't have turned and sat sideways, just as you were coming under the archway from the entrance hall. If it hadn't been for that I mightn't have noticed you.

Think of that, Phil.

Rounded wicker-chair, and the mantelpiece, white and empty. If he did come I shouldn't have a cigarette for him. Why didn't I bring the box from my room? I'm sorry, Phil dear, I can't get

21

at anything, shut away in here. Empty, white mantelpiece and rounded chair-back and the limp flap of curtain.

If only he were. If only I could tell him.

Phil, I must talk to you: I never could talk to you properly. Just stay there, keep still. No, he mustn't talk. Keep still and listen.

Phil's smile. Phil's shoulders above the low, rounded chair-back; Phil, keeping still and listening.

You'd have had to find me sometime, all the same. Even if it hadn't been like that. Yes, you would. Because you had to; because we belong to one another. We always have, somewhere, in space. Through the ages. I've been calling you, Phil, through the ages. No, beyond that: somewhere timeless, beyond space: always. And you had to come.

But you don't believe in that, of course. You hate anything like that, timeless and spaceless: anything that isn't here and now. Things like shining touring cars.

Oh my goodness, I wish I hadn't.

Well, why shouldn't he have it. If he wanted it. Anything he wanted. Anything, anything.

Touring cars and racehorses and slim, racing yachts. Things that are physically splendid.

Oh.

No, don't think about that.

Besides, you don't believe that people go on and on. So I never said much to you about that: about our having met before, and my calling to you. And when I did say something about it you only smiled — you remember — that slow smile that seemed to pick things up and weigh them and find they weren't worth your while and put them down with gentle derision: knowing it was nothing, but not wanting to hurt too much.

Though you could hurt. Oh, could you not?

And you didn't mind, then, did you?

But that was when you were threatened. When your life was

22

threatened. I see that now. I ought to have seen it. When you saw you might get tied up to an old woman, and not be able to get out. Then....

Oh, no doubt you did the wisest thing. The very wisest course you could have taken.

But not wanting to hurt, really. You didn't, did you, Phil? Just knowing it was nothing: not worth your taking in your hand with that slow, derisive smile. Putting it down gently as if it were something a child had brought you, some treasure unearthed in a corner of the garden: and while you stood there with it in your hand, turning it over, and the child was panting with excitement at the treasure it had found, you didn't want to hurt too much, as you said it was only a pebble.

Except that once. And then you didn't say or look anything at all. You just weren't there.

Oh, my dear, my dear.

"Phil."

No, I don't mean that.

That was the kind of look you used to have. But did it mean anything? Or didn't you mind, really, how much you hurt?

Queer, those little things, how much they matter. Now if it hadn't been for that wicker-work shelf under the table, if I'd been able to sit comfortably with my feet in front of me, I don't suppose I should have seen you come in. I should have drunk up my martini quickly, as I always did, and put out my cigarette and picked up my bag and gone out of the conservatory place into the hall when they began to dance, and not noticed anybody. I never did notice people much. And as the band was playing I shouldn't have heard your voice.

Because I think that would have told me you were there. Even if I hadn't seen you. I should have known it was you and that we had to meet somehow.

But I might have gone straight out into the hall and up to my room and never met you at all. Or would you have noticed me as I was sitting there, even if I hadn't been looking at you when you came in? Would you have come to that side of the room, I wonder? And would you ever have spoken if I hadn't looked round for a match? I suppose you would. I suppose it had to be.

Had it? Or did I make it?

It had to be, of course: that moment when I looked up and saw you coming in from the hall, between the palms. I must have known it all the time, all those years. All those years I'd been walking alone in the park and along the streets, among all the people. I must have known there was somebody somewhere who was you. That moment had been there all the time, waiting for us to live it. It had, Phil! Existing somewhere in the eternity you don't believe in, waiting for us. That moment when you came in between the palms and stopped just for a second, looking round over the tables, and nodded to somebody you knew among the dancers, and then came and sat alone, near me, without seeming to see me. That had existed: those events, in just that sequence, forever. Only it hadn't happened.

Little tables, all around, quite empty; mirrored walls of the lounge; people dancing, in a heap, beyond the tables. The polka. They've just begun the polka. Feathery leaves of palms spreading under the glass roof.

Giant pineapples in green wooden tubs on the tiled floor: black and white tiles in squares spreading out between the tubs, and people dancing in the ballroom, beyond the open door of the conservatory. And little, empty, wicker-work tables. An envelope on the table. Pen moving.

Envelope addressed: ∪⌣⌣⌣, ⌣⌣⌣ ⌣⌣ ·.
That's writing. I'm writing.

Sliding the celandine into the envelope: dried, yellow celandine flopping sideways from its flattened stalk. Celandine in the yellow envelope: that's a match.

Greyness; greying walls and grey blind, half drawn, and vague laurel bushes beneath the blind.

It's getting dark. I must have been to sleep. It must be nearly tea-time.

The door opening and a light switched on.

"I th-th-think I've been to sleep."

A good thing Sonia didn't come to-day. It's bearable here, so long as you're left alone. But nothing homely. Not like my room. I like to be able to potter round among my things. What's happening to my room? Might have asked Sonia.

Don't want to ask her anything. Don't like the girl. Thinks I don't recognize her, just because I don't want to see her. Conceit. Conceited little chit. Thinks I'm wandering, I suppose.

Hope somebody's had the sense to lock that room. Don't want the chambermaids poking round among my things. Mine, after all, as much as if I had a house. More mine than Chesborough: more of a home. I always felt Chesborough was Harold's, not mine. Suppose it was, in a way. His family's, after all.

And now it's let. Well, I can't help that.

But it was that way of appropriating his surroundings; everything having to fit into relationship with himself. My house. My wife. Yes, that's it: Harold's wife, not myself. That's what I felt, all those years. My wife, my dog: though he was courteous enough: I'm not fair to Harold. Never could be fair to him. He was too fair himself in that cold way. Not that I ever wanted him to be anything but cold: it was just that which made things bearable: that routine of courteous remoteness we'd settled into. I wonder whether it wasn't I who made it, though, in the first place? Harold didn't want that, really. He wasn't like that to start with. But I couldn't have stood anything else, not from Harold. Nor from anybody. Not then.

No, nor at any other time either. That is....

Oh well, that was different. That was just.... Phil wasn't like other people: just 'Phil'. That doesn't count. You can't argue from that. Besides, I don't know how it was.

Then why wasn't Harold just 'Harold'?

I don't know, he wasn't. That's to say, he was; but in the wrong way. He was too much Harold. But I wasn't Millicent, I was his wife. So he stopped being Harold and became my husband. I suppose I escaped from him by pigeon-holing him like that. I suppose he did the same to me, when he found I didn't care much for him. I suppose all those courteous, frigid years were a mutual defence.

Against what?

Against an aloneness which would have been unbearable if we had admitted it.

Better have this tea, I suppose.

Oh well, she has poured it out.

Careful not to spill it. A sip, and the cup tinkling back into the saucer.

The tea-table at Chesborough, near the fire; the long room with its chairs and occasional tables, islands in the green carpet. What a stiff room it was. Stretching away to the piano and the tall windows; the elms beyond the windows. The log basket and Harold, and the back of his head in the mirror over the mantelpiece.

Not that I was lonely, in those days. It gave one plenty to do, being Harold's wife. He always wanted to entertain such a lot, and then with the local charities and one thing and another.... His wife had to be somebody in the parish. And then I suppose the war saved us: me, at any rate. I think Harold could have gone on like that indefinitely: he'd only have grown a little more punctilious and a little more distant as he aged. I don't know whether I should have gone on. Probably. There was no reason to stop on one day rather than on another. In those days one didn't separate so easily, and Harold was a model husband, I suppose. Besides, I was half asleep, I believe. I didn't know it; not until afterwards. I thought I was using my brain on charity reports and committees, but it was only the surface. The rest of my brain was asleep, as if I had been stunned. There was only a top layer racing. Like a frozen river with a surface sheet of water fluid on the ice.

But I do think I was using my brain to run the hospital, though, after Harold was called up. Poor Harold, how upset he was, that first leave, to find the beds in the drawing-room, and the smell of carbolic.[1] I told him, he'd made over the house for the duration, and I had to have a free hand. I believe it was the first time I'd ever asserted myself. And my uniform upset him, too. His wife, a Commandante. Poor, order-loving Harold.

Cup crooked in the saucer. Tipped up. Straighten it. Right hand, and a bitten slice of cake, hovering. Oh, of course, I forgot. Left arm, limp and unresponsive, laid flat along the sheet: limp, grey fingers on the white sheet. Time they managed to do something to that arm of mine. Can't say I think much of them. Limp and dead and unresponsive. Seems not to be part of me at all. Well, I never did feel much personal interest in my body. And that's all Harold ever had of me.

What would have happened if he'd come back? I suppose we should have aired the drawing-room and put back the suite with the green brocade. There mightn't have been so much entertaining, after the war, but more committees. Reconstruction schemes, and relief for the unemployed.

Well, I had to reconstruct for myself. I suppose that sounds heartless. Well, it's true. How many widows felt like that, if they were honest about it? A feeling of cobwebs swept away. Our life together belonged to the prewar years. I don't think it could have gone on. And Harold wouldn't have adapted. I wonder whether it wasn't the best thing.

---

1   Short for carbolic acid or carbolic soap.

Why not be honest? I know it was the best thing. You see, Phil, I know it. I didn't know how intolerable life with Harold was, until it was over.

Not at once, though. It was a shock when the wire came. I can remember now seeing them come across the lawn with it, while I was talking to that poor boy — what was his name — who'd had his leg shot away. One of the worst cases we had there. There I was, standing facing the house, out on the lawn, talking to him in his wheel-chair. A nice boy, with blue eyes and light brown hair: just the young wounded officer of the stories. He was telling me some anecdote of the trenches and laughing up with the sun in his eyes, and just that little wince in the laugh that they had so often. Of course he didn't see the orderly come out of the house. I wanted to stop the story, because I wanted to get ready: I could see the orange envelope on the salver: I knew at once what it was. I wanted to be ready to take it in the right way. I felt the Commandante of a hospital, whose husband had been killed in action, ought not to let her private grief interfere in any way with efficiency and cheerfulness: the boys oughtn't to know, or learn only obliquely: they oughtn't to see any sign of my feelings.

But if I'd had any feelings I shouldn't have been thinking that just at that moment. I hadn't any at all, I believe. Under the surface thoughts I was telling myself what feelings I ought to have. But I hadn't any. I was making abstractions just as Harold used to do: seeing myself as a Commandante, grief-stricken but courageous; not as Millicent who had lost Harold. Not that I ever could think of myself by that name. Always hated it. I think that's why I dislike Sonia so much: she says it as Harold did. But I ought to have been thinking of Harold. I told myself I ought to. I tried to picture him in the trenches: mud squelching and bodies dangling from the barbed wire. I tried to make it as horrible as possible, just to make myself feel. But all I could really see was Harold polishing a button of his tunic with a thumb and flicking a speck from his trousers while he talked. He'd never been a dandy, but he did like to be immaculate: everything in order. In the end I believe I smiled at the boy with the blue eyes, and muttered something, and met the orderly half-way across the tennis courts.

"Nurse, what have they done with my room?"

Not this room, idiot. Standing gaping at the furniture as if you expected it to turn upside-down. Bulging blue eyes and starched cap and pink cheeks. Antiseptic, like everything else here. Looks as if they gave them a morning bath of carbolic and ironed out their aprons on the operating table. Nobody's done anything to *this* room except sterilize it till it's as impersonal as a public lavatory. Might as well expect one to live there and feel at home.

"Don't g-g-gape at me as if I were wandering. What have they done with my room at the hotel?"

Well, if you don't know, why couldn't you say so before?

"Just raise these pillows a bit."

I wonder what you do know. My tea was cold again this morning, and it's no good saying I waited an hour before I drank it, because I didn't. You can't expect somebody to open their eyes the minute you choose to put it down. If you had any sense at all you'd know that somebody who's been tossing about for half the night wants to wake gradually, not as if they were going to leap out into a bath of carbolic. No business to be a nurse at all. Only fit for an attendant at a public lavatory. What are you gaping at now?

"There, we're feeling better now, aren't we?"

Oh we are, are we? Now why, I wonder. Just why should you think it necessary to use baby talk. One can't understand plain English, I suppose, after a week or so in bed. And no wonder.

"Yes, tha-that'll do."

That's right. Now what's she left here? Plaice. I'm sick of plaice. Shall have to ask Sonia about my room, I suppose. Days, since she's been here. The my-aunt-in-a-nursing-home excitement worn off, no doubt. Just like Harold. No, Harold would have been fussing round all the time, seeing the sheets were straight.

Well, that's one good thing.

That room must be kept aired; shall catch a chill when I go back. And the trunks ought to be locked so that nobody can get at them, before the room's cleaned. Wonder whether I locked them before I came away. No business to rush me off like that: can't think how it happened. Just like Sonia to interfere at the wrong moment after leaving me alone for years. Can't think who got her there. I'm sure I didn't ask her. No reason why I should come away at all: much better there, where I could heat up something on the gas-ring if I didn't feel like going down to lunch. Can't move hand or foot here. Can't even wash out anything I want to. Ridiculous, not being able to get at my things.

Prong of a fork picking at the golden, bread-crumbed skin; white flakes of fish, parting.

Mrs. Caruthers will be wondering at my not coming down to dinner for so long. Won't like the empty table next to her. Always said it was brighter the days I came down. Might go up and see; not likely though. Glad I never encouraged people in coming to my room. The hotel people will be wondering, if Sonia didn't tell them. I'd be away for some time. Interfering little chit. Been much better there. Nobody to fuss.

I must say, I shall be glad to be back. Philip always said it was a pokey little room, but I'm glad I didn't move when he wanted to. Oh no doubt, my boy, you'd have preferred a smart suite in a big hotel: somewhere more central: more convenient for your lordship to pop in when you felt like it. And where should I be now, when you've suddenly taken it into your head....

"Phil, Phil."

No, I don't mean that.

I ought to have moved, though. He might have gone on coming to see me. Longer. Yes, that's it. He'd have gone, in any case, sooner or later. Oh yes you would, do you think I don't know? You think I don't know you? Oh I do, only too well. Oh yes, only too well. Well, it's a good thing you went when you did.

I suppose if I'd taken a smart flat somewhere you might even have come and lived there. Though there was never any question of that. Yes, I ought to have done that; my money would have held out for a few years. But it would have gone by now, and so would you.

No, I mustn't think things like that, it isn't fair. Phil wasn't like that, really. It's only that he was young. You couldn't expect him.... Why were you so young? If only we'd met when you were older, or I was younger. I wonder whether you'd have stayed then. Well, it had to be like that. I suppose it had to be: that I had to call you, all through time, just for those two years. Well, it was worth it, wasn't it? No. Yes. I don't know. I was an old woman when you'd gone. You finished me, Phil. I suppose I was one before, only I didn't know it. It took you, to point that out to me. Well, what's the good of being bitter about it.

Thick, grey under-skin stabbed and impaled. Plate jerked back, against the wooden edge of the tray.

Finished.

I don't think I was, though. I didn't feel old in those days: those years after the war, when Harold was killed. It was like a new life, being on my own. I think I'd always wanted to be alone, really. Being able to go out when I liked and come back when I liked: look in the shops if I wanted to, and it didn't matter being late for dinner. I believe I used to go down to dinner every night then, too: it was pleasant just to nod to people one knew and yet feel secure in one's own privacy. If someone asked Where have you been to-day, they could always be evaded politely. They didn't expect to be told. Only asked for something to say. Not that there was anything to hide, but one has a right to the little privacies of life.

The same in the streets: being able to walk without meeting a soul one knew. Something secure in a crowd, when you're not of it. It used to be torture sometimes, at Chesborough, meeting one after another. The tautening at a corner for the next encounter. Even though they meant to be pleasant; though they couldn't have helped speaking to Harold's wife, if they'd wanted to ever so. But that feeling of relaxing one's face, ready to smile, and wondering how soon to begin, and then the smile that felt stiff and carved on: and wondering how soon to stop. And all the time that feeling that one was impersonating someone. As if there were a shell, dressed up and marked Lady Chesborough, and one were something very small huddled away inside it and pulling strings to make it smile at the right moment and say the right thing. A feeling that they must see through one: sooner or later they'd find out they were being duped, were speaking to nothing.

Speaking to nothing. And they didn't know it. That's it: it took you to see that. That's how you treated me, didn't you? As if I were nothing.

They must have suspected something. Even they must. Even then. That Miss Platt: I always met her with her shopping bag at the corner of the Market Place, between the butcher's and the Church House. Grey, uneven, paving-stones, stretching away, empty; the distant shout of a drover; bobbing oilcloth bag against a black skirt, and heelless, black shoes. She always looked at me as if I were an impostor. It might only have been her way; that vague, staring goggle from under her ridiculous sailor hats with the flowers on them. She may have stared like that to fix the goggle, because it might have strayed otherwise. But I always felt she was trying to see through me. And I felt my voice going dead when I spoke to her. I wanted to put expression into it: sympathy for the poor thing's neuritis[2]: but my voice was quite dead and flat. The sentences came out mechanically, all on one note. And when I did succeed in forcing some expression into it, it burst out as if it had broken through a mask. 'Oh how *dreadful*. I *am* so sorry. How *trying* for you.' In a torrent. Ridiculously exaggerated. And the poor thing looked surprised, suspicious sometimes, as if she thought I were laughing at her. Or she may only have been grateful. Flat, hard, black straw and red bobbing roses. Were you, I wonder? But I wonder why, though I was quite sure you were Miss Platt, life-size, I always felt I was something very small cowering inside a figure labelled The Squire's Wife.

And Harold never would believe me when I told him I disliked meeting people. Not that it would have made much difference if he had.

Why can't that girl bring my pudding? Doesn't imagine I take all this time over two inches of fish, does she? Not that I want her messing round, but I want my pudding.

Sweetness withheld; slow, searching twist of the tongue.

But things weren't so bad after I came to town. It didn't matter so much. It was like a tonic, sometimes, to stroll along the High Street in the sunshine and hardly be glanced at. And in a 'bus one person is very much like another. I remember being grateful, even, to a 'bus-conductor, when he punched a ticket and pushed it at me, looking the other way. Just the right amount of notice. One must have a ticket: one exists. But not expected to *be* anything. To be, in a 'bus, would be an offence.

I wonder why I've always felt like that about people. You know, Phil, it isn't a sense of inferiority: even when I despise people it's the same thing. Just a feeling of being different; of not being there, where people think me. No, not even that. Of being there, but not

---

2   Inflammation of a peripheral nerve or nerves, usually causing pain and loss of function.

in the body: watching it from the outside and feeling responsible for it, without having it firmly in hand. Having to creep back into it to pull the strings.

But it wasn't always like that. There were days when I didn't think about people at all, in that way. When it was quite pleasant to nod to acquaintances across the dining-room, and there was a feeling of excitement, almost, in going out, without any particular purpose, just because it was a nice day. And pleasant to stay in, too, in my room, with the rain streaming against the window, and a bright fire, and little jobs to do among my things. Yes, those were pleasant years, before Philip came: the pleasant years. But you couldn't leave me those, could you? Not even those little things. One would think they were simple enough. You'd think any living creature had a right to the sunshine on the pavements, and casual acquaintanceships, and toast by the fire. But you poisoned it all. Yes you did. You couldn't leave me even that. I suppose it wasn't your fault. I suppose if I hadn't gone down to Brighton that summer — to enjoy all of it more when I came back — I might have escaped you: I might have cheated fate and been free of you forever. But it had to be. I couldn't have prevented it, it had to be. It had always been, like that: coming under the archway, between the palms, and smiling without smiling.

Oh yes, you left me those things, right enough: the sunshine was there, and the fire and the toast and the what-not: but there wasn't any peace in them.

"What's this?

"A book, Aunt Millicent. I thought you might like..."

"H'm. Don't c-care much for reading. Never have time to read much, nowadays."

With one thing and another. So many little jobs.

34

No. No, that's not it, is it? Plenty of time *here*. Not like... Never seem to have a minute, when I'm up and about. Always something or other to be done, when you're living in a self-contained way as I am. Oh well, may as well look at it.

Green, shiny cover and thick leaves. Smooth boards. Sonia arranging her hair, across by the dressing-table, tipping the mirror back so that it shows nothing but the ceiling.

Might show a little more interest.

"What's this. I don't want it. I don't like these modern books."

Sure to be something unpleasant. Disgusting, most of them. Wouldn't have been allowed, when I was a girl. Now when I could get out to the library I let them know....

The assistant, suave and expressionless, and the long, varie-gated shelves. Smooth boards of a rejected volume on the assistant's desk.

'I want a nice book. Can't you find me a *nice* book? I detest this modern stuff. Most of it ought to be burnt.'

The assistant, expressionless, suavely soothing: 'Oh yes, Madam? I think you would find this quite...'

No. No, of course not.

Sonia and her powder-puff and the slick tilt of her little hat. Shiny green boards on the white sheet.

"Very well, leave it here. I don't suppose I shall read it."

Good-bye.

"Oh yes: thank you."

Well, she might have saved herself the trouble.

For all the trouble she takes.

But coming along here every day, nearly: must be a bore for her.

Well, I didn't ask her to come. Rather she stayed away. Might have left me alone in the first place. That's what she gets for interfering.

Green, shiny boards on the white sheet. Pages fluttering. Black print in lines on the thick, white paper.

Sex, of course. You'd think there was nothing else for people to think about.

Well, I suppose I can't talk.

"Phil."

No.

Well, that was different. No, that was totally different. I should hope so. There wasn't anything like that about Us.

Green boards slammed angrily together.

I hate this modern attitude. Cynical. I could never be like that.

What about Phil?

No he wasn't. He wasn't like that. No, of course he wasn't.

Heat, and the sheets twisting.

How could I. How did I ever let myself. Phil being cynical and my not seeing. Or did I see. I suppose I was as cynical as he was: I saw it right enough and I didn't mind.

But I didn't. I didn't see it at all.

I liked it. That's the truth.

But he wasn't. Phil wasn't cynical. He didn't see it at all like that. There's nothing in all that, it's only in my mind. So I must be more cynical than he is.

He isn't. He wasn't. I'm not going to think about him.

I wish I could stop thinking.

Smooth, green boards and the crumpled sheet.

Suppose I may as well read it.

Black print jigging between the swiftly turned pages.

It is like that, of course. I can tell by the look of it. And they call that 'love.'

Ours wasn't like that, was it, Phil?

It wasn't fair: circumstances were against us. It oughtn't to have been like that. Phil and I ought to have been married. Phil ought to have been working in a bank, and we should have lived in Putney or Surbiton, in a little house, and he'd have gone to work every day, and I should have got everything nice for him while he was out. Taps shiny and a boiling kettle. Have the place as neat as a new pin. And then we'd have had a little car and gone away for week-ends and it would have been different. Everything might have been all right then.

A slim figure in an overall, with waved hair. And a hoover. And Own Your House. Trim and red and a green lawn. And Phil coming from the city, an attaché case, and Phil striding up the path, and Phil's smile.

But Phil could never have been like that.

He could have, if he'd been born in those surroundings.

But then he wouldn't have been Phil.

I don't see why not.

And Phil striding up the path. And the trim overall. And a tea-table. And Give the Kiddies Hovis.[3]

Oh. I suppose we might have had children.

Oh. I don't know. I don't think I should want....

But I shouldn't: I shouldn't mind. I never have wanted it, but I shouldn't mind if it were Phil.

Phil, I don't see why it couldn't have been like that.

I never thought of it, but I wish I had.

But even if we'd married it wouldn't have been quite like that.

I don't see why. I suppose we ought to have been the same age.

Well, you'll be as old as I am, one of these days, won't you? And I doubt whether you'll wear so well. Not if you go on the way you're going now, you certainly won't. I'd just like to see you when you're my age. Yes, I would. And then you'll be sorry, perhaps.

Phil, old; thinning hair flattened by the brush. Bald streaks between the plastered strands.

It'll go away from the temples. It's that kind.

And pouches under the eyes.

And serve him right too.

---

3   Hovis (brand) bread.

No, no. Phil, I don't mean it, really I don't. I should hate you to be old, Phil. Just stay as you are: it's your nature to be young. I don't want you to change, ever.

But we ought to have been young together. We were meant to be. We ought to have married. Still, it wouldn't have been quite like that in any case.

But it was, in a way. When I used to get my room ready it was as if he were coming home. It was our home, wasn't it, Phil, my little room?

What's happened to my room.

It was like being at home, Phil, wasn't it? When we were there? Just Us? Only it couldn't last.

I don't see why it shouldn't have. I can't see.

Well, I don't know.

I don't want to think about that.

Now if I thought about the time when he was nice, I might dream about him if I dozed off. One wants to get a clear picture and hold it. Hold the image.

Warm and heavy, and the blackness of closed lids.

Phil, I'm going to think about you the way you were when you were nice.

"Phil."

How is it, I can't see him. When he smiled, now; and the way he used to stand up, with an elbow on the mantelpiece. 'Funny ickle thing.' Yes, say it like that, Phil. Be nice to me Phil. You are nice, aren't you?

Phil being nice and Phil's smile. I ought to see him like that and go on thinking. Hold the image. Go on seeing and being nice and hold the image. You want to hold the image, you want to hold. You see you want to hold the being nice. You want to hold you see. You see the thing is you want to hold. You want to hold what do I mean you want to hold.

Long, white corridors and a turn and a dark staircase, curving up. Where is he, he isn't here. Where is he?

Up and around and a long corridor and a door open and a long corridor, where, where.

Urgency and speed and the passage running on and a swift bend and up and where, where. On and on and someone following. Quick, quick. Emptiness and on and a following unseen.

Long, long corridor and the unseen following. Quick, he's coming, quick. Feet dragging and a turn and a breach the height of an arm in the wall. Quick, quick and crouch and struggle through and a narrow staircase. Where, where is he, where? And a corridor and the unseen fled, where, where? And fear. Quick, he'll come, quick.

The small, sunny morning-room with the great bowl of lavender misty blue and sunshine on the peonies beyond the window; the swish of the portière as it swings to. Papa coming to the fire-place, rubbing his hands, and small hands flitting beside the lavender: Mamma's hands flitting in and out over the tatting; the moiré bow on her hair and the hair brushed back, smooth, from the forehead. But where is he, where? Have you seen him, where is he?

All in good time. You'll know that all in good time. Mamma's hands flitting in and out and the blue lavender, where, where? All in good time, but it isn't, is it, Phil. Where are we going, Phil, where? All in good time. And the smooth motion of gloves on the steering-wheel, and Phil's head but he won't look. But he must look, where, where? The road gliding on, white and straight and a swift bend in the road.

We're going the same way, the same way. We can never meet because we're going the same way. Of course, we're going the same way.

And the road gliding up and gliding on and Phil's face never turned and the same way. Phil, stop, stop, we're going the same way. Stop, we're going the same way. Don't you see, the same way, stop, you must stop.

39

And the road gliding up and gliding on. Stop stop you must stop. And a square placard in the white road and a map of Cornwall in the square, brought up close: NO MEETINGS HERE.

A jolt and a gasp and the starting-out of sweat, and eyes straining. White walls and the fire quietly burning and the wicker arm-chair and the glass of the dressing-table tipped back, reflecting the ceiling.

No meetings here. But why? I was asleep. What does that mean?

Phil was driving.

Phil, driving, road, placard. No, it was on the map. The map of Cornwall. But what happened before? How did we get there?

"Oh, yes, why d-d-don't you put it down."

White apron and starched cuffs and a tea-tray lowered.

So it was you who woke me, was it.

"Yes, that'll do. I'll have it when I'm ready."

All the same, it meant something. They always do when they're like that. But why Cornwall. It was the map of Cornwall: I can see it now. Wish I could remember what went before.

Phil and driving and the road.

But how did we get there?

It doesn't really matter. It's only the last bit that means anything, isn't it? Words that are spoken or written down, or a sudden, clear picture like that. Very queer. I suppose about a dozen times in my life it's happened. As if somebody outside the dream were speaking, or holding the thing up.

Oh well, I may as well have this tea, I suppose.

Chink of china, and steam misting the glassy green of the tea-pot.

Green. The map was green. But then, maps generally are.

Oh, well, of course, we did fail to meet that time, in Cornwall. Mentally, that is: the way I'd hoped we should. That time we drove down, when I wanted Phil to see it: where I used to go as a girl. I thought it would bring us closer together than we'd ever been. But it was a mistake, we'd never been further apart than when we were out there on the rocks. I don't know why. But it was a mistake, I'm sure it was. I believe Phil was never quite the same afterwards.

Why, yes, I'd never thought of that. It was from that time that he began to change, wasn't it? Though I didn't notice at the time that he changed. But I believe it was. Now why was that?

Now why should it have been?

Phil, with his chin on his hands, staring out to sea.

And you were so sweet and thoughtful.

I wish I knew what you were thinking about, Phil. I never did know what you were thinking.

You hated it really, though; the wildness of the sea: that strange, far-away feeling it gives one: as if there were something too big to grasp. That was why I'd wanted us to see it together. I thought you might feel like that, too. But you didn't see it like that, did you Phil?

Or did you? Did he? Was that why?

Oh it wasn't, was it Phil? You didn't go because you saw, all at once, the bigness of it all, and that it wasn't worthwhile our going on, you and I? That it wasn't worthwhile; not worthy of you? It wasn't that, was it?

No, of course not. It couldn't have been. Why should it.

Well, I can't see much sense in this dream, in any case. They say a dream is the fulfilment of a wish, but I don't see how that can fit in here! What was the beginning of it? Can't remember.

Oh well; meant nothing, most likely. A pack of nonsense, these modern ideas about dreams. They always try to make out one wished for something disgusting one would never have thought of. Why can't Sonia come in and bring that book she promised me?

Green, shiny boards on the white counterpane.

Oh well, she did, didn't she.

Black print jigging between the swiftly turned pages.

I detest these modern books. Sure to be something unpleasant. It seems as if one couldn't get a really nice book, nowadays.

41

"What have you done with my rome, Phil?"

No. No, of course not.

"You, Sonia, can't you answer? What's happening about my rum?"

Rum? Rome? Rome? Room.

"My room, I said. Ought to be kept aired; shall catch a chill when I go back."

Did I lock those trunks when I came away?

"You'd better go and see. L-l-lock them and bring me the keys. I want to know whether they're keeping the room aired, or whether they've locked it up."

Won't have people poking round among my things.

"What's that?"

Oh, it's all right-Aunt-Millicent, is it. Yes, I daresay. Leave my things to the mercy of any chit of a chambermaid, sooner than cross the park and find out.

"What?"

Have my trunks here if I want them?

"W-w-what on earth should I want them here for? I mean the big trunks: all my things I brought from Chesborough. Why on earth should you suppose I want everything I possess brought here, and have to drag it back again. Do you imag-imagine I'm going to stay here forever?

Very well. Don't talk nonsense then. Besides, the hotel wouldn't keep my room if all the luggage were taken out."

What? Don't tell me not to worry. It's my business, isn't it?

I hate that pert, solicitous voice. Does she think I'm an imbecile who wants humouring?

"I tell you, I'll have the trunks left where they are. The hotel needn't think they'll give me a diff-diff-diffent room when I go back."

Diffent. Diff. Diff. Diffent. Difflent. Won't have a difflent room. Though they'd be glad enough to get mine, I daresay. I've had that room for the best part of twenty years, and I'll have it kept properly aired. Only place I can get any peace.

"Yes, well, you may as well. No, I'm not feeling worse. You tire me."

At last.

How did I put up with Harold all those years?

What? What's that?

Oh, so they think they'd better shut the door. Go on with their whispering outside, I suppose. Now which nurse was that? The pink-cheeked booby, I know. So it wasn't 'quite such a good night'? Oh, *quite*. Wasn't it, indeed? Not quite so good as which night, I wonder.

I won't have Sonia here anymore. Tires me.

How on earth did I come to marry Harold at all?

There was nothing else to do, I suppose. I'm sure I never wanted to marry him. I just drifted into it.

I think I only realized it on the morning of the wedding. Even when they were fitting on the dress and going-away clothes I had a feeling it was only pretence, that the wedding would never really happen. As if it were a story I was telling myself. In the way one does. Stories about impossible things. All the more amusing to make them happen in one's mind, and it's of no importance, of course. So easy to go back a few stages and alter a point, and the whole thing goes off on to other rails. Harold, refused. Trousseau and trunks swept away: the empty floor. Harold, mournful, in his big tweeds, and his luggage stacked up in the hall: a long journey abroad, to forget. Poor Harold, poor boy. One's sorry for him, of course, but one couldn't have married him really. Quite impossible. But one was very gentle and sisterly. So it was only when I was standing in front of the glass that morning — smooth, close satin, down and down and sweeping out over the carpet, and a face staring back — and they were fitting on the wreath and veil as they'd done several times before, only more carefully, and this time Harold's sister came in with the bouquet — Sonia's mother; now that's a queer thing — and put it into my hands to see the whole effect in the glass: I believe it was only then that I knew I was really going to marry Harold. It was the arum lilies. Stiff, white curves of the lilies and their thick, yellow pollen. And the heavy scent that seemed to be cloistered in them: caught and shut away. Expensive lilies, trained to guard their expensive scent jealously from the air. Perfume in gracious drops: deliberate bounty. The restraint and poise that ought to belong to Harold's wife. I really believe it was that. I don't believe I thought of Michael at all, that day.

Oh. Well. Yes. Of course. I suppose, when you come to think of it, Harold was just a refuge from Michael.

Not from Michael, that is, but from the fact of Michael. The fact that there had been Michael. I wonder, now, whether I didn't marry Harold just to prove to myself.... What do I mean. Oh yes, prove. Prove, that's it. Just to prove. I think I must have married Harold just to prove. To prove that I never really loved Michael, that was it. Or else that I didn't care that I'd let him go like that? Or that I could marry somebody else if Michael wouldn't ask me?

Was it that, I wonder?

No that wasn't it. I don't think it was that. I think I knew even then that it was my fault. I don't know whether I knew it, but I must have felt it. Michael would have asked me, but I never gave him the chance. Oh, there were plenty of chances. Oh yes there were, Harold. We were alone often enough: during the shooting, and at picnics in the summer when the others went on ahead. I wonder we were allowed to be so much alone. But something always went wrong; I don't know what it was. Whenever I felt he was going to say anything, there was something which made me draw back and close up into myself. I don't know what it was, but it was always like that, after we grew up.

44

Why was it? I'm sure I don't know. We didn't talk about complexes in those days, but I suppose I must have had one. I don't know. But I did know, in a dim way, even then, that I was holding him off against my will. Though it was only later, when we heard he had married.... Oh dear, how upset I was. You wouldn't think a young girl like I could be so upset. And I suppose it was a feeling of failure, of something lacking in me, that led me to encourage Harold as I did. I must have gone to the other extreme, then. That time — you know — when I put the flower in his button-hole, when we were in the wood that time. I'm sure I don't know what I possessed me to do it! One of those yellow things: celand-ine, wasn't it? And looking so small, too, on his big tweeds! How angry I was, with myself. And I'm sure I was never more surprised than when Harold asked me to marry him. I believe I must have accepted him out of fear of that coldness in myself.

Or was it just hurt pride, because Michael hadn't asked me? It may have been that. Now I wonder whether it wasn't pride that made me mind so much about you, Phil.

No. No, don't want to think about that. No need to think. More than twenty years later, think of that. But that was quite different. That wasn't pride. It wasn't pride even about Michael, I'm sure it wasn't. I accepted Harold in sheer desperation, as a defence against myself.

And it was so dull at home.

And I always had that feeling that it wasn't real. And by the time I realized it, it was too late. The arums were there, lying along my arm. Waxen lilies, sliding over the thick, smooth satin. And even then it wasn't quite real. It wasn't a woman Harold married, but a shell: that's the truth of it. Something correct in white satin, labelled The Bride. *I* was never married to Harold at all. I wish you knew that, Harold. I wonder whether you did know it. I was huddled up in a corner somewhere, very small and remote: something small and shivering, like a startled mouse. What a little thing I was

45

in those days. Still am, I suppose, though there's no one to say it. Something small, that stared horrified at that straight figure in satin and heard it make the vows that I, little and frightened as I was, had to enter it and keep. No, Harold,

I never did marry you. If I was married at all it was to Phil.

Well, if that was a marriage, the divorce came soon enough. Oh well, no need to think about that.

And afterwards, it wasn't so difficult as you'd think, being married to Harold. No. It made it easier, you know, that you had such a definite ideal of a 'wife.' It was easy enough to find out what you expected — like taking a situation, almost — and fall into a routine, perform one's duties competently. You expected a good deal in some ways, you know, but you never looked very deep. I was a good wife, on the whole: I kept up the position your wife ought to keep up in the county. I don't think it ever occurred to you, even, that I mightn't love you. That made it easier. And I daresay I behaved as if I did, for a time. You weren't to know that that was Michael, like a cancer in me. And when I let myself go, as I did in Italy, that must have been a revenge upon Michael, because I'd kept him off.

Queer. Queer, isn't it. So many years ago. I wonder what made me think of it now. It gnawed for a time; but it died, like everything else. Except…. No, that won't die. That'll outlive me. Just as Philip will. That's different.

I never loved Michael. No, I didn't. I did not. I never loved anything but Phil.

It's true. Well, it just shows: I haven't given a thought to Michael, for years. I don't know why I should think of him to-day. It was thinking about Harold, and how I tried to take it out of Michael for my own stupidity in letting him go. Until, later, he got numbed. Well, yes, I did love him, I expect. But it passed; more than twenty years ago. Anything can pass in twenty years. Time passing: a long, low, flat lapping sea. But there won't be twenty years for you to pass in, Phil.

You oughtn't to have treated me like that, Phil. You knew I was an old woman, didn't you? Well, not old, but twice as old as you. You knew that from the first: I didn't try to hide it from you. Well, it's true, I did dress younger than I had before, but that was your fault: you shouldn't have told me I looked like a girl. I didn't believe you, of course: I wasn't such a fool as that. But I didn't think you were so conscious of my age as you must have been. I thought I might look ten or fifteen years younger than I was, to you. You oughtn't to have pretended: it wasn't fair. But it was my fault, really. I ought to have known you didn't mean the things you said. I did know it, but I didn't want to recognize it. I wanted to be deceived into happiness, just for a time.

Well, I was, wasn't I? I ought to be grateful, I suppose. Only I hadn't reckoned what it would cost.

I suppose it was my fault. I ought to have moved to a better hotel, or into a flat, and let you have the new car when you wanted it. I suppose I got careless: too sure. I did have my hair retinted, but I might have taken more trouble about clothes. And massage, too. But it took up so much time, and I wanted to be with you whenever you could get away. I wonder just what you were getting away from, though. I ought to have gone oftener, but it meant the afternoons lost: if I hadn't slept in the mornings I couldn't have kept up. I got careless, I suppose, but that was your fault: you lied so well. If you hadn't pretended you liked me as I was I should have known I looked as I did. But you deceived me. Yes, you did. Or did I deceive myself?

I suppose I was a fool to spend so much on keeping my hair tinted. If I'd let you have that new car, you wouldn't have minded if I'd let my hair go grey. You might even have put up with a few more wrinkles. Because that was all you wanted, wasn't it? I suppose I did know it instinctively, even then, and that was why I wouldn't let you have it. Though at the time I really couldn't see that you wanted a new car after only two years: not even that. And

47

things were difficult at the time, and it did seem.... I suppose if I'd been honest with myself I might have kept you. But I hadn't the courage to admit that that was all you wanted.

Well, I'm glad I didn't let you have it, then. I'm glad I didn't get you on those terms. I'm not such a fool as that.

What a fool I was, though. I might have had you like that, and I'd have been sure of you then. So long as my money held out. Yes, that would have been amusing, wouldn't it? To hold you like that, and let myself go to pieces: let you see how grey and wrinkled I was: if I hadn't had my face lifted again. That would have been funny, my dear Philip: to watch your repulsion struggling with your greed. Oh yes, wouldn't it?

Oh, wouldn't it.

Oh.

Oh Phil, but I wasn't repulsive to you, was I? Not really? Phil, say I wasn't. You know I shouldn't want to keep you like that. You know I don't think you're like that really. But I wasn't. You know I wasn't. I wasn't repulsive to you, Phil.

But don't you remember how he said.... But he did. And he couldn't have said all that if I hadn't attracted him just a little. All the things he said. And the way he used....

Phil, you did love me for a little bit, Phil, didn't you? You did. You know you did. Just for a little while. Only I was so tired and I couldn't hold you.

Just so tired. So tired. Just tired.

And a coal dropping into the fender. And silence.

Brr, brr, brr. You know. Brr, brr. You know how it is. Brr, brr, brr. You see, don't you, Phil. And the bells ringing out, and the white clergyman. He's put on his best surplice. And the bells and....

Coldness and tossing. Limp arm heaved up and dropped over; a hand dragging at the sheet.

And the bells and, the bells and, the bells....

Eyes heavily opening, and a cold room.

The fire must have gone out.

"Nurse."

Oh well, she isn't here. They never are.

What was I dreaming about? It was a nice dream. What was it? Something about a wedding. Being married to Phil! Why did I wake up?

Well, I'm sure I can't think what made me dream that: it's the last thing I should want to do! Oh well, I was thinking about weddings, wasn't I. Just before I dropped off. My wedding and Harold's. That's all: it didn't mean anything.

But what happened before the wedding?

Now that's strange, I can generally remember my dreams. I know there was a lot of it. It might have been amusing.

Oh yes, of course! We were in a room: no room I've ever been in. And yet I seemed to know it: a feeling of having come home. Now why? There was nothing in the room, though. Nothing at all.

Quite empty except for ourselves: quite small and nearly dark. And no furniture, that I can remember. Except that we were sitting on a kind of couch: of course we were. That is, we must have been, though I wasn't conscious of any couch there. But we were sitting, in a way: half sitting and half lying, and Phil was saying something. And then it changed to the church.

No, there was something before that. In between. Now what was it. It's funny, I can't remember.

"Oh, there you are. I've been c-c-calling for about ten minutes. I wish you'd see to the fire."

Rattle of tongs; clash of poker against the curb.

Clumsy. Idiot. Goes through my head.

What was I saying? Oh yes, Phil and I in a little room.

Why, of course, I remember! I was wearing a white frock. So I was. The muslin kind that one used to wear, with open-work.[4]

---

4   Ornamental work in cloth with regular patterns of openings and holes.

One hardly sees it nowadays. Why, I haven't seen that since I was quite a child. Quite a little girl's frock, with frills. How absurd! And Phil was kissing my hand. 'Beautiful. Quite, quite beautiful.'

Why, of course! Think of my forgetting that! He was saying that, of course he was.

'Ickle Marcia. Quite, quite beautiful.'

Of course: it all comes back to me perfectly clearly, now. Now fancy my not being able to remember that!

What? What do you want?

"Yes, of c-c-course I heard you come in. No, I don't want to be washed."

Why can't you go away. Can't leave me in peace for a moment.

Oh, so it isn't the pink-cheeked one this time. Thin and sallow. Dark. Sister, that's it. Scrubbed all the pink out with the carbolic. Suppose a Sister's been scrubbed longer than a nurse.

"Oh, Nurse is having her day day day off? Well, she's got a fine day. A fine day. Yes, it's quite bright isn't it. Yes, I can see quite a bit of the garden when I sit up. Yes, it's a nice, bright room."

Oh, you surely don't want to talk to me, do you? Can't you leave me in peace.

"No, I had it pulled down on purp on purpose. The sun's too bright when the blind's up. Yes, very br-br-bright for the time of year. I can't stand so much light. No, it doesn't hurt my eyes, but it tires me. I hate an unshaded lie. Light I mean. A s-sign of age, I suppose."

Oh, you take that seriously, do you? Well, you needn't snigger, you're not so much younger than I am. You're the best part of forty, *I* know.

"No, it wouldn't do me any good at all. To get some light and air. There's plenty of air and t-too much light as it is. With all this white paint. I like it left like that."

Like that, like like that. Well, you take a lot of telling, don't you.

"And I do *not* want to be w-w-washed."

You're no chicken. Look at those wrinkles under your eyes.

"Oh well, h-h-have it your own way."

And you needn't pinch up your mouth like that: only makes the wrinkles worse. The only mark of expression you're allowed, I suppose. If you'd thump the basin down and swear, now, you might be a bit more human. Instead of sliding the water in and wringing out the wash-cloth with that smooth efficiency of yours. Flat slap of the cloth on the water and the water lapping up against the sides of the china basin, lap, lap; and the drip and squish from the wrung cloth. You're forty-five if you're a day. How'd *you* like to be stripped and washed as if you were a dog getting ready for a show. A nice show you'd make, I daresay. Daresay you're not so firm as I am.

I'm not so bad, considering.

"That'll do. D-don't make it any colder."

One would think in these places one's body wasn't one's own. What business have you got. It's lucky, I've never felt much personal interest in my body: don't care whether it's mine or not. Never could feel it was myself: lucky, isn't it. I don't feel *I'm* exposed to you, in the least. Always thought of it as something I happened to be inside of by accident. Phil used to laugh at me about that.

Dull flump of an arm on to the rubber sheet.

Queer, to think this used to belong to Phil.

Well. Well, you've done with it, haven't you? Just a bit of wreckage you've left for this hatchet-faced automaton to swob with her rag. No more to her than so much mutton on a counter. Well, I don't suppose it was much more to you. Some rather old, tough meat you had to take, thrown in along with what you wanted. Well, why not admit it? May as well admit it. Lucky I can see the funny side of it.

"I'm not wrig-wrig-wriggling. Haven't you done yet?"

Slap and lap, lap, and the grey, twisted cloth, and drip and squish.

That's it, isn't it. I'm glad I've realized that, at last. I'm glad I know you, my good Philip, at last. Because now I shan't worry anymore about you.

Queer to think that what she's rubbing at.... You used to say my legs were a good shape. Well, I suppose you may have meant that. I always had a slim ankle, and I expect that's one of the things that don't change. I suppose that's one of the few things you could say that were true. That's why you repeated it so often. To do you justice you didn't enjoy lying. You only lied when it was necessary. Oh yes, I'll say that for you: you were honest, essentially. You never told a lie when you could help it: when it was possible to act it. And when it ceased to be seriously worthwhile, you stopped.

I ought to have known. I don't see how I could look at myself and not know. I suppose I did know. Oh, I don't know.

"Is that all? Th-thank goodness. I ought to have a clean night-gown. In the top, right-hand drawer."

That's right. Cover up the skin and bones. Tie them up in their bag and wrap them round with the sheet: bundle them out of sight, *I* don't want to look at them. I suppose they're mine, but they're not I.

They were to Philip, though. That's the tragedy of it. That's what's so unfair. My mind was as young as ever it was, but he didn't care anything for that. He didn't know it was there. People were bodies to him. He'd have laughed if I'd told him I was young though my body was middle-aged. I think I did tell him, and he did laugh. He said of course I was young: I didn't look a day over twenty-five. That was in the early days, before he got tired of lying. But he didn't see in the least what I meant. It didn't convey anything to him. He was quite sure he and his body were one, so I must be one with mine: just a middle-aged body, sagging in the wrong places.

No, I won't think about him.

"Yes, that'll do. You might fix the pill, pill, the pillows a bit higher. Thank you, Sister."

I don't want to think about him. I don't know why I keep on thinking about him. I wish I could stop thinking about him altogether. Think about Harold: Harold didn't find me repulsive.

But you didn't, Phil, you didn't.

No, I *won't* think about him.

Harold thought me attractive. But then, I was twenty years younger for Harold. What irony.

No, I *will not* think.

I wonder how I seemed to Michael, now. Perhaps he didn't think about me like that, only as a girl he used to play with, grown up and grown dull. I certainly didn't think about him, in that way. I should have thought it indecent if I'd thought of it at all.

Indecent: how odd.

Oh my goodness, there isn't much decency left to me, is there? Perhaps if I'd had a bit more, things would have been different.

No, I *won't*.

Michael. I was seventeen for Michael, when he went away. Why wasn't I seventeen for you, Phil?

No.

Seventeen. I daresay I wasn't bad-looking, then. I suppose I had a complex. If I hadn't had, what would have happened? If I'd married Michael? Well, I don't know. I should have been a different person. You can't argue like that: you can't say What would have happened if because if you'd acted differently you'd have been somebody else. The person I am is the person who acted as I did: that's it, isn't it? Then what sort of person should I have been? I shouldn't have been at all. Or should I have been, and now I'm not? Is that why I sometimes feel I'm not quite a person, only pretending to be one? In 'buses, for instance? Because I oughtn't to exist? Because I ought to have married Michael and been somebody else?

No, I don't suppose it's that. I used to feel like that before, even, didn't I? Most likely there was something in me already which made me take the wrong turning with Michael. Just as I did later with Philip. Only it was a different turning. If I'd felt a closer kind of relationship with my body I suppose I might have understood Phil better. I might have known how to keep him. Or else I should never have dared to love him.

I oughtn't ever to have let you know it. I ought never to have looked at you in the first place and called you across the lounge to sit near my table. And then looked round for a match. I think I knew it in that moment: all that was going to happen. Except the end. If I'd been one with my body perhaps I should have known that too, and never let it begin.

It wasn't fair to you. I wasn't fair to you, Phil. I couldn't expect you to feel anything for a woman twice your age. I think I knew it in a way, even then. That's why I wanted to give you things: to make up for what I couldn't give you. I never thought you'd take it in that way: I should never have done it if I'd thought. I don't think I did. I don't think I really meant it, like that. I don't think I should have done that to you. Though it didn't trouble you much, if it's true. But it ought to have. Or was that why you suddenly felt you couldn't go on with it any longer?

Phil, I didn't mean it like that, really I didn't. I wanted you of your own accord, only I could never have got you in that way. I didn't do it deliberately, but I must have known how you were taking it when I offered you the car: the first car. No, I don't really think I did. I only wanted you to have it because you wanted it so much. I believe when I refused you the second one it must have been that I had a faint suspicion.... No, if I'd known, you should have had it if it took the last penny I'd got.

No, I don't, now. I wish I knew. I don't know.

I don't know.

Well, I'm not going to worry about it, I don't see why I should. I'm going to try to get a nap.

I'm going to make my mind a blank. They say you should make your mind a blank. Look at things around, and don't think. And then you drop off.

It's a square room. What a very square room this is. Most rooms are square. It's because there's so little furniture in it.

The fire-irons are steel: some kind of grey metal. Why don't they have brass? Looks cheerful. They don't want the trouble of cleaning it. I like to see well-kept brass. Now the bits of brass in my room.... No, I mustn't think.

Think of the brass at Chesborough, now. How Harold....

No.

The mantelpiece looks odd with nothing on it. That's what gives the room that bare, unfriendly look, not like....

Why do they have a white shade for the electric light? Green would be more pleasant. Less tiring. Tiring. I'm tired. Even the flex is clean; how do they get up there to clean it?

Bottles on the dressing-table: my silver-topped bottles I always had. Had them for a wedding present. I remember how small they used to look....

Mustn't think.

Rugs on the linoleum. The one by the door is crooked. Somebody stepped on it and it slid. Corner of it showing around the screen. Green tiles in the fire-place. Blind half drawn: they never can draw it properly. Grey metal poker; shovel turned the wrong way up; white curtains hanging straight to the floor, and the green linoleum and the small table with a fruit basket and a jug of water, and the unbleached linen screen with the light wood frame, and half the door handle showing around the screen.

The fire going down. Whiteness and chill. Slipping down under the sheet, and a corner of the screen and the white, dangling cloth of the bed-side table.

55

The long, white road like a ribbon going on ahead and the car going on and on and the car made of brass and somebody running ahead in the road, wrapped in a bath-towel: Phil's sister: running, and the car catching up.

Sheep in the fields on either side of the road, and on and on, and Phil's sister in a bath-towel, running, and a milestone: Toddingham 17. And the car moving swiftly, without effort, I didn't know it was so easy to drive, going on and on, and Phil's sister running and the car catching up, almost over.

Run, run, he's coming. Running in the road and the car coming on and feet heavy and Phil in the car, waving a hatchet — no, it's a telephone — and coming nearer, run, run, and legs won't move and running and the hammer beating faster and faster and the car there....

Oh.

Light, and the quiet, tilted mirror ahead on the dressing-table.

How my heart's beating.

Now whatever was the point of that?

Of course, I woke up suddenly like that because the car was going to run over me. You always do, don't you? You're never quite killed, in a dream. But before that I was in the car myself, driving quite easily, too! And there was somebody else.... Oh yes: Phil's sister.

But he hasn't got a sister!

Well, it was Phil's sister, sure enough, and I was chasing her in the car. I believe I was just going to run her down. And then all at once I was in the road myself and Phil was driving over me.

Now what on earth can *that* mean? Not much of a wish about that. I don't particularly want to run over Phil's sister — supposing he had one, which he hasn't — and I certainly don't want him to run over me!

And she was wearing nothing but a bath-towel!

Oh well, I'd been washed just before: it's nothing but that. And the milestone: Toddingham: seventeen, wasn't it? Now why

Toddingham? What a very peculiar thing. Like the milestones I used to watch as a child, driving home in the governess-car. But they never got so far as seventeen. And why Toddingham should pop up like that, out of nowhere, after the best part of forty years....

Well, well. There isn't much sense in it, I expect.

"See, seek, seek of it. Seek to death."

Sick: that's it.

"Sick of it. Tell you I'm sick of it. Sick of your fussing."

That's right. So you took the hint, did you?

Sick of it.

But how did I get here in the first place, that's what I can't understand? How was it?

Neat bed-side table with carafe and tumbler, and the smooth, swept floor and clean hearth and small, bright fire in the sunken grate. White, empty mantelpiece. I don't see why I shouldn't have brought my things. She might have given me time to collect my things. And the blank, yellow blind.

Sonia, of course. But I can't see, now, what she was doing there. Fussing. And hadn't been near me for years.

But what happened, exactly?

I was just going to have a cup of tea — I remember, the kettle was boiling — and there was some little job or other I was going to do. No, of course, I'd just been washing out a few things. And then she had to come and interrupt.

But how did I know who it was? Shouldn't have known her from Adam. Hadn't seen her since she was a little thing. She must have said who she was, I suppose. But I can't for the life of me think how she persuaded me to come here.

Let me see, I was just going to make the tea. Been too busy at lunch-time, to go down. Hadn't felt up to it, most likely: the

57

noise and so on. I was just taking the kettle off the ring. And then she must have come in, and there was something about being ill.

'Well, *I'm* not ill, what's the matter? Even if I do feel a bit out of sorts lately. There's nothing wrong with me. What are you fussing about?'

But what exactly was I doing when she came in? How was it I let them bring her upstairs? Don't remember her being announced at all. Very careless. I know I was just going to make the tea, and then there was some talk about going away for a change....

'Oh well, have it your own way. If I'm ill I'd better go, I suppose. But I warn you I shall want time to see to my things.'

Then how was it I came away without seeing to anything? Most annoying. Just like Sonia to interfere. That's Sonia all over. And then when I got here I wasn't ill at all, and a nice state my room will be in when I get back.

"Why h-hasn't my niece been to see me?

Two days ago? N-n-not, not..."

Not. Not-sense. What's not-sense. Nonsense.

"Nonsense. Hasn't been near me for weeks."

All those years. Since she was a little thing, and Harold would have her here to stay. She never really took to me. Yes, Aunt Millicent; no, Aunt Millicent: always a pert politeness. Made me hate the name. Always had disliked it; it never belonged to me. Too big a name: I was a slim little thing as a girl. Well, I'm not stout, now. I've got a good figure still, when I'm dressed.

Never could think of myself as Millicent. It never suited me, except perhaps when I was with Harold. Harold and Millicent. Yes, I expect it was right for that. But it was never my own.

Hadn't thought of it for years. I don't believe I had a name at all, all those years after Harold was killed. It was Sonia who

58

brought Millicent back: with her 'Aunt Millicent.' Strange to walk about all those years without a name, but there was no need for one, particularly. I remember, when Phil asked me I had to think a minute before I could tell him! And I hated saying it, too. It's so old-fashioned, nowadays, it seemed to date me. 'I haven't really got a name!' Now what an absurd thing to say. 'Mine doesn't belong to me. It's Millicent.'

I was so afraid you'd laugh. But you were so wonderful. 'Such a big name for one little woman. We're going to call you Marcia. And that's our very own name: just for Us. Little Marcia.'

Oh Phil, where are you?

Say it just like that, Phil. Just sit here and stroke my hand, just softly, as you always do. 'Such a little hand. Little Marcia.'

Just stay like that. Just Us. Stroke it and make it well. Ickle wee thing. And then we'll go out, shall we? Right away somewhere. Where there'll be just Us. You'll like that, won't you, Phil?

Phil, Phil.

No, not really.

Why don't you come? Why don't you? What I want to know is.

No, I don't mean that. I want you back, Phil. I don't care what way it is.

What?

"No, there's n-n-nobody here, why should you think there was? No, I didn't call you."

What she want? Fussing, fussing. What was I thinking, when she came in? What was it?

Can't she go away? What's the matter: fiddling about with the brushes. Not doing anything. What she want?

No! I didn't call out, did I? I didn't say anything aloud, did I? I don't think I ever do talk to myself. I was thinking something, what was it? Oh, about....

Oh, I wonder, now....

"Yes. Yes, of course I c-called you. Want the fire made up.

59

Chilly in here, lying still. And this sheet is in a muddle, just st-st-straighten it out."

I must be careful. Mustn't do that. I didn't say anything that matters, did I? What was I thinking, exactly?

Yes, that was it. About the way he used....

"Phil."

There! There, that's it. I must have done that before. Something like that. She can't have heard this time, can she? Making too much noise with the poker. Don't know what's the matter with me: used not to talk to myself, that I know of. Or have I been doing it for years? Philip would have told me.

Better not think anymore. Wait until she's out of the room.

"Oh. Yes. That's quite com-comfortable, thank you. No, I shan't want anything more."

I'm not going mad, am I! Well, that would be a nice ending, would it not! Quite fitting, Philip, I'm sure. Quite what one would expect. But as it happens, my dear, I'm not. I'm in complete possession of all my faculties. Or I shouldn't be able to remember everything so well: only too well.

Only too well. Only too, too. Too? Only too well.

I wonder, by the way, why I didn't kill myself. It must have seemed the obvious thing to do, at the time. But one doesn't like to be so obvious.

There was really no reason to go on living. But then, so far as I can see, there was never much reason to live at all. The world would have got on quite well without me. Harold would have married somebody else: there were plenty of people who would have married Harold. And he wouldn't have been any different, I never had the slightest influence over him in any way. He'd hardly have found anybody else so passive. Perhaps, then, I hindered his development? If it hadn't been for me he might have married somebody who'd have jerked him out of his routine? But I don't think so. If he had come across somebody with a personality he'd have broken her, quite courteously, of course. Just worn her down with correctness and consistency. Or politely disposed of her. A judicial separation: the very term would appeal to Harold! Perhaps on the whole it was a good thing he found somebody like myself who wasn't really a person. But it wasn't of great importance.

And as for Michael, I never had any effect on him at all. Unless it was that I showed him how silly a young girl can be; and that maybe was why he went off and married a widow ten years older than himself. I don't know that even that was due to me: he might have done the same if we'd never met. And in any case that's not much of an effect to have upon anyone.

As for Philip....

No, but I don't want to think about him.

Well, yes, I expect I had an effect upon him, right enough. Oh, no doubt that was an effect. That was well worth living for. Oh, was it not. He'd have been better off if he'd never seen me. Though he wouldn't have had his car and a few other things. But he wouldn't have spent two years hanging around after an old woman he despised, pretending he wasn't nauseated....

Well, nobody made him. And he didn't do so badly out of it.

But I oughtn't to have put temptation in his way. Old enough to be his mother. I ought to have realized.

Well, he'd have found somebody else fast enough, if it hadn't been I. Oh yes he would. Why should he have thought I meant that, if he hadn't had it in his mind? It wasn't the first time he'd played that game, *I* know.

I wish I knew where he was now. I wish I knew whether I'd really done him any harm. I wish I knew whether that was really what he meant.

That was when I ought to have killed myself, I expect: after those first days at Brighton. Before it had gone any further. Before we came back to town. If I'd done it then it would have settled everything: it was no good, later.

But I couldn't have died then, could I? I should have missed it all. It wouldn't have been fair, when I'd waited so long to know what happiness was. I couldn't be expected to: not death.

What do I mean? Death.

Not death: not just then.

Why death? Death at the end of everything? Death, so horrible: all one's pitiful little defences torn down, all one's little evasions and vanities and reservations; not even a body to hide behind: pushed out, to stand alone in a naked light.

Oh, it isn't like that, is it? It can't be. People think of it as darkness and rest, but I've never been able to see it like that.

But it's horrible, I don't want to think about it. Of course it has to come sometime, for all of us, I suppose. But there's no need to think about it, that I can see. Besides, I suppose ultimately death is the only solution to any problem: anything else is no more than a compromise, you know. You do see that, don't you, Phil? Even life, only a compromise between being and not being. So one oughtn't to mind about death, ought one?

Wish I knew what they're doing with my room. Wish I could remember whether I locked those trunks. I don't believe I ever took down that nightdress that was drying: I'd only just washed it out, I remember; hung it over the chair by the window. It'll get dirty again, hanging there in the dust. Don't suppose Sonia thought of it.

Rounded, white wicker-chair with the curved seat turned, empty, to the steel fender, and a piece of cushion sagging through the open wicker chair-arm.

Wish I knew. Wish I knew.

Wish Mrs. Caruthers would slip up and see. Wonder she doesn't come to see me. Now if she were to come to see me, to come, I could mention it.

Mrs. Caruthers and her waved, grey hair and her cameo brooch, and the ferrule of her umbrella poked against the grey steel curb.

Mrs. Caruthers, I wish you'd just slip up and have a look at my room. You might take down the nightdress that's drying by the window, if you don't mind. Just slip it into a drawer: I can put things straight when I get back. You might turn the key in the drawer when you've done and put it. Put it. Let me see. Put it. Put it under the gloves in the box on the dressing-table. I shall know where to look for it. I don't like that new girl they've got: sure to be trying on my things. Very trying. Don't you find things have been tried on?

Would you really? That is nice of you. Nobody I can depend upon, nowadays. Sonia — that's Harold's niece, you know: my husband's niece, I mean — can't depend upon her. One of these young things. Yes, didn't you know I had a niece? No, I don't have her here very often: no use, like most of these young people. Shouldn't like to send her to see to my things, she'd be looking round to see what jewellery I've got. Thinks she'll get it another day. Ha-ha, well, she'll find it's all been left to Phil, what little I've got to leave, and that's not much. Nephew? No. What, did I say Philip? No, a friend. Just a friend. One must have friends, mustn't one? Somebody to depend upon?

Depend? Did I say depend? If she only knew.

Phil.

But what I wonder is, how I could ever have felt as I did. It isn't like me. I can't understand it at all.

Well, that's all over and done with. No need to worry about that anymore, I'm glad to say.

But I can't understand how it happened. How was it. How was.

Well I don't know. I don't know. Such a mess: I don't know. Such a mess.

Such a mess my room must be in. If I could only make sure....

Last few stairs, and the door opening.

63

Well, it isn't in so much of a mess as I should have thought. Glad they've had the sense to keep it aired.

There, to think I left this nightdress hanging here all the time! I wonder it didn't get more dusty, by the window. Just fold it up and slip it into a drawer. Shall find it when I get back.

What was I saying?

Do sit down, Mrs. Caruthers. No, take the chair, I'll sit on the divan. No, really, I prefer it. Creak of springs; an elbow sunk in the yielding down of the pillow. — Do you like this divan arrangement? Yes I do, don't you? Yes, I like the cover. I got it ... where was it now? Yes, it's Persian, I believe. Oh yes, I brought it with me from Chesborough: thrown over a couch in the drawing-room. Must have been brought there in Harold's father's time, he was a great traveller you know. Or was it a wedding present to Harold and me? I remember it never went with the room, but it's perfect here, isn't it? Just what was wanted. Odd, the way things have their niche if one can only find it. Nothing quite wasted. A lesson to one, isn't it, to look for the pattern in life. Nothing useless, if one considers it. I like this divan arrangement. Dislike a room to look like a hotel bedroom. After all, this is my home, you know. Always feel I've come home when I've shut the door. Key turned; take a look round.

Empty wicker-chair, and the fire, and the steel fender.

Oh well, it's no good thinking, I suppose.

If I could just get up to my room for a minute or two: soon put things straight.

Just get up to my room.

The swing-to of the hall-door, and across the hall. Are there any letters? Green baize and the letter-rack.

Wonder if there are any letters there, waiting for me. Of course not.

If I could just get over there for an hour or so. Don't see how I could.

Just get out of here — give them the slip — and take a taxi across. Just slip upstairs.

Click of the lift-door. Press the button.

It wouldn't take any time, in the lift.

Downward slide of floors past the grating. And a downward jerk, and stop. The landing carpet. Red; small, blue flowers. It's so simple: I wonder why I didn't think of coming before.

So simple, so simple, so simp. No, what do I mean. So delightful, that's it. It's delightful to be back. In my own arm-chair, delightful. Friendly: nice, friendly, solid chair. I'm glad Mrs. Caruthers didn't come up with me. She's pleasant, but there's a lot to do, putting things straight. When you've been away as I have. I wish they wouldn't put books upside-down in the shelves, it always annoys me, doesn't it you? And these taps aren't very bright: that new girl. Get out my own little pot of polish and give them a rub. If one must have a wash-basin in one's room it might at least be an ornament.

Don't think I'll bother to go down to dinner to-night. I wish this paste wouldn't so soon grow dry in the tin; but the taps only want a hard rub. These modern girls are bone lazy. Where's that glove I tore the other day getting on to the 'bus? Waste not, want not, as they used to say. It'll be pleasant to get into a dressing-gown and have a quiet evening for once, I seem to have been doing so much lately. There! That's coming up beautifully, only wanted a good rub: elbow-grease as we used to call it. There's one thing in a hotel, you're not bothered by servants. How annoyed Harold used to get when they would try to dust his study. As I told him, it had to be dusted sometime!

White, empty mantelpiece, and the empty wall.

Well, they haven't got much dusting to do here, I must say.

So empty. Now if only I'd brought my things. Don't suppose they've dreamt of keeping things dusted.

The marble clock under its glass dome; photographs in their twin, silver frames and candlesticks with dangling glass prisms;

and all their backs in the mirror. Content.

I should think these ornaments haven't been moved for weeks, they never think of cleaning underneath. It's a good thing I don't mind doing it. Once I'm in my dressing-gown I quite enjoy my little bits of housework! There isn't much tea in the tin, by the sound of it. Didn't I get some yesterday? It must have been the day before. Before I came, came away. No, what do I mean. There, Harold: I can't imagine why I keep your photograph up, collecting the dust, but you may as well have your frame polished.

Companion frame out of line, pushed back to make way for the little mosaic box with the blue flowers on the lid.

Empty, I should say. Must remember to get some more cigarettes, or there won't be any for Phil.

Oh well, no.

Wooden click of the box back against the mirror.

Where did it come from? Italy, I believe. Didn't I get it in Italy? Harold got it for me, I remember. Well, that was a good time ago.

Frame dragged forward, into place, half-way between the clock and candlestick.

And I was good-looking as a girl, wasn't I? Well, there's not so much difference as all that. Well, that's to say, I'm untidy now, with the housework and one thing and another. But it's the same face: one would have thought I should change more. The hair isn't quite right, though. These stiff waves don't suit me: it's the permanent. Must try another shop. Yet I paid enough, goodness knows, this last time. I was so anxious Phil should be proud of me.

Oh, yes, that was the time before, wasn't it. Yes. I expect it doesn't matter much now. I expect I needn't bother.

Well, I'm not going to let him think I've let myself go all the same. Not going to pay him a compliment to that extent. Oh no no, my good Philip. Besides, if he turned up suddenly; you never know. I don't like that last place I had it done; find somewhere else and make an appointment to-morrow.

Don't like the way they've done the lifting, either. Gives the face such a stiff, arranged look. The skin doesn't seem alive, as it used to. Yes, I was a good-looking girl. And to think all that was wasted on Harold.

I expect I was wrong to keep this photo up. I wanted to show Phil I hadn't changed at all. There's hardly any difference, when you glance quickly. I defy anyone to tell my age, in the right light. But he must have noticed those little things. I expect the photo was a mistake: he mightn't have noticed so much if I hadn't shown him the difference. Put it away: shouldn't like him to see it if he came in.

Creak of a drawer, and the frame slid out of sight.

There. Now if he did turn up.... Well, Harold, and you may as well go back up there. You may as well be there as anyone else. You had my youth, didn't you? So you may as well stand by me now.

Ought to wash out that nightdress. Shan't have one for to-night.

"Not so well to-day."

Who isn't so well? Who said that? I'm imagining things, lately. Need a change. Where did I put that nightdress? If I hang it over the chair by the window it ought to dry by to-night.

Don't make so much noise. What are you talking about.

Oh it's you, is it. So you have turned up, but I've put it away, so there. Oh, no. No, what was I saying.

Empty wicker-chair and steel fender and feet in front of the fender. And leaning against the mantelpiece: broad shoulders in a grey suit and fingers jingling a seal.

Oh it's you, is it. May as well save yourself the trouble. And that pink-cheeked booby fussing about. Don't make so much noise, I'm busy. And there's too much light, draw down that blind. Must wash out that nightdress, it won't be dry in time. Wish you wouldn't make so much noise. If I wash it out now it ought to dry while I'm out. Just hang it over the chair by the window.

I won't go so far as the Serpentine to-day. It's sheltered here. I'll just sit for a bit and watch people and then go back and get some of those odd jobs done. There was something I thought of, just before I came out, that I ought to do. What was it.

Now look at that couple over there. What are they whispering about? Now what's she trying to wheedle out of him. The way she's digging patterns in the path with her umbrella, and looking up at him now and then: outlining some scheme. I don't think you'll get it, my girl. No, I don't think you will. Doesn't look to me as if you would: much better be resigned. You don't look as if you'd be resigned, either. You've thought it all out carefully, haven't you? You want him to see how reasonable it is? But he won't. It's wonderful how little reason a man can see if a woman shows it to him. No no, my dear, you'd better make up your mind to it. Much better let him go his own way, and you go yours: save a lot of trouble in the end. You won't believe it, you young things. You don't even *want* freedom: don't know what it is. Look at me, now. I can go in and out when I like: nobody to ask questions. And nobody to worry about. Ah, that's it. It'll take a lot of life to make you see that. Oh yes, it takes a lot to make one see the value of independence. But ever since I haven't allowed Phil to worry me anymore I've been a different woman, I have indeed. Why, I don't know myself! Able to sit in the air like this for half an hour without anything troublesome to think of. Just able to look at the flowers and the dresses and one thing and another without having to think anything further. They're pink and white, aren't they: rhododendrons. Huge, waxen clusters. They're as big as I am. Blossoms crowding up, suffocating: huge flowers, white and huge and waxen, flushing to pink. Flesh, they're like flesh. Dwindled away: rhododendron bushes, on the far side of the path. Great bunches of pinky-white among the leaves: beautiful, beautiful. And that's a daring dress over there: that dark woman in the yellow, coming up past the rhododendrons. Very daring. But then with her colouring.... Now it's a pleasure to see somebody well-turned-out like that. She must have given a lot of thought to it. Now there was a time, not very long ago, when it wouldn't have given me the slightest pleasure to look at her, or at the rhododendrons either. I should have been thinking of the time Philip took me down to Kew, and wondering whether we'd ever go down there again, and if I hadn't better look for some clothes in case he rang up suddenly. Being in a fret in case he should come along. But now, you see, I'm perfectly free to enjoy the afternoon. Perfectly free! I can't think why I was ever so stupid as to go on worrying about him in the way I did. It must have been so obvious from the first, that he'd gone for good.

Well, that's one good thing, I needn't bother anymore. Now that I've made up my mind. Think I'll go back now, it's getting chilly. And the door closed. Turn back.

Oh dear, I oughtn't to be stiff, at my age.

Almost like a convalescence, being able to enjoy this beautiful afternoon! Don't think I'll go any further now, I'm rather tired. Feeling a bit fagged lately: well, no wonder! With all these worries. Still, that's finished with. And there was something or other I meant to do, back there at the hotel. Shall think of it in a minute.

Beautiful, those waxen bunches. Smooth to the touch. A long time since I've been able to take pleasure in things that were growing.

Think I'll go straight back and tackle some of those odd jobs I wanted to do. There was something I wanted to wash out, wasn't there?

It's really a pleasure to walk like this, with a sense of freedom. I don't believe I should mind in the slightest if I were to meet him this very moment! I only wish he *would* come along, with his jaunty walk. So that we could pass here, by the rhododendrons. Ha! you'd see then, wouldn't you, just how much I care.

"W-wouldn't you!"

What?

What's the mat, the matter?

"What are you doing here?"

What's she doing, making up that fire? I didn't ring, that I know of. I was asleep, wasn't I? Oh, I was dreaming, I think. No, not exactly: thinking. Can't one even. Can't one even, even, what do I mean. Can't one even think without being disturbed.

"No, I d-don't want any. Anything. Why? I didn't ring for you."

Or did I say anything, as I woke up? I seem to remember hearing.... Mustn't let her think. Suppose I really must have dropped off.

Oh yes, I remember, wasn't it.

"Where's Sonia gone? My niece? Well, she was here, a few min-minutes ago, but I fell asleep I think. Wha-wha-what's she gone. Gone for. Wanted to ask her something."

You don't know? How's that? It's only a few minutes ago that she was here.

"W-what, nobody's been but the doctor? Not, not nonsense. You must be dreaming."

Or have I been to sleep for some time? Must have dropped off while she was talking.

"Oh, the doc-doctor was here, was he. Then he might have waited till I woke. W-what does he think is the use."

Oh, don't shake your head at me like that, idiot!

Suppose I must have. Must be careful. Must have dropped off. Mustn't let myself drift like that or shall be saying something I don't mean to.

Quietness.

Quite, quite, what do I mean. It's quite in here. No, quiet. Quiet here.

Sizzle of gas-fire and pressure of friendly chair-arm. Solid, friendly chair.

Well, I'm sure it's nothing to me whether he comes or not. If he doesn't choose to come he's quite at liberty to stay away, so far as I'm concerned.

The ticking of a clock, under its glass dome.

You needn't think I care. No, you needn't.

Phil.

I'm not going to think any more about him. I don't see why I should. I've got enough pride left for that, I hope. I'm not going to think about him anymore.

Quietness and warmth and the friendly chair.

Don't think I'll go down to dinner, just for to-night. I feel so tired. Quite fagged out. It's this weather. I really don't want any dinner: couldn't eat if I went down. Nothing but a waste of time. I really must get that little saucepan, to be able to warm something up now and then.

But why should it have been that particular day, that's what I can't see. Why should you have gone then, more than at any other time? I could have understood it if we'd had a tiff, but there wasn't anything, was there? I don't see why it was, I wish I could make out. You see, we'd been talking that evening, in quite an ordinary way, and it must have been just after that that he....

Well, it doesn't matter why it was, after all. It makes very little difference. He's gone, hasn't he? Very well then, what does it matter.

Doesn't matter. It doesn't matter. And a good thing too. A good thing he did go.

I'm sure it makes no difference to me, whether he chooses to go or not.

Not the slightest difference, and a good thing too. And a good thing, a good thing, and a good thing.

Sun and sea; leaves in a great, green tangle, streaming down, and the white terrace. And a good thing. Sun on the terrace, and Phil. Phil, you're so splendid.

Peace and quiet heart-beats. Peace, peace.

71

Sea and the sun and a heart beating.

So you're here. I knew you'd come, Phil. I knew you would.

A lovely day. She said it's a lovely day. Well, so it is, I suppose.

Half-drawn blind yellow with sun; sunshine on dark laurels and a sycamore bough with limp, yellowing leaves.

What did she say? Quite warm for the time of year. Quite warm.

Fire pale in the grate, and the smooth sheet, and light, white walls. An arm laid quietly, long and quiet, along the quiet, white sheet. Quite warm. It's a lovely day. And the right hand tapping: grey fingers trot-trot, picking at the sheet.

It's a lovely day. I like to see the trees like this, with the young leaves. They're hardly green yet. A kind of yellow. It's a lovely day. Trot-trot: smooth horses trotting past, and the broad, brown belt of earth. I suppose that's what made me turn into the park, I'm sure I didn't mean to. I don't care much for this kind of thing, even though it's a lovely day.

The kind of day it was when I was here, just before.... You know, before I went to Brighton that time. It must have been this kind of weather that made me think of going away. And that would have been, let me see, three.... No, January he went. Frost on the road, that day I went out to 'phone. They can hear every word you say, there in the hotel — green baize letter-rack, and a door opening — with the 'phone in the hall. The summer before, that was when we drove so much: the time we went down to Cornwall. And the summer before to Brighton. No! No, that was only in the autumn. That same autumn. I thought it would be nice to see it again. Where we'd met; though it was only a few months later. It was very warm, and we went out on the pier, but it was late September really. I remember I'd taken my fur coat, and then it was so warm.... But is it really only two years, then? It can't be only two years. I suppose it is. Just about this same spot, two years ago, I thought of going. And then it just happened.

I wish I didn't think so much about him. I ought to have more proper pride. I don't know what's happened to me. I suppose that's gone like everything else.

I wonder what would happen if he came along now.

Nothing, most likely.

Well, it's time I was getting back.

I wonder how I can let myself feel like this about him, when it's so obvious he feels nothing at all. And never did.

But I don't know about that.

Crunch of gravel, and the path stretching ahead, straight and empty between the neat grass edges, to a distant gate.

But he must have felt something. I don't see how he could have said all he did and not meant any of it. That first time in Brighton....

Well, I don't care. I'm not going to think about him.

But he must have. I don't see why, if he had no feelings at all.... I don't see why he should have taken the trouble.

Narrow tape of path drawn back from under the feet and the gate growing larger and the shriek of a horn and a high-powered car whizzing past.

Heat and hurry.

There's no reason whatever why he should have.

Persistent crunch of gravel and the open gateway and screech of traffic and hurrying pavements.

I don't care. I'd do the same again. Yes, I would!

I tell you I would. I don't care. Yes I would.

I would, I tell you. I would.

Twisting, rumpled sheet.

Yes I would. I don't care. I would.

I don't care.

I don't care, I won't go down to dinner to-night.

Sizzle of gas-fire and friendly warmth of chair-arm.

I really don't think I will. There are quite a number of little jobs to do up here, and it doesn't seem worthwhile. It's so cold, down in the dining-room. White-clothed tables sprinkled over the room, each with its centre vase and three asters, one pink, one white, one mauve; the swift, surprised glance of the waitress, and the manageress in her blue dress waiting in the doorway for the girl to pass out with her tray, and a whispered remark. Mrs. Caruthers bending, in kindly enquiry, from her table in the corner by the fire-place: I wondered what had happened to you last night. She knows I never go out now. I suppose they all know it. They must have noticed. Mrs. Caruthers' white hair and cameo brooch, and the lamb and mint-sauce, and the new arrivals at the middle table glancing round. I don't want any dinner; it's nothing but a waste of time to sit in that room and watch people eat. I've got plenty up here for what I want. I don't see why I shouldn't get myself a little saucepan and be able to warm things up for myself. They make up such a fire, down in the dining-room, it gives me a headache. Sooner stay up here in peace.

Peace. Peace and the safe dark. A little room, safe and dark, and Phil. They won't come, will they?

Voices. People outside. But they can't come.

Voices going away, and the long beat of the waves. The long, long beat of quiet waters.

Voices. Walls opening out, falling back. Phil, Phil, don't let them come. People pressing around and pointing, and Annie in her black dress and white apron with the frills over the shoulders and cap with the floppy strings: Annie saying you didn't ought to do that. People pressing up from behind, staring, crowding up, filling the paths. People seeing, crowding up to see into the shop: the horribly light shop, and Harold, and the shiny counter: in the shop, with Harold.

And Annie — no, Phil — walking away. Phil walking away delicately, very straight and slim and walking on his toes: Phil walking away because it's nasty.

I don't see why. I don't see why.

What do I mean.

I don't see why I should bother about him. If he chooses to go he can go, can't he? Well, he's gone. Well, I'm not going to bother about him, he needn't think I am.

A lot he thinks about it.

Well, he needn't think it. Look here, I'm going to look at these hats. I'm not going to think about him anymore. I'm going to think about something quite different. That's a sweet little hat: that little black one with the stiff bow. Why, that would just suit me, wouldn't it? Just my hat.

No, it wouldn't suit *you*.

'Excuse *me*. Oh, *thank* you.'

A nice figure of fun *you'd* look in it, so you needn't push like that. Standing so close. Pah! Disgusting. How can people *like* to push up against other people? Pigs. Gross. No fastidiousness.

Now I'll tell you what it is, why shouldn't I get a hat? No reason, just because I'm not going out with him.... Serve him right. I wonder how much that one is. Yes I will, and I don't see why I should stint myself. Done that long enough. Besides, I needn't get it: no harm in trying it on.

'Upstairs? Paris models upstairs? Oh yes.'

That'll teach him, won't it! What a pity he can't see me. I wish I could just pass him somewhere in that hat and not take any notice. I would! Yes I *would*.

What's *she* staring at.

Ah, that's done it, has it. Sent you off in a hurry. The next one who stares at me I won't only stare back: I'll put my finger to my nose! I wonder what people think they are, staring at one like that.

'The little black hat in the window. With the stiff bow.'

Well, and if I have taken my hat off, what of it? Nothing to stare at in that, is there? Yes, I expect you *had* better try the next stand. Your hair won't be so good as mine when you're as old as I am, I can tell you. The same with all you young things, with all this bobbing. I could sit on my hair, when I was your age.

'Yes, that's the one.

There, I knew it would suit me. Just my style.'

How Philip would have loved me in this hat! I can just see....

What a waste. You'd have liked it Phil, wouldn't you?

Well, it's no good thinking; he's gone. Well, I may as well have the hat.

'This is a model, Madam. Just in. Four guineas.'

'Oh, that's rather a lot.'

'If Madam would care to look at others? Inexpensively priced little models?'

I may as well have it. Why shouldn't I. I've got nobody to think of but myself, now.

'No, I'll have this one. I'll wear it: you can send the other. Where did I put my bag?

Oh. Oh, you don't think it's too young for me, do you?'

'Oh *no*, Madam. Not at all too young. It suits you perfectly.'

'Well. Well it *is* nice, certainly.'

It's come to something, when one has to feel grateful to a shop assistant.... When one has to ask for compliments. Not that I care, how old I look. What difference does it make. I wish I were as ugly as sin.

'Oh yes, here's my bag. Four guineas you said.'

'... just fetch your change, Madam.'

It wants to be tilted a bit more, doesn't it? Like that. I need a little more make-up, with the black.

Oh I hate you, Philip! I hate you! I hate you! I wish I could meet you when I was got up so that you'd want to know me, and cut you in front of everybody. I'd like to see the smile freeze off your face. I wish to goodness I could look twenty and have everything perfect and just give you the look you deserve. I wish I could come into a fortune and take a place in Mayfair and let you know I'd got everything you want. And then slam the door in your face. I suppose you might feel that. Just about the kind of thing you'd be capable of feeling.

'Oh. Oh yes.'

'Your change, Madam.'

'Oh yes. Thank you. Good afternoon.'

Mustn't get into a state like this. I feel quite shaky. People will be looking at me if I'm not careful. Well, I look better than when I came upstairs, and a lot of good it'll do me. I wish my knees wouldn't shake so.

A nice girl, that. What are those imbeciles staring for? Well, they can, for all the difference it makes. I've got a better hat than anybody in the street. I suppose it was foolish to spend so much. But what else could I have done with it. I think I'll go home and have a cup of tea in peace.

Not worthwhile taking a 'bus. I hate having people crammed up against me. What are you doing, leaning against my shoulder? What do you mean? Take it? I don't want it. What is it. I said I'd go and make a cup of tea. I won't take it. It isn't worthwhile, taking a 'bus.

What's that you're putting in my mouth, take it away, what are you doing. Tea, I said. Hot, with a bite to it: clears away the fog. I don't want you pushing, putting something cold.... I don't want....

"D-d-don't want your beastly or-orange-juice! I've told you I detest the stuff. Can't you leave me alone? Get me a c-c-cup of tea, if you must do something. Yes, I should like that. Don't be too long, or I shall go to sleep."

I do feel as if I might drop off. And yet my eyes feel stuck open, how is it? It's the fog. Where's that tea, haven't you got it yet? Clears the fog. Think I'll go home and get a cup of tea in peace.

I don't know why people should look at me like that. I suppose they can see I'm not anything. I don't see how they can see I'm not anything. They're all solid and I'm hollow, but they can't see that.

I don't know why I should feel like that. I suppose I've been hollow like that all the time, but he put a kind of artificial life into me. It didn't belong to me. I danced so long as he pulled the strings and when he dropped them I went limp. It must be that: I feel limp. I don't think I can get to the end of this street. Better wait for a 'bus.

'Oh, it's you, Mrs. Caruthers? Fancy meeting you here. Are you waiting for the 'bus? No, I've got some shopping to do, good-bye.'

I don't know why she wants to talk to me: I don't want to talk to her. I suppose she's got her 'bus by now.

Oh there I am. I don't like the kind of shop-window you can see yourself in. It's like meeting a ghost. I look awful. I look hollow, don't I? No wonder people look at me. The eyes look like that: there's nothing in them, you know. It doesn't matter what I look like, he must have got his 'bus by now.

I'm not going to take a 'bus, I don't see why I should. And I don't think I'll go in the park to-day. People stare so. It's so open.

One's less noticeable here, where there are people.

Hurry up and get to the shops. Where there are people. So open here.

Wide, grey road with high, withdrawn buildings on one side, and the open park beyond the railings, and people loitering.

Oh dear, this must be a 'bus stop.

Tap-tap on the pavement, in a flurry, and breath coming quickly.

There, you see. Now what did they turn round for? Nobody could look more ordinary than I do. Oh well, they've nothing else to look at, I suppose.

78

There, that's better. There's nobody now for quite a way, and then the crowd beginning, all at once, by the shops.

Oh. Oh, isn't that...?

Just coming round the corner. There. Coming round the bushes at the edge of the drive.... No, what's the matter with me. Coming round the corner, just before the shops begin.

But it is, isn't it?

Halt; the racing of a hammer, and a swift going on.

I'm not going to turn back. I'm not going to let him see I care.

Oh, well, no, it wouldn't be, would it. He wouldn't come along here. Never did.

I'll just buy that tea and get back to my room. Anything will do. I won't bother to go to the far shop to-day.

There, that's better, now the shops are beginning. If he did come along now, he mightn't notice me.

But he wouldn't come. Never did.

I wonder what I look like, if he did come along.

Awful.

Well I don't care. Why should I.

It would serve you right if I made you stop and speak to me when I'm looking like this. I don't see why I should bother.

I suppose I ought to have bothered more.

Phil, do come back. I'll be more careful, really I will. I suppose I haven't been doing you credit, and that kind of thing. But I will, really Phil, if you'll only come back.

Well, I should just like to see him come back, after this. I just should. I suppose he'd have the impudence. But you needn't think it. No, no, my boy, you needn't imagine.

Oh, there you are, so you haven't gone have you. Come back to see what you've made of me, have you. Oh yes, I remember you all right. It isn't likely I should forget you, is it.

"No. No, it's you, is it. Then w-w-why did you say...."

Wish they wouldn't put these pillows so low. How can they expect one to see. Yes, yes of course, Sonia.

"Th-thought you said you were somebody else."

Doctor? Doctor? Oh, the doctor. What does he want: nothing wrong with me, only, only. What is it: not very. Not very. No, what do I mean. Not very well.

"Not very well to-day. Can't you shut out the sun? Oh, well, you might have thicker binds, blinds then."

They ought to shut you in better; not leave you exposed like this. Not fair, putting you in a shop-window with everybody looking in. Everybody seeing you're an old woman and he doesn't want you.

Oh. It isn't that is it. It isn't that, is it Phil. It isn't, is it?

But it can't be that. I don't see why you should have said, if you meant that. What did you mean. What do I mean: you can't put on all the lights like that.

No, what do I mean. The window.

No, but you can't. Not all the lights like that, in the window. You can't, Phil, you can't.

Lights. The hideously staring, unshaded lights, and space, huge and empty. The huge, dark window with faces pressing: pressing up, rank on rank, white against the glass, and fingers pointing. Dark shoulders jostling up and faces white and staring; pointing fingers white, blunted by the glass.

Phil, I can't, I can't. You can't do this to me, Phil.

Staring and a shout, and a lighted window, very far below. A huge, light shop-window and a little woman in black and they're pointing. The huge, dark crowd pressing up and pointing. It isn't fair, they're safe. Safe out there in the dark.

The dark crowd surging up, far below, and the huge, blank window. She's old, you know, that's why. She's old and he doesn't want her. She's old. And the fingers and the lights.

Oh but it isn't. It isn't that, Phil, is it.

Oh.

No it isn't. Say it isn't.

It's only that you were busy last night. Somebody came in and kept you. It isn't that you didn't want to come, is it. It's only two days, after all.

I know you don't like my ringing up. And I've been good now, haven't I: two whole days without ringing? But I do so wonder what's happened. Would you be very, very cross with your ickle Marcia if she rang up just this once? But anything might have happened, Phil. I must find out, mustn't I? I do so want to know what's happened. I know you're busy, Phil; I don't mean to be impatient.

'Two nine double O. Yes, that's it. Two nine double O. Are you there? Yes, I want to speak....

What! I can't hear you.

What!'

Phil, what is it? Phil, come. You must come. What? What was it?

'What? Impossible. Why, I saw him only two days ago.

Gone abroad? But it's impossible. It isn't possible. You must be making a mistake.

Oh. Oh, very well. Oh, I suppose it is, then. Oh, thank you.'

Gone? But he can't have gone. Impossible. But he can't have. But it isn't possible. But how can he have gone without saying anything. It's impossible. It's a mistake. They thought it was somebody else. They'd written it down wrong. Impossible. He can't have. Why should he. He wouldn't have gone without saying good-bye to me.

Then he has. Then it's come.

Phil! But you didn't mean that, did you? To go without letting me know. Slipping away so that I couldn't say anything. Make a scene or anything. You hate scenes, don't you Phil. You thought I shouldn't understand. You thought I shouldn't see. You just wanted to go away for a few days without any fuss. That's ail, isn't it. Just for a holiday. It doesn't mean anything else. And you thought I mightn't see: I might have thought you were trying to leave me, or something silly like that. That's all, isn't it. But you might have trusted me, Phil. You might have known I shouldn't make a fuss. We've always been so much to one another, haven't we. You didn't want to upset me. You knew how I should miss you, even for a few days, and you thought it would seem shorter like this: you thought you'd be back before I discovered you'd gone. That's all, isn't it. It isn't anything else. You're always so sweet to me, Phil. I oughtn't to grumble, ought I.

So it's come. So its like this.

I oughtn't to cry like this, it's silly of me. I do look a fright, don't I. If he came in just now it would serve me right, wouldn't it? I used to have a bottle of astringent, somewhere.

I didn't think it would be like this.

There, if I pat that in and leave it to dry.

Well, I suppose it might have been worse.

Well, you do look a fright, don't you? Funny, I haven't cried like this for years. I don't know when. Certainly not when Harold went. But then.

But you haven't, have you Phil. Not really.

And my eyes didn't swell up like this when I was a girl. Not so red and puffy. Puffy-feeling under the fingers. Cream might be better: this astringent only draws the skin. That's it: a gentle, circular motion. The idea is to make the mind a blank. Then the wrinkles go. I oughtn't to neglect my face like this. Smooth, slippery semi-circles. My hair's all right, but I haven't bothered enough about the skin. Round to the corner and back. Round to the corner and back. If he came in just now I should have to rub it off in a hurry, shouldn't I. Have the towel ready on my knee. If he came in just this minute.... Mustn't think. Round and back. Round and back. There's quite a lot in this jar. I ought to use it every morning till the jar's finished. That would make a difference. It's stupid to let myself go like this. No wonder Phil couldn't stand it.

Crash.

Oh! I didn't mean to break it.

Phil, Phil, but it isn't! It isn't that, is it? It isn't. Say it isn't.

Oh, I can't sit here any longer. I can't stand it.

Phil!

Well, opening the window won't make him come. You don't suppose he's coming in that way, do you?

You don't suppose he's coming at all, do you.

Oh, oh. Oh, I am a fool. There, now that's all wet again. Now it'll be just as bad as before. Now suppose he comes in.

Well, he won't. Don't be such a fool. You don't imagine he's coming back here anymore. He's done with you, you old fool: patting your face and pretending it looks twenty years younger than it does. You don't suppose somebody like Phil is going to put up with it, when he might have anybody he wanted.

But I don't, I don't. Phil, I don't, do I? I don't look old enough to be your mother? You always said I looked half my age. You did mean it, didn't you Phil? You weren't pretending, were you? But why should you pretend? I don't see why you should: I never asked you to.

Oh what a mess. Now all the cream's in the carpet. Leave it alone, it doesn't matter. What's the good of walking about, it won't do any good. It won't make him come, he isn't coming. He's done with you, and no wonder.

But you haven't, Phil, you haven't. Oh Phil, you are coming aren't you.

What a noise the springs make. Somebody will hear. I don't care. I can't keep on walking about. It won't do any good. It won't make him come. It doesn't matter whether anybody hears or not.

I don't care, you must come, you must come, you must come. Phil you've got to come, I want you.

Well he doesn't want *you*. So you may as well sit up and not make an old fool of yourself.

"There, we're more comfortable now, aren't we?"

Sheet smooth under the arms; cool slope of the pillow and clean, white walls.

But how could I have behaved like that, that's what I can't understand. But I'd never been that kind of woman. And for so long.

How long would it have gone on, I wonder.

No wonder Phil went.

But how could I. No wonder.

Walls closing in around. Dark, close walls and big furniture, close and dim. Fire-light on a rounded brass drawer-knob and the quiet, patterned chintz curtains, and the big easy-chair.

If I put the light on I might read.

And the clock ticking.

What's the use.

What's the use, Phil. It's no use thinking. What's the use.

Phil, how could I? How could you? How could you let me? Why didn't you stop me. How you must despise me.

Dark and small and safe: a quiet, dark room. Glint of light on the glass stopper of a bottle and orange light on the carpet; chair a dark island in the splash of light.

Safe. Nobody to see.

Oh my goodness, Phil, how could you. In shops and places. The way we used to go around, and people must have known.

Lights and a counter and staring, bored eyes. Taking us for granted. Yes, but I'm not. Can't you see? I'm not like that. Horrible eyes, taking it for granted; 'buses flashing past the shop-door and Phil's fingers stroking the silk on the counter: 'Quite, quite beautiful.'

But they must have known. I was old enough to be his mother. What must they have thought.

Small, safe, enfolding walls. Light fading from the drawer-knob, the chest falling back into the dark wall; circle of orange light dim and shrinking on the dark floor. — The shilling in the meter must be running out. And the smooth warmth of the sheets.

Small and dark and safe. Shut away. It's all right so long as I stay up here, in my own room.

How could you, Phil. But you needn't have come everywhere with me, like that. You didn't spare me, did you Phil. What must people have thought about us. About me. But I'm not. I wasn't like that really.

Well, you've gone now, haven't you. So I oughtn't to complain.

But I don't mean that. Come back. It doesn't matter, what they think. Really it doesn't, Phil. — Space opening out and fingers pointing. — But I don't care! I don't! I don't care what they think. But now they think you couldn't put up with me any longer. Well, it's true, isn't it. Phil, it isn't true, is it?

Faint, fading glimmer on the rug, and the close, quiet darkness.

Phil, don't let them come. They can't come here, can they.

But you don't care.

Darkness, closed in. Safe and quiet. Gently swaying darkness and quiet warmth.

But I don't care. They can't come. They can't see.

It's the white walls, they can't help it. The blinds are down, but they're yellow. That's the sun. Yellow with sunshine: square suns, burning, crackling. No, that's the fire. Why did they light the fire. So hot. It's so hot. Too many clothes, and the sun's burning.

Oh, it's you. Oh yes, I know.

"You, Sonia, w-w-wanted to ask you something."

I said: want to ask you something. Can't you answer? Don't say Yes Aunt Millicent; so irritating. And there's no need to whisper. Listen to what I've got, got to say. Wanted to ask you something. What was it. Wanted to ask you. It's so hot.

That's better, but there was something. Something I wanted to ask.

Well, if you can't stay to listen I can't help it. Can't keep on re-re-reaping. Only wanted to know. Reaping. Reap, reap, repeating. Can't keep on repeating, only wanted to know. Phil, I think you might have told me. I only wanted to know. I think you might have told me. I only wanted. It wasn't that, was it, Phil. I only wanted to know. Of course, it wasn't. You haven't gone, have you, or you wouldn't be here.

Small, dark, safe room, and Phil.

Let's not think of anything bothering to-night, now you're here. There isn't anything bothering, is there? Not now.

'Great, big bothers!'

Oh Phil.

Steel fender and small, crackling fire and the curved, low back of the white wicker-chair.

No, that was when he said, wasn't it. No, that was it: great big bothers. When he was standing up tall by the fire, and I was sitting on the divan.

Phil's smile, and the glass dome of the clock behind his head.

'Oh Phil, I love the way you say it. Big Bothers, with great big B's, as if they were big and bumpy and full of feathers!'

'Big, bumpy bothers for baby Marcia!'

That was it! And then he came over, by me, and I looked up; and then he sat, in that quiet way he had.

'Phil, you do spoil me. No, stay there. Like that. Don't move, I want to rest my head. Your shoulder's so safe, Phil.'

'Why, what's the matter, little one? Not anything really?'

Call me that again, Phil.

'Nothing, now. Don't stop. I like it when you stroke my hand, gently like that. No, nothing: nothing at all.'

'Such a little hand. Little Marcia.'

Just like that.

And I don't know why I had to go on talking about it.

'It's nothing, really. Only some silly bills, but they don't matter. I've been forgetting I'm not a rich woman, that's all. But nothing matters now. Now that you've come.'

And his poor face so funny and sad.

'Why, Phil dear, it's nothing! We're not in the workhouse! Silly boy, it's nothing to be upset about! It only means cutting out one or two little things, just for the present. There are one or two little things I should have liked to do, which will have to wait, and that made me a tiny bit sad, just for a minute. But it was silly. Because those things don't matter, do they? Not when we're Us? When we're together?'

'Isn't little Marcia a funny little thing?'

'What is it, Phil? You're not moving away? Oh, how dreadful of me: I forgot your cigarette. There, where did I put the box? Up there, dear, on the mantelpiece.'

And that was when he got up, wasn't it? When I said that? No, it was just before. When I said 'we're together'; and that was why I said…. And he had the far-away I smile. Oh Phil, I do love your far-away smile. It gives me such a queer, sad feeling inside. And then he reached out for the box. Blue lacquer box, and Phil's slim, white hand lifting the cover. And that was when I remembered I hadn't given him his cigarette. And then he said….

'But you don't sound quite yourself, Phil darling. You aren't ill, are you? Tired, that's it. There, let me stroke the tiredness away. Right away.

There now. Now Phil isn't tired anymore. Now we'llgo out, shall we, and dine somewhere? You'd like that, wouldn't you? Better than staying here? Now be a good boy while Marcia changes.'

'Is little Marcia going to wear her best lace pinny?'

'Phil likes that, doesn't he? Oh dear, that's one of the things that will have to wait: a new frock for when we dine out. But Phil doesn't mind, does he? He likes his Marcia in the lace?'

'He adores his Marcia in the lace!'

And that was when he came over, while I was standing by the mirror....

'Oh Phil, how can I get dressed?'

'But suppose we didn't go out, just for to-night? I should so like to stay here.'

'Oh Phil, but I thought you'd enjoy going out. Why?

Oh, you dear boy! But you're not thinking of horrid economies! But that doesn't count: our little outings. We're not going to cut *them* out, you know.'

'But can't we be all by ourselves, just for one evening? Can't Phil have little Marcia in her best pinny all to himself, without horrid, jealous people looking at her and making him cross?'

'Phil, you naughty boy, you don't mean it. You're dreadful, Phil. A dreadful flatterer. Well then, let me powder some more. There now, Marcia's all ready.'

Oh, like that, Phil. Stay like that.

'Is the fire too high? Turn it down just a scrap, it's so hot.'

So hot.

Phil, where are you. Phil.

There, stay like that. Just like that.

'Why can't we stay like this forever and ever? There's not the remotest reason why we should ever move.'

'Not the very slightest!'

'Oh Phil, you do laugh at me, I love it when you laugh like that.'

'Not suppose we hear all about the big bothers.'

'But they aren't anything at all!'

'Funny little thing, Marcia. The way you shake them off with one flick of those little shoulders.'

'I've always done that, Phil. Troubles aren't worth anything more, are they?'

'Not worth a shrug of those little shoulders. All the same, suppose we look at them together and see if they're such great big bothers after all?'

'Oh Phil, aren't you dreadfully serious to-night?'

'Am I?'

Oh yes, smile. Just go on smiling. Just like that. Do, Phil.

'Well, it's time somebody was serious about little Marcia's business. She's such a little scatter-brain, she'd leave herself without a penny in the world. And so recklessly generous. Talking about things like great big cars, when all the time....'

'Oh Phil, no. There's just that one thing. The car: you won't mind dreadfully? I did hope we could manage the new tourer this year, but it does seem as if it would have to wait, doesn't it? Will you mind dreadfully?'

'*Mind*, little Marcia? Why, as if Marcia could be allowed to spend her pennies on such foolish things as cars!'

Pennies, flat and brown and jingling. — Funny boy; your odd little way of putting things.

'I should be very, very cross! She's much too generous as it is: squandering all she's got.'

Dull metal drawer-knob; rubbing, and the shine coming up. I really must give the brass a polish.

'Oh Phil, I do wish I could, about the car. But it does seem just a little bit foolish.'

'Quite, quite foolish. Now we shan't say another word about it. That's quite settled.'

Poor boy, I wonder if I couldn't manage it. But I don't see how: not this winter. Even without getting the fur coat. I mustn't get the coat in any case, or we shall be short for our little outings.

'You're wonderful, Phil. But you do see my point, don't you? We should be so dreadfully cramped. And after all, the Bentley's only two years old. Why, he's a naughty boy, talking about a new car when he's had the other only just over a year! Come to think of it, he doesn't deserve it! There now!

No, let me light that for you. There.'

The match fluttering down into the fender.

'Seriously though, Phil, you do think I'm right, don't you?'

And Phil bending to pick it up. Little stick of match laid neatly in the centre of the ash-tray, and Phil dusting his fingers, flicking the tips together.

'Seriously, Marcia.'

Oh Phil, when you look right into my eyes like that I can't bear it. It seems to mean so much. I wish I could give you every single thing you want. I will: I'll manage it, somehow, about the car. But it shall be a surprise. When you think it's out of the question. I won't spoil this: your giving up. Phil, you're so lovely. Just like a little boy who can't have the toy he wants and is dreadfully unselfish. It's so beautiful, Phil; I can't spoil it. It would be like throwing back something you were giving me.

'Seriously, little Marcia is always, always right.'

Phil. Phil.

Phil, that wasn't really the last time, was it? Not the very last time: that evening we talked about the car?

No, I don't want it. Take it away. —

Why did you, Phil. Why did you make it the last time. But it can't have been that. You were so dear about it.

"I t-t-tell you I don't w-w-want. Don't want to be washed. Take it away. The sun's too bright. Oh, it's the light is it. Put it out then. Too dear: I don't want."

I'll have a shampoo and set. Phil likes my hair when it's freshly done. Don't you, Phil? Yes, a henna shampoo. It's quiet and warm in here. I like the swish of water in the other cubicles. Swish and drip and lap, lap. — I'm glad they don't talk too much. I don't mind voices conversing in the distance. They're not saying anything important. They're saying it's warm for the time of year and have you seen the film this week at the Palace: restful things that don't matter, and their answers don't matter.

It doesn't matter, I tell you, it doesn't matter. I like bending forwards with my hair in the basin and the towel tucked in snugly at the back. I wish the water weren't wet, but I like the swish it makes and it's warm. What I like about it is that while you're leaning forwards with your forehead on a smooth, folded towel to save the make-up, and the back of your neck snugly tucked in and the assistant's hands sliding in and out over your scalp and the water hissing you haven't got to talk. It doesn't matter thinking of something to say, there'll be plenty of time when she's combed it out and made the parting.

Swish and drip and the slap of water up against the side of the basin, and the cloth wrung out. Dull flump of a leg on to the rubber sheet.

Now I don't like that so well. I don't like being put back in the chair and having the towel taken from my knees and the hair rubbed. The hair's all in wet bits: it's coming back into a frizz now, even before she sets it. That's the permanent. I can't see very well, the glass is misty. It doesn't matter. There, I feel quite in a glow with the rubbing. Rubbing and the shine coming up. I ought to say something presently. It doesn't matter until she's made the parting, and if I talk to her while she makes it she'll make it crooked.

'Oh, thank you.'

Well now she's wiped the glass, but I don't particularly want to look at myself. She's a good-looking girl, I wonder why they generally have them good-looking. I wonder how she likes attending all day to middle-aged people like me. Well, when she's done with me I shan't look middle-aged anymore. It's being in these places that

91

makes you feel like that; I never feel anything but young when I'm with Phil, but he's so sweet. I wonder if they're amused to see people come in and go out looking different. Suppose they're so used to it.

'Yes, that's straight, I think.'

After all, plenty of people look worse than I. My hair's my own, after all; it's only touched up a bit.

I ought to say something now. People are talking in the other cubicles. I don't see why one should, it's peaceful saying nothing. It gives you time to think and see where you are. Where, where, where you are. I can't say anything while she's combing, wait till she begins to wave.

'Have you seen the film this week at the Palace Madam?'

'Oh. No. No, I haven't, have you? Do you go to the cinema often? No, I don't often go to the cinema. Yes, I like going to the cinema when I do go, but I don't often go.'

There doesn't seem to be anything more to say about that. She expects me to talk. People do talk to them, you can hear them in the other cubicles. It's so tiring thinking of something to say. I so seldom go to anything, because Phil doesn't care much for going out in the evening: he says he likes it to be Just Us, in my little room. Phil likes my little room, but I can't tell her about that, can I. I wonder what she'd say if I told her about Phil. She'd be surprised, wouldn't she, if she knew who she was making those waves for. Expect she thinks they're for nobody, if she thinks at all. Middle-aged vanity. Well, that's where you're wrong, my girl. You're a pretty girl — pink cheeks and blue eyes. Why do they make them wear those caps? So disfiguring — and you're not more than twenty-five at the most, but you haven't got anybody to do that hair of yours for half so wonderful as Phil.

Rub between the fingers, and the hand dropped. You needn't, I can do it myself. No, what do I mean. I can't set it myself, not well enough for Phil.

Oh, I ought to say something. Shall I say, what did you think of those disturbances in Trafalgar Square the other night? Or, were you in Piccadilly when? But if I said something like that I should have to give an opinion on what happened and the truth is I haven't any opinion, I don't care one way or the other. I wonder why I haven't any political opinions, everyone else seems to have. I never can see that it matters: what I think can't make any difference to the country, and it doesn't interest me. I suppose it ought to interest me, but I never seem to have time nowadays to think about anything. It makes far more difference to me after all whether Phil likes my hair when it's done than it does whether we reduce unemployment or have a communist government. But suppose there was a war, Phil would have to fight. But I wouldn't let him, I'd take him away somewhere. It's the same with most people only they aren't honest about it.

The waves are coming in nicely now. Lap, lap, and the long, flat waves. Phil will have a surprise to-night, I don't often have it done at the beginning of the week. I really must say something, I ought to think it out and then say it when she begins on the other side. But the noise of the dryer's so soothing, and she may not hear what I say so that I shall have to repeat it. I wish I could say things spontaneously like other people without thinking them out beforehand. Like a set-piece: get all the bits together in a pattern ready to be lit up, and then hold tight on to the first remark so as not to forget it. Wish my mouth didn't feel so stuck, know I shall gulp when I try to speak. It's quite a long time since I said anything I suppose.

There, now I've cleared my throat she knows I'm going to say something, she looks inquiring. Suppose I shall have to.

'Do you go into the country at the week-ends?'

It sounds idiotic.

'Not very often.'

'The country's lovely, isn't it.'

Wish my voice didn't sound so toneless. Oh dear, now she's

looking scornful; afraid the set-piece didn't go off. Well I shan't bother anymore, it doesn't matter. Go to another shop next time, I hate having the same girl every week, you don't know what to say to her.

It'll be half-past twelve when I get out of here. I think it's too noble of me to get up like this and have it done in the morning. But I didn't want to waste Phil's afternoon, I thought we might go down to Kew. He likes going out into the country with me and he doesn't much care for town because he has to be in it all the time and the poor boy's so dreadfully busy. And then we'll come back to my room, or we might dine somewhere first, but it's nice in my room. Phil likes my little room, but I can't tell her that, can I.

Push of an arm upwards, into a starched sleeve, and the arm dropped.

I ought to look for a new frock for the evening really. I've had the lace one such a time. But Phil likes it and it all means money, it doesn't really seem worthwhile.

Towels tucked in firmly under the chin, smooth and tight.

What she mean. Don't want the towels again, what you mean. If I get out of here by half-past twelve there'll just be time to get his cigarettes for this afternoon and go back and polish my nails before lunch. Mustn't forget to get. Get the cigarettes and polish my nails. She doesn't look as if she expected me to talk anymore, she must have given it up as a bad job. Wonder how they manage to get their basins so shiny in these places. Shiny: smooth, round shiny leaves, round and smooth and cold and flat and bright green. No, of course not. More than shiny, it's as if they put some sort of transparent polish on top of the china, and rubbed. And the shine coming up. I suppose they do. Mustn't forget to get.

I might go along the High Street and look in the windows, if I saw a frock that suited me and wasn't too dear I might get it. If I let Phil come with me he'd make me spend such a lot, and he won't know the difference.

If she doesn't finish soon I shall go to sleep, it's as much as I can do to keep my eyes open, I'm glad she's given up wanting me to talk. I've got to get those cigarettes and polish my nails before lunch. Mustn't forget.

I don't think I'll bother about the frock there won't be time to-day, I shan't get out of here before half-past twelve.

I mustn't keep my eyes shut or she'll think I'm ill, I look so silly shutting them but it's the warm air. Get cigarettes and polish nails. How do they get so much shine on china, you wouldn't think they could.

I don't see what's wrong with the lace frock I've had it a good time but Phil always liked it. It isn't as if we were going anywhere special it seems a waste just for ourselves.

There's a brush in the corner, that's to sweep up the pieces when they cut your hair. I don't want mine cut, it looks nice like this, I can comb it out and it'll just be right by the time Phil comes. Get cigarettes and do nails, it's the hot air, it's so quiet in here and warm, and warm and peaceful.

It isn't as if we went about a lot as we used to, I don't know why but we haven't been about so much lately, so it doesn't really seem worthwhile, and it's so hot.

Hot. It's so hot.

Don't make it so hot. It must be dry by now. Damp and hot, it's the steam, you ought to turn it off.

Never get dry. So hot. It's all these towels. Take these towels off me, so damp and heavy. Too hot. Take them off me, I can't stand it. Can't get out. So clinging and hot. Too high under my chin. I tell you take these towels away. I tell you it's

"hot."

Take these towels away, it's so

"hot."

I tell you take these

"t-t-towels."

95

Don't talk so much, what's the good of bending over me, take it away, why have you put all the lights on, what's the little light over there, there there can't we sleep, no we can't these towels are so damp and

"hot."

Oh it's you, is it, how did you get here. Can't you do anything. Oh,

"is it night then?"

"No, I c-c-can't, it's so hot."

Cool: cutting a way down. A nasty taste, what is it. It's cool, it's better isn't it, we shall soon get off again, it isn't quite so hot, we might get off this afternoon if you brought the car round, Phil. We might get off for the week-end, somewhere it isn't so hot.

I like it when you drive, Phil. I like it like this. I wish we could go on and on and never go back. I want to stay like this and not think and hardly breathe and not see anything but the road.

White road, unwinding, on and on.

Like a clean scroll we write on and forget because there's more to write. On and on, and your hands on the wheel. I'm glad I got you those gloves, Phil, they look nice don't they. Such fragile-looking hands, Phil, and yet they're so strong. When you drive like this I feel my life is in your hands, quite truly. It's a lovely feeling. I love to watch your hands and think you could send us both to death with one little movement. I don't want you to die, Phil, but I should like to die with you.

Where are we going? Oh, not to Brighton. Let's go somewhere wild where nobody's ever been. There must be some little scrap of sea somewhere that's been left for us. Just for Us. Don't laugh at me, Phil, I mean it. There's something unworthy about a shore that's been trodden by so many people. It has no life of its own: nothing left to give us. Don't you feel that? No, you don't of course. You want to bathe, don't you Phil. It's selfish of me dragging you off into the wilds. But why don't we go down to Cornwall. You could bathe there, and there are patches of coast very few people have walked on. The earth has had time to renew itself, and the sea's dark and wild.

Oh Phil, I did think we should crash that time, didn't you? Turning so suddenly. That was wonderful, Phil. Why do you smile? Do go on smiling.

'Morbid little creature!'

Oh, say it again Phil. Do say it.

'Going round looking for wild, dark shores. Now *I* like a nice, friendly sea that doesn't play tricks with you. What's wrong with Brighton? Wild and savage! Isn't that just like Marcia, now!'

'Oh Phil, you're sweet when you try to be contemptuous! But do turn back, then. Let's go to Brighton after all.'

'No, no. Dark and savage scenery for little Marcia, the morbid little creature!'

'You're sweet, Phil. Let's go down to Cornwall, then. Where I was, years ago. It isn't really savage. Just a friendly little harbour, winding far up into the land. You'll love it, Phil. Unless you walk out over the cliffs you can't see the sea at all: no wildness! Now isn't that just right?'

'Whatever Marcia says is right.'

'Phil, don't laugh at me, you're horrid!

There, don't you love this? Don't you love the little harbour? Isn't it like a river, winding out between its high cliffs? But don't be silly, Phil, of course there's a harbour: over there, on the bend half-way to the sea. No, I know there aren't many boats, but they're out fishing I expect. It's years and years since I was here; not since I was a girl. It makes me feel like a girl to be here again.

Oh Phil, but you know that isn't true.

We'll have to walk down, along the cliffs, to find the sea.

I wish they hadn't put a path here.

Not much of a path, but people walk on it. And oh, Phil there are even seats. I wish they'd left it quite, quite wild, with just the heather. And I wish there were fishermen down in the harbour, the little quay looks so dead and lonely.'

'Contrary little woman!'

'No I'm not. Don't you see? Let me hold your arm: it isn't really *very* much of a path, and I suppose I'm not really so young as I was.

No, but don't you see, the fishermen wouldn't matter. They're not people, in that way. They're themselves. They live here to live, and they don't spoil things even when they throw bait about and it smells. It doesn't matter. They're part of the earth. It's the people who come here just to look who are people. They're not part. They stand outside and look. Like people everywhere: so safe in themselves, looking out at you.

'Oh Phil, you do like this, don't you?'

'Quaint little place. Quaint and little, like Marcia.'

'But you'll love it more, Phil, when we get out to the end. It's so far. I didn't remember it was so far.'

'Oh, look. We'll sit here, shall we? On the rocks. Where nobody can see us. Isn't it tremendous. I've thought of this so often.'

'What, little Marcia?

'All this: the bigness. Wishing we could be here and be in it. Oh, I can't explain: the sea's too big to talk by, the wild, open sea like this. One ought to be quiet and wait.

When I was a girl, Phil — no, listen, give me your hand — I used to come out here all alone, to this very same place on the rocks. We used to come here in the summer, and I used to get away from people whenever I could, just as I do now except for you. It must be something wrong with me, Phil. No, listen. I used to think that this point we're sitting on would soon be cut off, as that one is over there: see that deep gulf cut into the rock, and the island further out. That must have been joined on, once. The headland stretched right out there, and perhaps people like us walked on it and looked at further islands that have gone now altogether into the sea. And thought as we're thinking. Or perhaps there were no people to think, then. Then the sea made a little bay in the side of the cliff, and there was a cleft in the rock. Then the cleft widened into a gulf; and now there's a broad stretch of sea so that nobody can reach that point anymore. It's quite alone: given a little time alone to think in, before it's swallowed up. And this point we're on: there's a neck in it. There was one already, when I was a girl. I used to think that very soon it would be cut through; but I can't see any difference, Phil. There's a difference, of course, but I can't see it. It takes so much longer than that. Perhaps a couple of inches worn away in a lifetime. That's all a lifetime is: we're so small, Phil. Does it frighten you, how small we are? I don't think it frightens me, really. I've never been afraid of being nothing: only of having to be some-thing. A feeling of inadequacy. I suppose I was born inadequate.'

He's bored. I'm boring Phil. I oughtn't to talk so much about myself. I oughtn't to talk about when I was a girl: it makes a gulf. A cleft and then a gulf and then a broad stretch of sea and nobody comes. Odd, to think Phil wasn't born when I used to come here and think. I don't think I thought very much; I felt. I didn't think very much in those days, but perhaps I felt more. Oh no, I didn't. I couldn't have felt more than I feel now. I've never felt half so much as I feel about Phil: never. But I oughtn't to talk about that time. I oughtn't to let him see I'm conscious of my age. Only.... Well, I like him to contradict me. I suppose it's that.

Oh, Phil, I love you when you're thoughtful like that. I haven't often seen you thoughtful. You're so gay, always.

Tremendous: it's tremendous. Wash and suck of the tide. That slow, slow insistence. Forty years: it must be quite forty years. But it hasn't stopped for one moment. And it's made no more differ-ence in those forty years than you could measure with a pin. The terrible, slow patience of it: it's annihilating. It's the insistence and the slowness and the immense force held in. The terrible acceptance of order. When it might rush upon the land: content with an inch in a lifetime. But unrelenting.

Oh, Phil, it's something bigger than we are. Why can't we enter into it. We'd be eternal then, Phil. Can't we be part: not always separate and struggling. It's the being separate, the having to be, which is so terrible. Having to be, and somehow stand: somehow maintain one's place with sufficient courage and yet know it's useless. Such a tiny, disregarded scrap in the pattern. So helpless.

Phil, I wonder what you're thinking, staring out to sea with your head in your hands. Phil, Phil. Can't we draw closer? Can't we be more worthwhile? Can't we be part of it all, you and I? I wonder if you're thinking something like that. If only you'd say something, but you've got to be the first to speak. You're thinking, I won't break it. But I want to be part, Phil. I want to be part of your thoughts, and us to be part of all this: you and I together.

Wash and suck and backward sweep of the tide.

It's tremendous. It's like you, Phil. Strong and strange and unknowable. Phil, you're so splendid.

But I thought it would bring us together, being here. I thought we should be together in a different way. But we're apart. We've never been so far apart.

So slow and steady and unturnable. It's life and the world. No, eternity. Oh, I don't know.

It's nothing but itself.

But why is there such a gulf, Phil? Such an ache?

I don't know. I don't know in the very least what he's thinking. It's strange: although he means so much to me, the whole world, sometimes, I can't realize him, I can't grasp him, he's a shadow.

'I don't like this.'

'Oh Phil, I'm sorry, I thought you were liking it. We'll go back, shall we?'

How is it: you love somebody and you can't realize them? One can't. One becomes part. He's too near to me, that's what it is. When you're close to someone it's like looking at a face on the screen: big and vague.

Huge, light screen and a face looming up. Huge and blurred. The texture of the skin and a crease at the corner of the eye when he smiles.

But I can't see it as a whole. If I could only stand away and look at him it might be different.

'But do you really not like it? But just see how immense it is, something beyond us, something.... It makes you feel terrible. As if you wanted to be more worthwhile, somehow.... Oh, I don't know. It's so tremendous.'

'I call it depressing.'

Oh Phil, I love the way you shake yourself, as if you were shaking something off. I ought to have known you wouldn't like this wild country. You like safe and pleasant things, don't you? Let's go back, my dear, and be together again where everything's safe and pleasant. Let's go back where we can dance and have people around us: little, safe people: people who are secure in themselves. We're together there, in the noise and the music, aren't we?

This music is too big: it's something we mustn't understand. It drives a wedge between us and leaves an ache. I can't reach you. It's as if we'd been washed apart by the sea.

Let's get back into the car. Take the wheel into your hands and make it obey you. There's a big force there, too, but it's chained. It answers your will and becomes part of you. It's like a great beast you've forced to obedience, and you're master.

You're splendid in the car, Phil. All that speed and strength is your will: you hold death in your hand. Go on and on and on and never stop. Go faster and faster, so that the wind rushes by and the whole universe is speed and it obeys you. Go faster and faster and faster until breath stops. Let us die now, now. Crash over the side into this wild valley or suddenly against a stone wall, but let us die. Only let us die. We shall never be closer than now: for the whole of me is in your hand.

Dark box of the crawling taxi, closed in, shut away from the light and noise.

As if we were in a box, you and I, Phil; shut away, safe. We're together, aren't we. Safe together.

Phil's arm, strong, and the smooth cloth. Strong and dark.

Packed away in a dark, safe box, slowly moving. Light in patches; a flash of sequins as knees move. Come closer, Phil. Closer. And light on the plated vase with its nodding paper carnations.

Dark taxis slowly moving past the window, passing and repassing: the glimpse of a shoulder, or a gleam of silk, or nothing. Other people like us, Phil: safe and together. But not quite like us. We're different.

And not one of them could be like you, Phil.

Pressure of hand on knee and tingle of skin at the swift contact. Like electricity. It's like electricity.

Flesh leaping to flesh through the thin, sequinned gauze.

Lights, shop-windows; a jerk and swift onward movement. Lights jolting past and the honk of cars, and dark taxis drawing alongside and passing and falling back. The dong-dong of a bell somewhere, and horns, and lights racing, Late Night Final. Late Night Final-1-1. Final Star-r-r. And Phil's hand, and flesh burning to flesh, and jolt — oh Phil — and the lights of the Circus ahead: red and green and yellow electric signs jigging above the driver's cap, and slowing down, and wait.

Phil, Phil.

Jerk and start and a slow crawling onwards. People jostling on the light pavement, forwards and back and across and on and on, and the glitter of windows cut by jostling heads. People in a dark, rippling ribbon frayed at the edges on to the slimy road, and a honk and a jump back, and a dark, rippling ribbon on and on and the twinkling lights of the advertisements.

What would it be like if there were no people?

People in waves: dark, muttering waves beating up against the light windows. Mutter and boom and crash and the spray thrown out, glittering in the lights; a backward suck and mutter and the grey oncoming wave.

Mutter of waves; lights jigging and twisting, green and yellow and red, high up over the dark waves. Slow, onward movement and the dark taxis passing and repassing, and the glow of flesh in its dark box, and the dark, smooth cloth. Late Night Final-l-l, and crimson letters ablaze on the tide: DEATH OF....

Death of. Late Night Final-1-1; and the jerk and onward leap and the warm leap of flesh against gauze and answering flesh, and searing crimson letters like a scar on the tossed pavements. Late Night Final, Death of... and the yellow and red and green flares astab at the swaying night.

Death of whom? It doesn't matter. It doesn't make any difference.

Death. Isn't it strange: that matters a lot to somebody, and to us it's nothing but a word on a poster. Part of it all.

Hand on hand; pressure; the tingle of fingers intertwined, and a smile in a patch of light thrown back by a passing car.

It's nothing to do with us, is it? Death, and horrid things like that?

Dark, swaying crowd and a beating up of voices; voices in a tide ebbing and flowing: suck and mutter and boom and crash, and the shrill spray flung up and hovering, and the mutter and boom and the flashing spray. Death of. Death. Late Night Final-l-l.

Phil, you'll be there, won't you? When I die, I mean? Because, I suppose, one does, sometime. But we'll be together, won't we?

The suck of bleak waters, and chill, darting lights.

So horrible. Alone. And not knowing. We don't know what it is: nobody's been able to find out. Emptiness, and wandering on and on. A going on and on, always, through space. Phil, you'll come, won't you? I can't go out alone, out there, not knowing.

But it isn't like that, it can't be. I shall never be alone, there'll always be Phil. Nobody can separate us now.

Hands interwoven and the warm clench of fingers. Mine and yours, which is which. It doesn't matter, does it.

Phil, let's always be together. Not only like this; always. Really together. We are really, aren't we?

Groping of hand on hand; desperate clutch, and knuckles straining. Ache of slackening muscles, and the grip retaken. But we are, Phil, we are. Together really, aren't we. The ache of tired muscles relaxed; fingers agrope and a strained, aching grip. But we are. Say we are. Strain and ache of flesh; blind outward strain and drive of the spirit, bruised against flesh. Phil, we are, we are.

'Of course we are.'

'I know. You're so sweet to me, Phil.'

Smooth cloth against the cheek; cheek digging in, and the muscle of a shoulder, and a beat, beat. Strong and still. Beat, beat. We are, aren't we. We are together. Peace, peace; a still, steady beat. Phil, you're so splendid.

Beat, beat, and a strong shoulder. Dark taxis lurching up sideways and passing, and oblique patches of lit window; lights twinkling and jigging, on ahead, coming nearer, and the tide of voices: dark, ragged waves, muffled and booming, and a dark, quiet, beat.

It'll be like that, death. That's all. Just like that.

It won't matter, dying. It'll only be like this. Quiet and safe and being together.

Beat, beat; deep and still; and the cloth of a sleeve smooth under the fingers.

Being near, and never going away anymore.

Stroking, and the firm arm under the smooth cloth, and a dark, steady beat, and peace. Steady onward movement and voices in a far-off muffled roar, and all at once the full glare of lights, red and yellow and green letters — words, but they don't mean anything — shifting and jigging and flickering high up overhead.

The centre of the world. We're alone, at the centre of the world.

The world, radiating outwards from Piccadilly: fields an low-roofed farms quiet under the drifting clouds, and an owl in flight through the moonlight over a black hedge, and angry furnaces and the sky red and sullen, and black hills of slag and people like ants toiling to and fro in swarms beneath the tall chimneys, and valleys with the moon asway on broad waters. The sea, foaming and breaking up against cliffs, eating far into the land and lying at rest in small harbours; fishing-boats putting out into the dark-ness, and dim cottages, waiting, and the lap-lap of waves on the quay. Islands flat and white under the moon, and liners like sleeping cities ploughing the waters, and land, and the dark, sleeping fields of Europe, and rivers in broad ribbons and great cities alight in the darkness, very small, like distant stars. And the great, black steppes and cold wastes of ice, and sea and land and huge, vague forests and the black jungle, and deserts blazing under the sun. And pyramids and tents and temples and white palaces and on and on, and the fortresses of savage tribes and mud huts in clearings, and on and on and on, and swamps and ... and palm-trees and things, and smooth cloth under the fingers, and a firm shoulder and a strong, steady beat. Peace, peace. And the red and green and yellow lights circling and prancing overhead, and the far-off, muttering crowd.

Near. Perfect. Complete.

It'll always be like this, now.

Together.

Death will be like this. I know now. But no people. Just you and I, together. All alone. It will be like that, won't it, Phil. Warm and safe and dark and together, always.

Safe and quiet, and people all shut out.

Don't put the light on, Phil. I like it to be dark.

Dark and quiet and close: the dark tent of the sheets. We're in a tent, Phil. It's as if we were in a tent. Dark and safe and alone, and all the people shut out: shut away outside, on the blazing sand. And the light hurts so, Phil, but it can't reach us in here. All the light shut out, and the people.

People: what would they think of me.

Safe, dark tent, and quietness, and quiet breathing.

Phil's asleep. Stillness and warmth and a heart beating: warm and strong and safe and quiet. Strong. Phil's so strong.

What would they think?

Nothing. They don't matter. They're shut out.

Beat of a heart under the fingers; sigh of relaxed limbs, and soft, yielding warmth.

But I wish you weren't asleep, Phil. Why are you asleep. There's something … Something I wanted to say. Something. Can't we be together? Can't we be together really?

But why don't you come. Why don't you. Why don't you come.

Sheet tangled and strangling, and light rushing down.

Where are you. Why don't you.

And a clutch at the heart.

What is it? What woke me? I was asleep, wasn't I?

There isn't anything. No, I don't think I was. I don't know.

The white, light room; electric bulb bobbing in the mirror of the white dressing-table, and a round, white, empty chair, and the fire burning quietly in the grate.

But you aren't. Why aren't you. Why don't you come.

But he hasn't come. Why don't you come.

An hour and a half. I needn't get ready yet. He won't be here before the half-hour, he never is. Now where did I put that nail varnish I got yesterday.

Where on earth did I put it. I'm sure I put it here, I always do. Now who can have had…? That girl. She's been poking round again. I did get it, didn't I? Yes, I know I did. Yes, of course, when I was coming back. That shop by the 'bus stop. Counter piled up, dentifrice, smell of soap. 'I want a packet.' White coated assistant. Vacant eyes. 'No, rose-colour.' A 'bus rattling past the door. Of course I did, and then I remember throwing away the empty bottle and putting it.... Small, rectangular, white-coated packet sealed with red wax, and a bunch of keys. No, of course, I left it in my bag.

Oh well, I needn't do my nails yet. There's plenty of time. I've a good mind to have some tea before I dress.

Bright brass tap turning. Gurgle of water; kettle atilt in the white enamelled basin. Pop of the gas-ring.

I don't know how it is, I've felt so fagged the last day or so.

Better get my frock out; which shall I wear? Phil likes the brocade, but I've had it such a time, he's seen it so often lately. The new lace. May as well. No point in keeping it. Now where did I put the slip that goes with it.

I'll tell you what: if I put that cream on my face now it could stay on while I have tea.

There. Must allow plenty of time to take it off. Oh well, there's plenty of time. I do hate to look fagged for Phil. Oh dear, what a rush everything is, nowadays.

That's better.

Hot, sliding sip of strong tea.

That's quite cheering.

Now rest a bit. No point in getting in a flurry. Time for two cups, and then get on. Give the cream time to work. There's plenty of time. He's sure to be a bit late, only I must be ready.

An hour and ten minutes. Quarter of an hour for nails and twenty minutes for face. That leaves plenty of time.

Click of cup in saucer and a brisk getting-up.

Now, let's get on.

Now if I do my face first it won't be fresh, only suppose he came and found me like this.

Oh well, there's an hour yet, and he's sure to be a bit late.

Better change first. Now where's that chemise I washed out last night. The pink one. Oh yes.

Soft, sliding silk.

Face next. Twenty-to. I'd better not do it before six. Oh, well, that'll be a rush. Do it now; can always powder again. Mustn't put frock on first, it'll mess it. Better have the light.

Kneading fingers; cream smeared in circles, up and across and round the eyes.

Now towel.

Wiping, and the dull, faintly lined skin.

The lines really don't show.

Now where did I put the rouge.

Only ten-to, that's good. Then there's only frock and hair. Find frock first. Sure to mess hair putting the frock on. Now if I left my nails till the end: they aren't very bad. But there'll be plenty of time.

And now powder.

There, now there's only put on frock and do hair. That won't take a minute.

Chair scraping back.

Why, I never drew the blind. Not like me to forget it.

Broad, grey ribbon of Bayswater Road with its high, following string of lights: yellow beads threaded on the darkness, winding, smaller and smaller, away into distance. Lit, lumbering 'buses and the swish past of a car and the shadowy park beyond the railings.

Wouldn't it be funny if I saw him coming now. And he might see me! Well, I've done my face, that's one thing.

A single, loitering figure on the opposite pavement, alone with the railings, drawing near to the lamp.

There, isn't that!

No, of course not. Besides, he'd come in the car.

Dark figures hurrying past and a crawling taxi.

Oh well, perhaps I'm rather obvious here, with the light on.

Well, they don't know who I am.

Pink, frail silk and powdered chest, smooth to the chin.

It wouldn't matter if the whole of London was out there, not one of them could get up here, except Phil!

I wish he'd come. Why doesn't he come? Oh, I wish he would: now that I'm ready.

I must look nice from down there!

I wish he'd come along and see me like this, at the window. Phil, Phil, do come along.

Dark, loitering figure and a cap tilted back; blurred white face uplifted under the lamp.

Well really!

Click of the blind, sharply drawn down.

Why, I believe I'm a shameless woman, Phil! You've made me that, I believe!

Why is it. Why. I wish I knew why. I wish I knew.

What is it. Why you said. That time you said. You didn't mean that, did you, Phil? Why did you say? That time you said I was always right.

Quiet, meditative smile. 'Little Marcia: always, always right.' And the faint, faint stroking of a shoulder.

Phil, just once. Just for a minute. It wouldn't hurt you, Phil, just for a minute. Just once.

But you didn't think I meant, did you? You didn't mean I thought. You didn't think when I said that that I meant. That wasn't why, was it? But when you said. But why did you say? But it wasn't that, was it, you didn't think....

"Oh, w-w-what is it?"

What do you want. Why can't you leave me alone. Just when I was thinking out; when I'd just thought out.

High, starched cap and collar bending, cut grey out of the yellow blind; a stiff, white garment efficiently shaken out and the sheet turned back.

Clean nightdress? What do you think I want that for What do you think it matters. Go away. Don't worry me. A lot of difference it makes, nowadays. A lot of diff.

Mustn't say that. Would shock her.

And a good thing too. A good, a good thing. Take some of the starch out.

"Oh, very well."

It doesn't matter. You tire me.

Crackling of a starched sleeve and dull flump of an arm on to the firm bed.

Funny how easily I was shocked myself, once. Remember when we used to go....

Phil always would come with me to buy things, and it was dreadful sometimes. Though it's wonderful how quickly you get used to things. But it was dreadful at first.

'No, really, Phil, you mustn't. Now you just wait outside and be a good boy. Why, it's downright indecent!

No, of course I didn't mean it. As if I would. Poor boy, you didn't think I meant it, did you?'

Oh dear, I must try not to be old-fashioned. It's dreadful having these feelings, and Phil doesn't seem to expect it at all. I suppose nowadays.... But Harold would never have dreamt.... Oh dear, I should hate him to think me old-fashioned.

Red 'buses lumbering, jolting past; people hustling and jostling, and the shop-door.

And we were in the way. People began to look at us, and Phil said....

It was that time, you know.... I believe it was the first time we went shopping.

'But I don't like to, really Phil. It looks so peculiar.'

Padded swing of the door; noises of the street sharply cut, shut out, and a soft, menacing silence. The warm, carpeted shop with its high display stands: embroidered, silken chemises and nightdresses and knickers. Oh dear, what am I going to do. And the counter, highly polished, across the carpet, and the assistant waiting, and polished nails.

Oh dear, this is dreadful. I can feel myself blushing. Ridiculous to blush, at my age. Well, that shows I'm not so old, after all!

Soft silk slipping between the fingers. Phil's white fingers and the shining silk, and Phil rejecting a design, gliding over the carpet, treading delicately, on tiptoe.

Why? Oh dear, is he embarrassed too? Oh no, it isn't that at all. I suppose he always walks like that, really, only I hadn't noticed it. Silk slipping from the metal stand, and Phil's white fingers caressing the fine embroidery. 'Beautiful. Quite, quite beautiful.'

But what will she think? What will the assistant think?

Broad, shining counter, and a figure, waiting.

I simply daren't look at her.

Oh, she's taking it quite for granted. Of course, she thinks.... Oh course, they must often see...

Oh, of course, she thinks I'm Phil's mistress.

Oh dear, I mustn't blush. That makes it worse. Oh dear.

Well, but. But you see. Yes, that's to say, I suppose I am. If you look at it like that. That is....

Oh but how dreadful, to think she knows. Oh Phil, how could you. What must she think. We're horribly obvious. But of course they take it quite for granted, that kind of thing. Yes, but to have her knowing.

Quiet, heated shop. Phil's fingers fondling the embroidery, and Phil's smooth head bent to the smooth silk.

Oh Phil, how could you do this to me.

Rush of blood to the skin, and the world opening out and pointing.

111

How dreadful.

The warm, hushed shop, and Phil, and the assistant: knowing. Knowing all about Us.

Well, I don't care. I'm glad. Yes I am. I don't care if people do know. I don't care if she does know I'm Phil's mistress. If that's what they call it. I don't care. I don't care if they all know. I am. I'm Phil's mistress, that's what I am. Phil's mistress. So there. I'm Phil's mistress, and I want the whole world to know it.

Phil, stroking, tenderly, the soft silk.

He doesn't care. He's cruel. He doesn't care.

Phil's head, sleek, intent.

He's cruel. He's brutal. I love him.

Phil, I want them all to know. I do. I want them all to know I'm your mistress.

Walls torn away: space agape, shelterless, and fingers pointing. Flesh seared by pointing fingers. Hot, shameful rush of blood and pulse racing and the brand scorched in. Phil's mistress. I'm Phil's mistress. More and more: burning and branded and bruised, and the sweet, choking flood of shame. I want it. I want it. I want to go out in the street. I want to stand naked in the street, I want to be stoned, I want to be called whore and spat on and flung in the gutter, for you, Phil, for you. Phil, Phil, Phil.

'Quite, quite beautiful. You must certainly take this set, my dear Marcia.'

Hot, hot. Hot and tossing. Sheet and pillow tossing; the drag of an arm, up and up, dead weight, and flump on to the other side. Burning; head burning. Hot and turn and drag and the dull flump. Burning the face; it's burning.

Burning: it's burning the sea. The sea shivering in the sun; great streams of dark leaves rushing down, leaf and blossom in a tangle, to the white sea. Burning, it's burning. It's their fingers burning. The sea falling back and fingers pointing: fingers in a tangle, pointing, and seared flesh. Seared flesh of the sea, and fingers like flames leaping up: leaping and burning, up and up. Flames all around leaping and pointing: like fire: it's hell-fire. Leaping, and the huge flames pointing; turning and twisting, and the pointing flames.

Cool.

The sea. They've brought the sea.

Cool.

And the flames burning, and the cool, lapping sea. And the flames dying down; the fire dying down, shrinking away. It can't get out, it's only the fire. Only the fire. High, black bars of the nursery fender: it can't get out it's only the fire; it isn't hell really it's only the fire. Little popping flames in the black grate, yellow and red: spurs of red and the black coals. It can't get out it's in its place. Dying away. It isn't hell, it's fire in its place. Red and black, dancing, and the flickering yellow flames. It can't get out it's in its place. And the dancing yellow flames.

Oh dear, but I shall never dare to dance in a place like this. Whatever possessed me to come to a place like this.

Lights and the glitter and rattle of jazz; red and black zig-zagging walls and the slippery, horribly empty floor.

Phil must be mad. I can't dance well enough. We haven't practised enough.

'Do wait till more people come. I can't. It's so open, and people will stare.'

People pointing, and the red and black flames lapping the walls. Rattle and crash and zig-zags. Noise. Chair held back and the little, safe table and a sigh.

'Oh Phil, this is dreadful. I don't know how I dared to come to a place like this.'

But I mustn't spoil it for him. Poor boy, he chose it for me, he thought I should like it. Oh well, I expect it'll be better presently.

Pop of a cork; gay, bubbling liquid, and a warmth.

Oh yes, it'll be all right.

Whatever would they say, now, the people in the hotel? If they could see me in a place like this, drinking champagne? I wouldn't have believed it myself!

Gay, bubbling zig-zags of sound, and Phil's half smile, and Phil getting up.

'Oh yes, let's dance. I couldn't with anyone else, but I can always dance with you, Phil.'

Floor gliding along, light and sliding underfoot; Phil's arm, and the crash of music a long way off.

Oh look, there we are. Isn't Phil wonderful. He's a wonderful dancer. I should never dare to dance if it weren't for him.

Gliding floor and rattle and bang and the swish of skirts; little tables gliding by and big, glittering space, but it doesn't matter.

I could go on and on forever.

There we are. Isn't Phil wonderful. However did I dare to wear a dress like this; I've never worn anything right down at the back before, but Phil liked it. Why shouldn't I, it looks nice. After all, you can only be young once.

Gliding floor and rattle and bang and smooth, gliding zig-zags through a golden haze, and Phil's arm and Phil's shoulder.

I never dreamt you could be so happy as this.

Gliding and sound through a haze, and Phil's shoulder, and golden mist against closed eyelids, and warmth and sound and the swish of skirts, and gliding and Phil.

'Happy, little woman?'

'So happy. It almost frightens me, sometimes.'

Gliding and Phil. And Phil and the smooth, smooth glide, and the yellow mist, and the pop and crackle of jazz very far off. They're going away. Why are they going away. Yellow light in a square; solid, white walls and the pop and crackle of fire in the grate. Oh no, it's here I don't want to be here. Why am I here.

Oh no, I was gliding, I'm gliding. Rattle and pop and the mist, that was it. If I close my eyes it's a mist. Gliding and gliding, no it's gone. Gliding and gliding. If I shut my eyes. Gliding and pop, and pop and rattle, and the floor swishing round, I'm not going to look. Gliding and gliding and Phil. Phil, Phil, so happy, so happy Phil. And the gliding and Phil, gliding and Phil, and the pop, pop, gliding and Phil. And the gliding and Phil and the gliding and gliding and glide.

'Phil, you mustn't make me laugh so much! What will people think? Oh, look, shall we go on the pier? I love piers, they make me feel so girlish and giggly. It's the springy feeling of the floor, and the slot-machines. Let's try all the slot-machines we come to. Isn't this fun, being here. I feel as if we'd run away on holiday. So we have, haven't we!

Phil, you're dreadful! You make me feel like a shop-girl on the spree. I love it, Phil! Is my hat straight, naughty boy? What must people think of me? But they're all too busy with one another. That's what's lovely about a place like this: they're all feeling silly, and nobody thinks you queer because you're happy. Let's be Of the People, Phil.

Do you think I'm silly?

You are sweet, Phil. It's lovely to be young and foolish: I've been sober for so long.'

'Poor little woman.'

Oh, you're sweet. Go on looking at me like that. 'But that's all changed now. Perfectly different. Since I met you.'

'Quaint little woman.'

Oh, smile like that again, Phil. Do smile again like that.

'Perfectly, perfectly different. You forget, I was a sober woman, Phil, and you've made me go stark mad on Brighton pier!'

And a smile. 'On Brighton pier: Lady Chesborough and friend.'

'Oh, don't call me that, Phil. I wish you wouldn't.'

Why does he say it? So often.

'She shall be obeyed,' — and a mock bow.

Well, it really doesn't matter, but I wish he wouldn't. Why does he.

'Another glass for Lady Chesborough.'

So unnecessary.

Miles of white, glittering table-cloths and glass and silver and pink walls, and lights and carnations in a pink cloud. The bustle of service and rumble of a hundred low-voiced conversations. Pop of a cork, across the room.

'No, I don't want champagne, Phil. I don't care for it. I never did.'

A woman in a backless dress at the next table; a cloud of gypsophila[5] blowing out in an over-bright green mist along the cloth; pink carnations, and the cloth smooth as glass, and the ranked glasses, and music, and the couple at the next table getting up to dance. The woman's broad bare back with a bar of black coat-sleeve across it. Disgusting.

'No, I'd rather not, really Phil.'

What a dreadful place. Whatever possessed me to come to a place like this.

Phil likes it, though.

But how can he.

Phil's quick smile above the gypsophila and the cool, pink carnations. His quick turn to the waiter; a consultation. Phil's head, with the dark, smoothed-back hair, bent to the menu. Immaculate. Phil's always immaculate. Of course one has to be, in these places.

'Lady Chesborough would like....'

Oh, I wish he wouldn't. It's so unnecessary. And there might be somebody here who'd know me, you never know. Not that it would matter, but still....

---

5   A flower: baby's breath.

'... for Lady Chesborough.'

Oh. Oh, he likes the sound of the title. Is that it? No, it can't be. How dreadful.

No, of course not.

The waiter moving off in suave haste between the glittering tables.

'Phil, I wish you wouldn't use my name so often.'

But why? I can't say, because somebody might hear. It oughtn't to matter. It doesn't matter, of course. Besides, it isn't quite that.

'I don't know why. It's just that I don't like it, from you.'

The florid moulding of a fork prodding at the white, immaculate cloth.

'It's just that there's too much of Harold about it, I think. Just that I don't want to think of Harold. Having been, before. Before Us.'

It must be that.

'Before Us? Naughty Harold!'

The brocade wrap flung across a pushed-back chair at the next table; the pop of a cork, somewhere; Phil's white fingers crumbling bread among the green, straying tendrils. What would Harold have said? And a lizard-swift dart of the thought, back into a dim, forgotten crevice.

Phil's smile; white fingers straying through the tendrils, and a meeting of finger-tips in the green shade.

Oh, suppose somebody saw.

But it's only his way. He's so sweet.

'Phil, you're so sweet. Let's go right out to the end of the pier.

Oh, look, do let's have our fortunes told. Don't you love that big chart of the hand? Let me look at yours. That's the heart line; now let me see yours, Phil. Oh no, do let me see.'

'Isn't it a persistent little woman? Dreadful place, this: regular dark and ghostly. Witch's den. Oo!'

'Let's go in together, Phil. I'd love to hear what she tells you. But it doesn't *matter*, not believing in it, silly boy! Do come.

Oh, don't be a great big, dreadful bully, do lets go in. I'd love to see if she gets it all right about Us.

But it doesn't *matter*, Phil. She doesn't know us. Well, perhaps you're right.

Well, I expect you *were* right. It's nicer to have tea out here in the air than sit in a dark, mysterious den as you call it! But I'm going sometime, I am really.

Oh Phil, look, it's lovely out here. How blue the sea is, and such miles of it to the shore. Isn't it queer to think it was only just over there across the water that we met for the first time. I can see the roof of the lounge from here, can you? That glass place at the side of the hotel. And I do so hate big hotels like that too, as a rule! Isn't it strange we should both have just happened to be there. It must have been fate. We were fated to meet, you know.'

'Of course we were!'

Oh Phil, so you did know it too.

'I'm going back some time to that palmist woman, Phil. I'm sure she could explain things like that about us: why we met and how it happened. I should just like to know what she'd say.

But do you really hate that kind of thing? But why? But it doesn't matter, even if it isn't true. It's only for fun. And I should like to know.

But of course I won't, if you really don't want me to! Though I don't see why. I don't think it's sinister a bit. But I won't. No, really, promise. There now!

Oh, but you mustn't hold my hand. No really, please! People are looking.'

'Let them look!'

'Well, it doesn't matter really, after all. Only I wish they wouldn't. Why shouldn't we, after all. Like other people. Everybody's happy here, aren't they? It's wonderful to be happy.

It's wonderful here. You did, really, want to come back here, didn't you Phil? I thought it would be so nice, to come back and see it again. Where We began. You did want it, didn't you?'

'More than anything in the world, little Marcia.'

Oh Phil, Phil.

Oh Phil, you're so wonderful. Phil.

Phil, you're so wonderful. How did you happen. Nothing so wonderful as you has ever happened to me before.

Phil, it isn't fair, my being so old for you. You ought to have come sooner. Why didn't you come sooner? You ought to have come before Harold. I hate Harold. No, I don't: I don't mean that. That was twenty years ago. More like thirty. Well, no, not quite. You ought to have come thirty years ago, Phil.

I'm going to see: I don't really look my age, do I? I like these hotel dressing-tables with the three mirrors, you can really see yourself. I hate smart hotels as a rule, but I like the mirrors. And if I hadn't come to this one I shouldn't have met Phil.

I like the way they show you back and front and side at the same time. Really, anyone might take me for twenty-five from the back, mightn't they? The short hair suits me: it waves in nicely at the nape. And they did the tinting well. Now wasn't it lucky I was able to get it done before Phil had really had time to notice. Lucky I had a hat on, that day in the lounge. And a wave before I came here. Why, it was almost as if I knew 1 was going to meet Phil! It's really very odd, because I'd never thought of such a thing before. Oh dear, I suppose I'm getting quite demoralized! But what a good thing I didn't meet him before, when it was straight and turning grey. I do believe it had begun to turn. Dreadful, the way one doesn't notice these things in oneself. He wouldn't have looked twice at me then, would he? Why, I must have looked almost old enough to be his mother, and that's absurd of course. I don't suppose I should have thought of him either, in that way. I believe it's given me confidence in myself, getting freshened up like this: quite a new lease of life!

It's nice from the side. I like the right side best, where there's no parting, but the other isn't bad. I shall have to have the mud-pack again, when I get home. Once wasn't enough; the wrinkles are showing up again, to-night. It's the fault of these bright lights. I don't think he can possibly have noticed it, out there on the Front.

I'm glad we went out after dinner, it was wonderful with the moonlight on the water. Phil, you did see what I meant then, didn't you? About our having been fated to meet? Those things are so much clearer in the moonlight, when everything's quiet. And I'm so sure of it. And it makes our love so splendid, Phil.

I'll have the mud-pack again when I get back to town. Must keep it up. Mustn't let yourself go; can't pull up again in a hurry. Besides, I shall be seeing Phil ever so often now. Should hate him to see me as I used to be. If only it were twenty years ago, though.

But after all I'm not any age to speak of. Not much over forty.

Well, nearer fifty.

Still, that's nothing: early middle-age. Many people are at their best, then.

Phil, I wonder whether you meant all you said to-night, out there on the Front. Phil, you did, didn't you? You do believe it, don't you: that we've always been meant for one another? It's true, I know it is. I feel it so surely. We've been looking for one another all our lives. And before.

It's such a strange, strange thing to think that in this life I was quite grown-up before you existed at all. Now if Harold and I had had a son he'd be just about as old as Phil.

But that's of no consequence, after all. Besides, that's an exaggeration of course. But even if it were true it wouldn't make any difference. This life doesn't count, you see, Phil. You do believe that, don't you my dear? You see, there have been such millions and millions of years that we've been looking for one another, somewhere. Only we just hadn't managed to meet until now. So it doesn't matter a scrap that this time I was born a few years sooner: that was just a cruel joke of nature's. And it might have been a great deal worse. But we've turned it to nothing, haven't we, Phil?

Oh my dear, my dear, I don't want to saddle you with an old woman.

But you said I wasn't old, Phil. You wouldn't believe me. I'm glad I told you, though it wouldn't have been fair, not to. But you simply wouldn't believe me. Oh Phil, you're so sweet to me.

I shall have to be patient. It isn't fair to expect him to spend all his time with me. I must remember.

But you want to, Phil, you want to, don't you? Don't you? Say you do, Phil. Say it doesn't matter. Say you really do. But you did say it, and you looked so dear, with the moonlight on your face.

'Yes, forever and ever, little Marcia.' And your dear, funny smile.

Phil you do, you do. I believe you, Phil. I must believe you. I mustn't spoil everything by not believing in myself. No, it isn't even you or myself, now: it's just Us isn't it? That's what you said: Just Us. You're so sweet, Phil. We're starting out on a wonderful adventure, you and I, now we've met. Now at last. So wonderful, and nobody's going to know. You were quite right: nobody ought to know. Nobody at all. Just our secret.

Oh dear, I don't know what's the matter with me. I've never done anything like this before.

But you see, Phil, if it hadn't been fated forever and ever that we were to meet, I should never have let you say all those things. Because I'm not that sort of woman: you know that, don't you, my dear? And it wouldn't have been fair. But it is fated, Phil, I know it. And we mustn't deny the truth.

You see, if it hadn't been fated, I should never have come here, I know I shouldn't. Because I'd certainly never thought of it before. Something in me must have known you were here.

And I shouldn't have had my hair done, and all that kind of thing, should I?

I wonder whether it would be worthwhile having my face lifted, now. It's terribly expensive, and once you begin it you have to keep it up, they say. Might enquire about it when I get back to town.

I wonder how it is I don't resent you, Phil. I used to resent Harold horribly at times. A sense of losing one's identity as a person: I think that was what I had, and I hated it. Although I never had felt strongly that I was a person. But perhaps that was why. I always had a horror of being absorbed by Harold. Not that I wanted to be myself, particularly, but I wanted to be Harold still less. I had to keep on saying: I'm Millicent, I'm Millicent. Because I was Millicent in those days, Phil: it's only you who've made me Marcia. I was reborn for you, you see. Why, that's symbolical in a way; you had to give me a name, because I was born only just now, when we met! But is it really only for a fortnight that there's been a Marcia at all?

It's queer, I don't have that feeling with you, Phil, in the very least, of not wanting to be absorbed. I am, and it doesn't matter. All I wish is....

Phil, can't you absorb me altogether? Can't you make me not be? Don't you see? Phil, Phil, don't you see? I don't want to be Millicent anymore, or even Marcia: only part of you.

And not even that. I don't want to be part of you, Phil. I don't want to be at all. Only for you to be, and I to be faded out into you: not there anymore. Only just you. It was like that the other day, can't it be like that always? Must we come back? Must you send me back into the world just to go on and have to pretend to be somebody? I think if I ever lost you, Phil, I should go mad. I couldn't bear it. I couldn't bear to have to be myself again.

Oh. Oh, yes, I'd forgotten the mirrors were there. Now how odd to see yourself suddenly like that: as you look only when you're not thinking what you look like. Oh Phil, why weren't you here just now? I didn't know I could look like that; I wonder if I do look like that when I look at you. I've forgotten just how it was. Like that. No, not quite; I can't do it again. You have to think the same thoughts to look the same way. They were lovely thoughts, too, Phil. — Phil, I don't want to be: I only want you to be: just you, Phil. — No, it isn't quite the same. I wasn't thinking about it the first time only being it. And it's so very, very rarely that one can just be. So difficult not to be conscious of oneself; not to know, now I'm feeling this, now I'm thinking that. Yet it's only when the self is quite forgotten that one can be beautiful. That's why you're so beautiful, Phil; you're so unselfish. Even I was beautiful then, just for one moment. Just for that one, rare moment. It may never happen again. And Phil wasn't there. What a waste.

Phil, why weren't you there? Why weren't you there all the time: all those years, so empty, such a waste. And if I hadn't come here I should never have found you at all.

I wonder why I did come here. It certainly wasn't because of Harold, after all that time: just because we used to stay here in the summer. Besides, I was so horribly bored when we did. No, it must have been that day in the park when everything seemed so young and spring-like. That was when I first thought of it, I believe. There must have been something in the leaves coming out which told me you'd be here.

And it was so lonely here at first, too. I hated that big lounge, and so many young people laughing together. No, that is, they didn't laugh, exactly. They used to do that when we were young: when I was, I mean.

— What does it matter? It's stupid to keep thinking about that. —

When I was young, young people laughed, but now they only smile in a sophisticated way: and so many of them, with their cocktails, in the lounge downstairs. All the better, perhaps: it's easier for people like us to smile than to laugh. It comes more naturally to us, and laughing calls out the wrinkles. I suppose that's why it's so much easier to keep young, nowadays. And it really isn't at all difficult to look sophisticated over a little cocktail glass with something bright-coloured in it, and a cigarette. I ought to get a holder, like the long, black one that girl has over there, with the little, red hat.

But I shouldn't dare, should I?

It matches the big onyx on her finger. The first finger: I must remember that. After all, there's no particular reason why I shouldn't get rid of some of this old-fashioned jewellery that belonged to Harold's mother and get a few really modern rings.

Well, I should like to know who would look at them!

All the same, there's no point in appearing old-fashioned when one needn't. This background shows one up so. Not at all the kind of thing I expected to find, of course, but still.... Now I've come, I may as well let myself go, as they say, and be part of it!

Such an extraordinarily good chance I have of being part of it.

Well, here I am. No doubt about that. Those big mirrors round the walls do show one up so dreadfully. I suppose that must be I over there, between the palm and that big woman in black with the pearls. Yes, that's it. Well, I might look a great deal worse, but this hat isn't quite young enough. So unpleasant to look like a relic of the past, in a place like this! It wasn't nearly so smart when I used to come here with Harold, before the war. But then, there wasn't the same kind of smartness about: not this bright, slick, up-to-the-minute smartness. They must have rebuilt a good of the hotel, it wasn't nearly so large, and I don't remember this lounge. But I suppose Harold wouldn't have brought me to it: it wouldn't have been correct. Poor Harold. I like the big, plain mirrors; they'd have had gilt frames round them in those days, if they'd been here at all. And the big, crazy patches of paint: jazz, they call it, don't they? Like the music. The jazz age, of course. They're not so solid as we were: people like Harold, at least. But they probably enjoy themselves more. Get more out of life, as they would say. Well I don't think I was solid, even then, so I may as well be jazzy as anything else. I suppose they've been like this for a long time now, only I hadn't noticed it. How does one set about belonging to a jazz age? Or any age, in fact? In my time one wasn't conscious of belonging to an age. At least, Harold wasn't. He was

Harold. And an age lasted so long that one didn't realize one was in it, just as you don't realize you're on an island, in England. Still, it's pleasant to belong to a jazz age and sit here drinking cocktails at a little table. And nobody seems to think it strange.

I wonder people don't think it peculiar I should be sitting here alone. One would never have thought of doing such a thing in the old days. But there are quite a number of people alone, here and there. Or perhaps they think I'm waiting for somebody.

What a pity I'm not.

Oh dear, now people are beginning to dance it'll be more noticeable that I'm alone.

I suppose there must be professional dancing partners in a place like this. The kind one reads about. How dreadful: I hope they won't come up to me. What a dreadful thing, to think one was paying a partner because one was too old or too unattractive to be asked. I wonder how people can: you'd think they'd have more pride. You'd think they wouldn't like to admit it, even to themselves.

I hope I look as if I were waiting for somebody. Perhaps if I seemed to be watching the door.... I can't be very noticeable over here now they've begun dancing. I wish there were a magazine or something to read. It would be such an insult, even to be asked like that. I might just as well go up to my own room. There's a clear space now round the door, if I could just get by.

... Now if I were waiting for somebody like *him*.

Oh, he's looking this way! Suppose he came over here!

No, of course not. Really, how ridiculous. Why, besides, I don't know him, I've never seen him in my life. I like the way his hair is thrown back. Not quite English.

No, of course, he's bowing to somebody over there: that stout woman, dancing with the Italian looking man. How strange, quite simple when he smiles: not at all what one would expect. Now you may just as well come over to this side of the room: let me have a closer look at you!

Oh, he is! Oh. I wish there were a magazine or something.
'Waiter!'

But do I really not know him? His face seems familiar. I'm sure I must have met him somewhere. Now where have I seen him before. Dancing here yesterday perhaps. Or is it only the kind of face I've sometimes imagined.

Really, I'm being quite ridiculous!

Of course, he must have crowds of friends here. I'm sure I've noticed him dancing. As if he would notice me, in any case. Why, besides, I don't know him. I shouldn't answer even if he did speak. People do seem to pick up acquaintances nowadays, but it isn't the kind of thing I've ever done.

He is! He's actually coming right over here. Oh a little table all to himself? Now isn't that strange. Yet he's bowed to quite a number of people.

Now I wonder.

Well, it isn't likely he would say anything. Whatever is the matter with me, thinking of such a thing? Even if this *is* a jazz age!

'Waiter, another martini?'

I wish my hat were a little more up-to-date. Of course, he's only waiting for somebody he knows. But I could have sworn he smiled when he turned this way. Just faintly. I oughtn't to have turned away so sharply. They'll be finishing this dance in a moment and people will be coming back to the tables in between.

I wish I hadn't looked away. It's so difficult to turn, now.

Well, really, I think I may as well be going up to my room. If it's clear round the door....

Oh, he's bowing to somebody again, across the room. Oh dear, I wish....

Where's my cigarette case.

I wish I had a holder.

There, now, before he gets up. Oh, but I can't. Really.

'Oh... Oh, excuse me, have you a match?'

126

Oh. Oh, I haven't done it, have I? And he's getting up. Oh dear, how dreadful, whatever shall I do now.

Phil, Phil, where are you, Phil.

Phil.

Such a little thing, Phil. Just a match. So many little things. Why do things happen like that: just through little things. If I hadn't asked you for a match. Or if you hadn't said afterwards — the next day, wasn't it, or the day after — 'have you seen Hastings and Battle Abbey, we might drive over'; and if I hadn't said, 'I was thinking of getting a car and going about a bit now and then'; and if you hadn't said, 'the ambition of my life is a really high-powered car'.... Or did you say that first? And if you hadn't looked at me like that, just at that moment.... But did you, or did I imagine it? Or did I notice it, I don't think I did, I only remembered it afterwards.

Phil, Phil, it wasn't that, was it? Say it wasn't.

I didn't mean that, did I, about the car? I couldn't have. But did you think I did. I only wanted to give it to you because you wanted it and you were young. And you'd been so sweet, I didn't mean anything else, did I. And you didn't. It wasn't that. It just happened, didn't it, Phil.

Just as things do happen: through little things. Just my asking you for a match, and my saying, and your saying.... And just through my going to Brighton, which I hadn't done for twenty years. And I should never have thought of Brighton at all, if it hadn't been for Harold. So it's all Harold's fault, whatever it was. So there, Harold, you needn't be so righteous about it. Now isn't that odd: if I hadn't been married to Harold I should never have met Phil.

That just shows it had to be, doesn't it, Phil?

Say it does. Do say it does. I know it had to be, but I want you to know it too. I knew it the moment I saw you coming into the lounge. I knew I'd always known you and had to know you again. We were meant for one another. It was meant, all through the ages. It was a beautiful thing, our meeting, Phil. Say it was.

Phil, Phil, where are you. Why don't you come.

Why do you say that? Don't mock me, Phil. Why do you say you're here. Why do you say. Why don't you come.

Oh, it's you. You've come, have you. Why do you come. Haven't been near me all these years, since Harold went. Might as well have kept away now. Why should you come to mock me.

No, no. I don't mean that. Harold's dead, isn't he? Been dead more than ten years. Fifteen, isn't it. Or more. Doesn't matter. Oh yes, I'm getting on quite well by myself, thank you. Just leave me alone. I like being alone.

Dear me, I haven't thought of Harold for years. How many years can it be? Peculiar how accustomed one grows to being alone. Quite pleasant: thinking one's own thoughts. It's only on a day like this when the sun's shining on the water — the Round Pond, and the sun cutting a path: bright ripples on the smooth water — that it might seem pleasant to have somebody to talk to. Might ask Mrs. Caruthers up to my room when I get back, and have a chat. She knew those Davises who were friends of Harold's sister's, didn't she? Wonder whether she has any news of the Davises. And that child, Sonia, must be quite big by now. Grown-up, even, I shouldn't be surprised. Strange to think one has a grown-up niece somewhere. Why, let me see: why, she must be thirty at least! A niece by marriage: that means nothing, of course.

Leaves and blue water. Grass, and the dark patch of a coat half hidden by a tree trunk.

And a quick step back.

Just look at that couple over there. What are the guards about? Disgusting behaviour. In public, like that. Or even if it weren't! People have no proper pride, nowadays.

Grass and the blue water.

I don't think I want to hear about the Davises to-day, on second thoughts. I'd rather meet somebody fresh. Now it might be amusing to go up to those children and talk to them, or ask that man why he's sailing a toy boat. I should really like to know! What can make a man of his age want to sail a toy boat? Spring, perhaps. The same kind of thing as makes me feel like asking him, I suppose! It gives one quite a feeling of youth, all these leaves coming out. I really haven't felt so young for years.

Most peculiar: it's ages since I felt I should like to talk to people. But really, one can't. Besides, they'd stare, and wonder at one.

All the seagulls have gone, now. Gone back to the coast.

Following steamers and waiting around harbours for the fishing-boats to come in, and screaming over the rocks where nobody comes.

It's years since I saw the sea.

Now in Cornwall, when we used to go there when I was a girl: that was real sea. Those tiny villages, and the great stretches of coast where nobody ever came, and you had to trample your way through the bracken....

A farm at the head of a valley, and the valley sweeping down with heather and bracken and river weeds, down to the sea; and the huge, tortured rocks, and untrodden headlands.

You could be alone, there. But it's a wild country: I couldn't do it now: the way you had to force a path through the brambles, and down and up and another valley ahead; and the farms and villages so hidden there was not a sign of life on the whole horizon....

Gulls, and the sea never still, and now and then a line of earth-works or a stretch of ancient wall grown over by thyme and the short, wiry grass.

A wild land. A scarred and savage land. It's not for me: I'm not so young now. I need a smooth shore: a pleasant sea, as Harold used to call it. How small and safe the Round Pond looks, with its little boats. We used to go out in little boats at Brighton, in the old days. It might be amusing to go back to Brighton now, to the hotel where we used to stay! It must have changed a good deal, with the war, and one thing and another.

129

Why shouldn't I go down there for a bit? It would be amusing to see how things have changed. Why, it might do me good to have a change. After all, you can't call me old, yet; but I've let myself get into old ways, as they say. Now look at that woman over there, taking her dogs for a run: she's no younger than I am. But her hair's nicely done, and face made-up. Well, I should hardly have thought of that kind of thing, in the old days. Still, perhaps I've not been taking enough trouble with my appearance: not necessary to let my hair turn grey, after all; people don't, nowadays. I don't care for much society, but one can hardly live without human companionship now and then. You never know whom you may meet in a seaside hotel, of course. Still, one is not obliged to know them. There might be interesting people, one never knows. I really ought to pull myself together and take a holiday, I believe it would do me good.

There really would be no harm in having my hair waved, just to see how it would suit me, you know.

After all, I'm no age really. I'm letting life go by: it's quite foolish. All very well and pleasant to live alone, but meeting people for a time would make it all the more enjoyable. After all, a life can hardly pass with nothing in it but Harold, and then a room in a private hotel.

I'll go to Brighton. Yes I will! I expect I shall thoroughly dislike it when I'm there, but it'll do me good. Nothing could possibly happen there, of course, but it does one good to be among people for a time, even if they're tiresome.

How quickly the leaves are coming out, they'll soon be too heavy. I prefer them like this, before the trees look weighted.

Now if I went out this way into the High Street I might find a hairdresser's, and then see.

Wanted to ask you. Wanted to, to ask. What was it.

Mrs. Caruthers, with her greying hair under a little hat, getting up from the white wicker-chair.

'Oh yes, Mrs. Caruthers, I wanted to... to what was it... to... to ask you, that was it.

Why do you stand there looking at me? About my room, I said. Wanted to ask you. What was it. My, my room.

Don't stand about here. This hall is one of the draughtiest places I've ever been in. We'd better go up to my room if you want to ask me something. Oh, of course, if you have to go. Come another day, won't you?'

A good thing on the whole she had to go out. Now what could she have wanted to ask me? What was it. Nothing of importance; a subscription, probably. So many good works. She has nothing else to interest her, poor thing. Good works are all very well when one gets to a certain age. I always say, I may take to them yet! But even so, one ought to have interests in oneself.

I'm quite glad Mrs. Caruthers didn't come up. So disturbing, having someone alien in one's room, and I've got quite a number of little jobs to do to-day. There was something.... What was it, now. Poor old thing, I must ask her up sometime; but as I tell them, I'm a busy woman. It's really surprising, how many little things there are to be done, when one's self-supporting as I am.

Of course that girl has taken my duster again. Really, it's too annoying. No, I remember, I slipped it into the shoe-box so that she shouldn't find it. Dear me, how glad I am not to be dependent upon other people for entertainment. Really, if one had to sit about in the lounge, waiting to catch someone for a conversation, like that Mrs. Jones.... But with my things to see to, and a book now and then....

'But can't you find me a nice book, for once? I detest this modern stuff.'

The assistant, suave and expressionless. Long, variegated rows of books on shelves and the smooth boards of a discarded volume on the assistant's desk.

'Don't give me any of these *sex* books, or whatever you call them. *Love-stories*, we used to say, when I was a girl. Things like this wouldn't have been dreamt of. But there's no decency about, nowadays. I don't get a great deal of time for reading, but I do like a *nice* story.'

No, she certainly has *not* dusted the mantelpiece to-day. Well, for all the good she would probably have done.... And the glass quite smeary. I really wonder why people have servants at all. So much more satisfactory to attend to one's own things. As I tell Mrs. Caruthers, I'm really quite a communist, in my own little way!

How Harold would laugh at me. I should never have thought of touching a duster in the Chesborough days. What would the servants have thought, I wonder. Besides, one was so crowded up with social duties. And an impersonal room, that drawing-room at Chesborough; even though Harold had insisted on my choosing the decorations, it never had very much of me about it. I suppose that's why I enjoy so much making my own environment here.

What a good thing I thought of keeping my own little tin of metal polish. These taps would be disgraceful.

Rubbing; arm-ache; the shine coming up.

Elbow-grease, they used to call it.

Bright yellow knob with a splash of light.

That's what I've always been looking for, I believe: a chance to make my surroundings to suit myself. And nobody to worry one. I must say, this is a pleasant little room. So nicely away from people, up here.

Dear me, Harold, how surprised you'd be to see me dusting your photograph, now, wouldn't you? Strange to think I'm here still and dusting this frame. And where are you, I wonder. I don't think it ever occurred to you I might outlive you. There was something so permanent about the life you'd made for yourself — for us. With your household and your wife. Well, I expect you hadn't exactly made it. It had been made for you: waiting for you to step into it. All but the wife, and that you had to find for yourself. Now I wonder why you chose me.

Well, you might have chosen worse, perhaps! I was a good-looking girl, I believe. I don't think I've changed very much, either, considering it's a good ten years that I've been living alone like this. Not so much colour, perhaps; but then, I never had much. The same round face: my cheeks haven't hollowed as one might have expected. After all, I'm not much over forty, there's plenty of life in me yet! No troubles, you see: that makes all the difference. And I don't allow myself to worry. Never trouble trouble, till trouble troubles you: there was a great deal of truth in these old sayings. Now many people would think they'd quite come to an end if they found themselves alone as I am. But I believe it saved me, losing Harold, I do indeed. There'd have been nothing left of me by now. One really might say it's been the saving of me, having peace like this and nobody to worry about.

I wonder, now, whether I mended those stockings I meant to the other day.

Yes, I suppose most people would consider their lives over, if they found themselves alone like this, with no husband and no children. But then, that was a thing I never wanted. And as for husbands, I'm sure Harold didn't keep me young. I aged more in those twelve years we were married than I have since. Oh, much more.

Oh yes, here they are. I might darn them now, before making tea. Oh well, there's not much the matter. But a stitch in time, as they used to say. I hope that girl has cleaned the kettle since yesterday.

There was that boy — what was his name — who used to stay up at Sibsley Court, when we were children. Michael, that was it. Now what a strange thing: I couldn't even remember his name, for the moment, so that shows he couldn't have counted for very

133

much! I believe I was fond of him though, at the time. I remember I was quite upset when we heard he had married. And he never came back after that, I think. Went abroad somewhere. Very odd: it must have mattered at the time, and just now I could hardly remember his name. That's how things are, of course: nothing in life is quite worth the fret we make about it, I expect.

Bright track of the needle in and out across the black wool; over and under, and the needle flashing out and poised, with the black strand taut.

Now if I'd married Michael I wonder where I should be now. In quite a different place, I expect: abroad, very likely. Or perhaps he would have died, like Harold, and I should be in exactly the same place as I am now. I never heard that he died; but there's no reason why he shouldn't have, in twenty years, and the war out of it. Now isn't that a peculiar thought: things might have worked around to exactly the point they've reached only by a different way. I suppose it might happen like that? Or does each event happen logically, follow on from what went before? Everything must have an effect upon one, of course: leave its mark.

Thread slackened; swift flash of the needle onward, in and out, through the neat, black criss-cross.

Not a great deal, though. Harold hadn't much effect upon me, that I can see. It's true he was killed, and I came here because of it. But should I have been any different at all if it had been Michael instead? *He* certainly had no effect upon me, even though I did once think I was in love with him! Just passed by — twenty years ago, isn't it? — and a minute ago I couldn't even remember his name! Yet he must have mattered at the time.

What a strange thing. It seems as if there were no logic or purpose in life. No doubt it's best when you can cut quite clear of people, as I have done, and plan your life with no risk of interference. Now what could be more logical than my life as I've planned it?

I'm old-fashioned, I suppose. But what people call *life*, nowadays...!

All these cocktail parties and this rushing about. Nobody can stay quietly at home. I'm thankful to say I'm satisfied to be where I am: it wouldn't give me the slightest pleasure to dash about the country in a motor-car or drink cocktails. I much prefer my cup of tea!

Twenty-past four. If I put the kettle on now it'll be ready by half-past, when I've done this heel.

No, you really couldn't find a more rational plan of life. No superfluous possessions to clutter one up and waste time. Just the things I need, in the smallest possible compass. There's certainly no space wasted here! But then, I like a small room: always have disliked large ones. My room at Chesborough, for instance: something so cold and hostile about it. I like to feel I'm in my own little castle, with everything around me. So compact and sensible.

Black wool taut over the curved wooden mushroom: smooth, brown wood in a patch between the torn strands. Flash of the needle; frayed edges gathered up, firmly held, and the healing threads tightening over the smooth wood.

And what could be more sensible than the way I live? Self-supporting; able to wash out things now and then when I want to; do my own little jobs in peace? And then there's the dining-room for meals. Still, it's convenient to be able to make tea for oneself.

Why, the kettle-holder's wearing quite thin. I shall have to look for something to cover it. There must be a piece of stuff in one of the trunks. Dear me, how busy I seem to be.

Oh I quite believe one should reduce the necessities of life to a minimum: the only rational way of living. I certainly wouldn't change my way of life for any other. Active, busy; if one wants a walk there are the shops. Quite entertaining to watch the people: such a rush and scramble for non-essentials. And then come back to one's own well-regulated life. There's something neat and compact about it. It couldn't be managed except by one person alone, of course.

The only sensible way. I certainly haven't the slightest intention of ever becoming entangled with another person!

Though no doubt I could have married again, now I come to think of it. Harold's widow could have married well, you know.

Ah, but then. I'm not in the least Harold's widow, I'm glad to say. I'm myself. Oh yes, I think I can certainly say that, more than most people.

This tea has no taste whatever. Let me see, where did I get it? Oh yes, I must remember.

No, I think I can certainly say that having ceased to be Harold's wife I have at last succeeded in being myself. And really not succeeded so badly, I think. Very few people are so definitely themselves as I am.

I wonder, now, how it would have felt to marry again: to be somebody else's wife after being Harold's. Well, marriage isn't the same thing nowadays, it seems. One hears a great deal about the freedom of married women. Marriage as it was in my time is out of fashion.

Not that that has anything to do with fashion. Oh dear me no. Or to do with laws and prejudices. It's a matter of people. I defy any modern young girl to marry Harold and keep her personality.

All the same, I much prefer Harold's kind to the modern type of young man. Insignificant creatures; and the women are as bad, with their make-up and indecent clothing and rushing about: the breaking up of home life. Nobody has any dignity nowadays. Now when Harold was alive there was dignity in our life together. Our marriage was an ordered, dignified thing: beautiful, in a way. I'm glad I was born when I was. I can't see myself going on in the slack, vulgarized way young people seem to now. It was worthwhile to lose something of one's individuality, when it could give one a dignified, orderly existence.

Besides, I haven't come out of it badly, on the whole. Not much over forty: and it only took a year or two to find my feet and arrange life to suit myself. I made some mistakes at first, no doubt, but I've got myself collected together now, and I fully intend to keep it so, thank you!

Friendly hum of the kettle.

Think I'll get ready for bed. Late, isn't it? But no hurry. Plenty of time.

Friendly, humming kettle. Warm, enfolding wool of a dressing-gown swung from its hook; nightdress on a chair, with sleeves dangling, outspread to warm.

Now the bottle.

Soft, limp rubber; hard turn of the screw; drop and jerk of the stopper at the end of its string. The pleasure in small actions performed in a familiar order. Pop of the gas-ring. Diminishing hum of the kettle as the ring cools; steam and hiss of water slowly poured; tug of the swaying stopper, and the kettle shaken.

That's enough. I think I'll have a cup of tea.

Screw turned: fat, hot rubber, and the sheets turned back. Scalding rubber and the cold sheet.

Why has this tea no taste? My mouth's horribly dry. I can't think, without some tea.

Fat, black tea-pot, and the mouth dry and tasteless.

I must have a proper cup of tea. It sounds dreadful, but I really think I couldn't get along without my cup of tea. It's a harmless pleasure, after all.

Why are you whispering like that. My mouth's so dry. I can't think. What was I saying. Harold: but he's gone, hasn't he. My mouth's so dry. No, it was Phil: I'd made my life and then he wanted.... No, I'd made the tea, that was it. And he wanted to upset it all. No you don't, Philip. Oh, you needn't think it. Not now that I've got free. Tea, I mean; made the tea. I'm all right as I am. Oh yes, I've made my life, right enough. I don't want any more life, thank you. But you might bring me a cup of tea.

What are you whispering about. Wish you wouldn't stand whispering there.

What do you want. You can go and fetch your uncle, he must be round at the stables. I want him to know I've made my life and I don't want any more of his tea. Go and fetch your Uncle Harold. Always a pert little thing, staring at me, with your thumb in your mouth. I wouldn't have you here at all if it weren't for Harold.

No, he's dead of course. Killed. They brought the telegram out on to the lawn.

Orange envelope; silver salver white in the sun, and the sound of liquid, poured.

Well, you might have brought it before. My mouth's so dry. Must have my tea. Don't mind about lunch, but I really can't get on without my tea.

What is it? What? What did you say? Harold's dead, is he? Then I'm free, I suppose. It's funny, I don't feel free, particularly.

So Harold's gone? Where to, I wonder.

Nowhere, of course.

Death: darkness and a sinking away. Noise shut out: noises oozing, sliding away, and the drip, drip of darkness.

Nowhere. Just gone. Gone into silence and darkness and nothing.

I suppose I ought to have a sense of freedom. No, I ought to feel sorry for Harold, that is. Harold had a great many good qualities. And he was killed in action. He was shot into the mud or blown in pieces or nailed up by a bayonet like a moth on a pin.

White butterfly on the grey cardboard, and the pin, and wings struggling, and Dick with his hair all rumpled sticking in the pin.

'You're not to, it's horrid. Mamma says it's horrid.'

Dick's laugh, and Hilda's, and the wings fluttering: Harold's arms struggling and waving and the pin going in.

I don't know which it was, but it doesn't mean anything at all to me. Of course I'm very sorry for Harold; but it has no meaning for me. I don't feel it. Just as I don't feel that I'm free: only that I'm in a street with a great many people around me, and am alone, and people are pushing me, rushing from behind in a most ridiculous way. Oh, it's because this is a 'bus stop? But there are a great many people everywhere else in the street, too, and most of them seem to be in a hurry. But I'm free, of course. There really isn't any hurry at all. Perfectly free. If I wanted to cross the road or turn round and go back through tile park the way I have come, or take a 'bus to Richmond or Hounslow, wherever that is, there's no reason at all why I shouldn't. There's no reason why I should get back by any particular time, or why I shouldn't go into one of these shops and buy the first useless thing I see: an inlaid, occasional table or a tree made of mother-of-pearl or a glazed boar's head. Neither of them would be of the least use to me; but there's nobody to say it's foolish and no reason why I shouldn't spend all the money I've got, except that then I shouldn't have any to live upon. But there'd be nobody to reproach me, or be sorry either, if I hadn't. So I'm free, I suppose.

Why are people in such a hurry? They all have to be somewhere by a particular time, no doubt. Harold was always annoyed if I was late for a meal. At first, that is; after a time I shouldn't have thought of being late. Some of them move slowly, but then they're carrying parcels, shopping. And they all have an anxious or dissatisfied look. They can't be anxious about what they're doing, not all of them. They have that expression because they've been anxious for so long, about so many little things that they must have forgotten: the meat coming late for luncheon, or the bathroom tap that won't stop dripping, or the hat that isn't quite right for tea this afternoon. Petty. Well, I'm glad to say.... Oh, they're not thinking about them now; they must have forgotten. People, looking into shop-windows or staring at fruit on barrows. But those things have happened and will happen again. They're not free.

I think I may say I'm free, in that way. I don't think any life could be much freer than mine is now. Yet I can't feel it, at all.

139

They're all anxious, you see, and they're all people. What do I mean. People. They're all people. They're people just because they're anxious and dissatisfied, I expect that's it. If they weren't they'd be like the wax figures in these windows. I expect I'm like that: that's why they look at me so often. They think there's something peculiar about me. I'm not quite a person, I expect: only a good reproduction, like these figures. Pretending to be a person. But how can they see that? I must look very much like anybody else.

They're not really looking, of course. Harold always said I imagined people were looking at me. Not really taking any notice. Quite restful to be in a crowd like this. Not like the empty High Street at Market Chesborough, where you saw people coming a long way off.

Bobbing oilcloth bag and flat, black shoes, and the paving-stones stretching away, empty. The distant shout of a drover. How soon shall I begin to smile? Flat, hard straw hat and bobbing red roses. She's got as far as the butcher's, shall I begin? And feet flap-flap on the stones. But they're not real people, they don't matter, they're not real. And the crowd gliding up.

These people aren't people, you know. They haven't any faces. They're only anxieties and dissatisfactions, busy with themselves. That's why they keep on whispering and whispering.

They're not really whispering about me. It's only their thoughts. They make a hissing sound: sinking, may be sinking. Sinking. Their anxieties hissing at them as they walk about. Now I haven't any anxieties. I'm free. I might go into a cinema. Sinking. Do you think she's sinking. Sinking, into a cinema. Pleasantly dark in a cinema, and people are quiet, looking at the screen.

Into a cinema. Sinking, into a cinema. I'm free, you know. I'm free, Phil's gone. No, what do I mean. He's killed, I'm free. Did you know Harold's killed. Harold's gone: I suppose, if you come to think of it, I'm free.

A cinema. They turned the County Theatre into a cinema. But this is a London cinema, of course. One's free in London, it's so big. People aren't people, they haven't any faces. And all quite quiet, looking at the screen. They've left their anxieties outside in the street, in that big, glaring porch with the big posters. They've chained them up. Anxieties, waiting and hissing outside.

So many people. That's why they come here you know. In here they needn't be people anymore. It's dark in here, it's dark in my room, I like my room. And I'm not separate. I don't think I am, I'm part of the darkness, and the people who aren't people. All part of the darkness.

I think I'm like them in here. I'm like anyone else. All alike and nothing, staring at the screen.

The people on the screen are so big and so bright. They're bigger and brighter than the people in the street. They're bigger than life because they've taken our lives on them: all our lives. That's why it is: they've relieved us of life. They've taken our burden for the moment: the burden of living, of being separate, of being somebody. They're bigger than we are because they're all of us. And they're pictures. No living being could endure that: to live for us all under the brilliant lights.

It's horrible to think of, and everybody stares. They stare, and the burden goes out through their eyes.

The streets so light, so horribly light. Cruel lights: and the dark crowd with their burden of lives. A little woman in black, and the light upon her. She's separate and they stare, they stare and whisper. She's sinking, sinking. They stare and whisper and the light is on her. Always the light. Shade the light.

Long, dark streets and the huge, light screen. I can't, I can't. The huge, open, light screen: open and light and huge all round: great, dazzling sheet of light, and they stare, stare. Sinking: it's the lives: the weight of their lives.

But I must, I must. They stare. I must. And the lights and the lives: the great sheet of light, blinding. Searing, unseen eyes of the dark streets.

And the crowd all around and the screen. The tiny, light screen far off above the heads of the crowd, and a little woman in black on the screen: it's I: they're staring at me. And the struggle out through the choking crowd and the eyes unseeing, boring the screen. And the long, long, lit pavements: streets horribly light and the silent, dark, moving crowd. And a voice close up, loud and clear: WHY NOT ONE MORE.

And a gasp and sweat and shivering, and the white walls closing in.

Where was I? What is it? One more what? How did I come back.

Where was I? No, it's gone.

And the white walls firm and still, closed in, and the hot, crumpled sheet and the light, shade the light.

Shade that light, I said.

White, quiet room, and Nurse, standing; starched, high cap and stiff collar and face bent, watching, and the high, glaring bulb.

What do you mean, staring at me like that. *Will* you shade that light.

Mouth open and struggling.

"Uh... uh...."

Struggling, and the tongue heavy as lead. But I can't. What is it. I can't.

"Uh... uh...."

And a cold, high wall. A high wall of glass. It's the window, the window. High, glass shop-window, and a figure beyond, bending. But I can't, why is it, I can't. It's the glass. Can't speak through the glass.

And the leaden, thick tongue: "Ah, ah... uh." And silent eyes, watchful, beyond the glass.

Cold, staring bulb and a high cap, bending, and the frame of the mirror, and a patch of curtain grey against the white wall, and the rail at the foot of the bed. White and quiet.

'Nurse, what are you doing? You mustn't waste your time here, attending to me.'

'Have you seen to the boy in Number Five? The one who came in yesterday?'

'Give me my torch. I'll go round the wards now, before I get out of uniform.'

How quiet it is when they've all been put to bed. The carpets on the stairs deaden those hospital sounds. I feel like a ghost, creeping about. We might have had the carpets taken up, for the duration, but Harold wanted the house left as it was as far as possible. How strange it'll seem when the war's over and we get things straight again. Oh. Well. But Harold's killed.

I mustn't show anything. Must carry on as usual. Carry on. Most of them must know it by now, but they're tactful. Nice boys, most of them; I suppose they only send us the nice ones. They must find it quieter here than in hospital.

Across the dark hall: the light from the electric torch a pale, moving circle on the dark parquet.

How many more times shall I do this? For the duration. How long is the duration? Twenty times or a thousand times. Must have been hundreds of times already.

Cold door-knob; soft swing of a door over carpet. Faint light from the sky beyond the high windows; vague, blurred shadows of elms against sky thrown on to high brocaded walls.

You see, they don't sleep, all of them; but they keep still. Be careful with the torch: the light on their faces. There's light enough. No moon: the grey sky.

'Yes, what is it?'

You see, he's awake, that one. Lower the torch, keep it from the others. Water in a glass. The queer, dull light of the bed-clothes. Restless. Hand over the torch and pass on.

All quiet. Vague stirrings in the shadows. 'Good night, matron.'

Back down the carpeted aisle, between the small, grey beds. How Harold would hate this.

You see, we left the mirror.

Big, mirrored wall above the fire-place. The back of Harold's head as he stands with his hands behind him.

But Harold's killed.

Softly on the deep carpet. Light of the sky in the glass: a lighter patch in the long, dim room.

He always stood like that, with his hands behind him. Rubbing them to the fire.

Door softly closed. Nurse will come presently. You know, they come round every hour.

You know Harold's killed.

Grey light from the high hall window, on the stair-rods.

The carpet's thick.

Harold's killed, you know. They brought the wire. I mustn't show anything.

You know I'm glad to be back in my room: it's ghostly, creeping about. They can't hear me from here. The walls are thick. This is an old house. I might take a smaller room, they could put three or four beds in here; but Harold wants it left as it is.

Dark mahogany around the cheval-glass.

That's I.

A small, round woman in matron's uniform.

A Commandante. This was her house, you know, and her husband was killed in action. It suits me, the cap. They won't want me again to-night, there are no serious cases.

Harold's killed: I ought to think about him.

Huge, dark wardrobe, and a dressing-gown.

Now there's no Commandante anymore. That's Millicent, and Harold's killed.

It was to-day, wasn't it. Or was it yesterday. If he's come back here he knows I'm not thinking about him. Why can't I? Why can't I see him? I did, didn't I, just for one moment. As he used to be; a long time ago; when we were married. But it's gone. And he isn't like that now. And he's killed. But I *am* thinking about you, Harold: I'm thinking how you were killed. I'm thinking terribly hard.

Dark frame of the cheval-glass and a knee and the arm of a chair and a foot in a blue slipper.

I'm thinking about you terribly, Harold. Mud, and the shot, and falling backwards. No, he'd fall forwards, they do, don't they.

Harold, you ought to be here. I want you here, I do. If you're here I want you to know that I want you, Harold. — A grey mist, and Harold hovering unwanted, and drifting away. — I want you here, here, here. Yes I do.

Veins on the forehead rising in the effort to want. Foot, in a blue slipper, gripping the carpet.

You ought to be here, you belong here, it's your place. You know he belongs here, not in the mud, not to the mud.

You ought to be here. I'm here. Why am I here. I'm alone, now. I'm Millicent, and Harold's killed.

Drag of slippers over the clinging carpet; dark wood; white, embroidered runner; silver stoppers of bottles, and the glass.

That's Millicent, and Harold's killed.

Pale face. That's the strain of to-day. And brown hair puffing up from the temples. I'm untidy, that's from the cap.

Quite alone, and not old. Now if I'm a widow I ought to be old. A widow ought to be old. Harold's widow. You know I'm Harold's widow, and thirty-two.

I might go away from here.

Can't leave Harold to wander about. A mist and Harold drifting

145

away. Don't go away, I want you here. Yes I do. Harold's widow and thirty-two.

Light, glinting on the glass, and dull eyes. Flecks of light on the walls, from the cut-glass bottles.

Might go away and be Millicent. Don't want to be Millicent. I'm not Millicent really.

'Such a big name for a little woman.'

You see, I don't want to be Millicent. Eyes shifting, and soft, puffed hair. Not Millicent. Something else. What is it.

Nothing. Not anything. Harold's widow and thirty-two.

Light glinting, and the bright, dark wood.

Might go away and be thirty-two.

Who said that? I didn't say that. What does it mean? Doesn't mean anything. Might go away and be thirty-two.

Might go away.

Darkness, and straining eyes.

Might go away. Might go to London. I'll tell you what I'll do, I'll go to London and be thirty-two. No, I don't mean that. I'll go to London and be free, that's what I'll do: I'll go to London and be free, and Harold's killed he can't say anything.

No, I don't mean that, I want you Harold. I'll go to London and be free, not Harold's wife anymore. Not anybody's wife; I'm going to be free. I'll tell you what it is, I'm going to be myself.

Are you there, Harold, I want to tell you; I'll tell you what it is. No, I don't mean that. They said you were killed, but you aren't are you.

Soft, green turf after rain. Cool air. Starched cap-strings blown against the check. Wicker wheel-chair and blue eyes.

Poor boy. Such a nice boy.

White orderly's coat on the high steps.

He's looking around. That's a telegram. He's got it on a salver.

'That's splendid. We shall soon have you running about.'

He's looking around. Looking for me. He'd bring it to me in any case.

It's for me. Harold's killed.

'That's fine. Well, I must go; they're looking for me.'

Soft, green turf. Tennis net sagging, caught up in the middle. Orange envelope.

Yes, yes of course. Harold's killed. — 'No, no answer.' No, of course not.

Soft turf; high steps to the door.

I'm walking steadily. There's no difference in me.

A small, plump woman in matron's uniform.

That's Millicent, you know, passing through the hall. Harold's killed.

Smooth, marble banister, cold to the hand.

White, gleaming balustrade and the blue, blue sea, and Harold leaning: Harold in white flannels, and the muscle of his shoulder straining the thin shirt; pale, nodding mimosa, and dark leaves in a tangle. Harold out there on the terrace, and the blueness of the sea, and the straining shoulder muscle against the thin silk: Harold's splendid. Harold! Harold! But you're not, you can't be, he can't be dead. Harold come. Come to me Harold.

The quiet hall: very quiet, with empty, shallow stairs. The ticking of a clock somewhere behind a closed door, and a click of crutches outside on the drive where a bright blue uniform moves painfully across the afternoon sunlight.

Broad, shallow stairs and empty corridor and a Commandante passing to her room. Smooth swing of the door and noiseless steps on the deep carpet.

For the duration. I shall keep it on, of course, for the duration.

A comb, and the starched veil straightened.

There's no difference in me at all. Nobody would know anything had happened.

Harold, where are you, I wonder.

Head turning, and the rasping sheet.

Where, where, what is it, where? Not here, then where? What I mean is, where is it? No, what do I mean. You see, Phil, what I mean is, where do we go, what happens? What I mean is, yes, that's what I mean, where? Where are you Harold?

Harold, where are you?

'Do you know where the master is?'

'Oh, very well, I'll go round to the stables.'

I wish he'd get harder gravel for the drive. It gets so soft in damp weather. The snowdrops are over, what a pity.

Damp mud on the small, long leaves beaten to t e ground.

I suppose Miss Platt will take the needlework stall as usual. I wonder what to do about the Perrits. If I give them the produce stall Mrs. Fox will be hurt, but it would be easier for them, a mother and two daughters. Newcomers are such a problem to fit in, but Harold will know. Mrs. Fox is getting old and rather deaf. She won't like it though.

The daffodils will soon be out, now.

Big, greenish yellow buds, boat-shaped. Hard and 1 cold to the hand.

I might suggest it to Mrs. Fox at the next sewing party. Oh dear, she'll think I want to get rid of her. She thinks I don't like her, as it is. I might wait until tea is brought in and then say something about it. She bends nearly double over her sewing. 'Mrs. Fox, we were wondering whether you don't find the stall too much for you.' No, that won't do. 'We wondered whether you'd mind letting Mrs. Perrit.' Oh dear, she'll see through it, whatever I say. Her work isn't worth anything, but it makes unpleasantness in the parish. The vicar ought to do it himself. 'Mrs. Fox, the vicar and I were wondering whether.'

Firm, slaty paving of the yard; gravel on shoes scraping against the pavement. Pale yellow wooden doors with black iron fastenings; upper halves open, flat back against the bricks. Horses' heads out, brown or black with white lights in the sun. Swish-swish of a groom in a loose-box in the far corner. Come over there, woah, and the rustle of straw. The tap of a hoof against the wooden door. Harold coming from the harness room, rubbing his hands.

'Did you have a good ride, dear?'

Harold, towering and solid, filling his pipe: a good landlord, Harold, efficient on his morning round. Sound observation; necessary repairs; improvements which will pay in the long run. Aglow with a canter back over the downs. The crunch-crunch of the drive under his heavy boots, and the crinch-crinch-crinch of feminine steps not quite in time: three to two.

'How did the meeting go off at the vicarage? Perrit business settled?'

Harold, never-failing in consideration; remembering with kind, unflagging interest the scarcely distinguishable details of one's daily round. To-morrow he'll say, 'And how did you find Orchard Cottages? Blodger keeping on the water-cart?'

Efficient and kind, always. Knowing the right line to take: just how to put things to poor old Mrs. Fox and whom to ask out of Market Chesborough to meet the new doctor and his wife.

'The daffodils will soon be out now.'

Hard, yellow-green lumps, smooth and cold in the palm.

'Hm, we shall have an early spring. Wants a load of gravel here.'

Cold, yellow-green lumps, sliding from the palm; momentarily a-quiver; still and patient on their stems.

Harold, patient and polite, broad shoulders bent over the drive, prodding with a heel at the sandy mud.

'Must get in and look over Denman's accounts.'

Stupid to keep Harold waiting. Stupid to linger by the daffodils. A woman's job, flowers. Very pretty. Must get in and look over Denman's accounts and see what can be done about the roof of Copse Farm.

Harold's the squire. He's a good landlord. His tenants love him. I ought to be proud to be Harold's wife. I am proud. There's nobody in the county who wouldn't envy me. Harold's a model landlord and a model husband.

He's generous. He had this room done up as I wanted it. It's the finest drawing-room in the county, even now when the heavy curtains are drawn and the gas lit. It was for me he had the gas put in: did away with the chandeliers, though he'd known them all his life. And it was I who chose the green brocade for the walls, too. But that's the family tradition: it didn't seem to shock him that I should change his mother's drawing-room. All the rest must stay as it is, of course, but the drawing-room is the wife's. Each wife chooses her own setting. Harold's wife, in turn, must set her mark upon Chesborough Hall: the mark of her temporary occupation: that's only right.

And in turn be swept aside.

By whom?

'The fire is going down, dear. Would you mind ringing the bell?'

Harold jumping up, his broad shirt-front agleam in the gas-light: broader, more solid even, than in tweeds. Harold, quick and courteous, breaking up a log so that the sparks shoot up the wide chimney and throwing on more wood from the log basket. Dusting his hands behind him, back to the fire: the back of his head reflected in the great mirror inset in the brocade.

Fire-light on the toes of beaded slippers crossed on the settee; a frail cascade of lace tea-gown over the deep carpet.

Harold likes lace and beaded slippers and a small hand holding needlework. He likes a woman to be frail in the evening but strong by day: strong enough to play her part in the parish and the county and supervise the household and take the carriage out for calls in the afternoon and dine at any distance up to twenty miles and take an intelligent interest in his interest in the estate and ride with him when he wants a morning's pleasure. It's not such an easy task as one might think, being Harold's wife lying on a sofa in a lace tea-gown for an hour after dinner, and talking pleasantly when he's tired.

'Are you tired, dear? You must have had a troublesome day with the Little Chesborough property and those tiresome commissioners.'

Harold opening the piano and asking for music. Sitting on the end of the couch with his seal dangling and the fire-light on it; shading his eyes from the fire.

'Of course, dear. What shall I play?'

The flat drag of lace over the carpet. Candle-light on the music and white, shining keys, and candle flames reflected in the dark, polished rosewood.

I don't think I'm a bad wife to Harold, now I know what he expects. Since I've discovered his ideal of what a wife should be I don't think I've often failed him.

Except in that one thing.

'Thank you. Very nice indeed. Now, let me see... Ten o'clock. Time to turn in.'

Except that Harold's wife should have had a child.

Harold, watch in hand, on the hearth-rug. Impatient to get away to the smoking-room. Impatient for his own hour. Harold's hour: wife and household packed away under his quiet roof, his farms and fields quiet out there under the drifting clouds — quiet, except for an owl in flight over a black hedge, or a beast restless in its stall — Harold can sit alone and be at peace. For an hour, in his smoking-room across the hall, with his pipe and his whisky and syphon on a tray under the college groups and the oar and the running-cups and the hooves of horses and the dark green rows of stud-books, and in the leather arm-chair by the fire that his man piled up before going off duty for the night, the squire can be at peace. Harold can forget, or remember, if he pleases, with quiet satisfaction, his sleeping farms and his sleeping tenants in their low-roofed cottages across the fields, and his sleeping servants in their comfortable quarters over the kitchens and offices, and his sleeping wife in her great, panelled

151

room overhead, with the great cheval-glass and the great, dark wardrobes and the great, half-curtained bed. Harold can forget, or remember, and be Harold. What is Harold? If I'd ever known, things might have been different.

Harold, impatient but courteous, gathering up wrap and beaded work-bag, holding open the door.

'Good night, dear.'

'Good night, my dear.'

The soft brush of a hard cheek, and the great, shadowy hall with its inadequate gas-light from the huge chandeliers, and the flat fall of lace from step to step up the wide, shallow stairs.

Harold will be himself now, for an hour: until he turns out the gas and leaves the hall dark behind him and tiptoes with his candle up the stairs and past my room, and closes his door very softly so as not to wake me.

Harold wants an hour in which to be himself. It doesn't occur to him that I might want to be myself. Why should it? Have I a self? Probably not. Most likely I'm nothing but this: Harold's wife. It's true I have no existence except in relation to him. Possibly that is why I've failed him.

If I had been more of a person I might have had a child. How can an abstraction have a child? Harold succeeded too well. Wife — estate — yes. But when it came to an heir.... And Harold is incomplete without: Harold has failed. But if I had had it, it would never have been a person. It would have been Harold's Child.

I never wanted it. It's strange, I never have wanted it. One ought to. Harold's wife certainly ought to. But I never have. Then why do I resent Sonia so much, and Harold's having her here so often?

'Sonia, don't make so much noise, you'll disturb your uncle. Play quietly. Little girls should be seen and not heard.'

Sunlight in yellow patches on the lawn; the trailing boughs of a weeping-willow violently shaken and a child's voice from its damp, leafy tent.

'Sonia, do you hear me? Answer when I speak to you. Sonia!'

"Uh… ah, ah… uh."

"Yes, Aunt Millicent, do you want anything?"

'Don't be impudent. Come out of that tree and play properly on the lawn, where I can see you.'

"What is it, Aunt Millicent? I'm here."

'Don't answer me back. Do as you're told.'

Harold's voice from the study window, behind the nodding Gloire-de-Dijon: 'Do as your aunt tells you. Look sharp, now.'

Light leaves parting; a bobbing, pink bow and a child's face, impertinent with mock obedience.

'But I'm an Injun, Uncle Harold. This is my tent.'

'Well, well. Suppose you come out of your tent and play on the plains, for a change.'

Harold turning from the window, back to his accounts and his journal.

'Sonia, you'll stain your frock. Stop rolling on the grass at once, and play properly.

'Sonia!'

Don't mutter to yourself. 'Wandering', are you? Harold oughtn't to encourage this kind of play. It isn't a suitable game for a little girl.

Harold's foolish with children. The notice he takes of the Smedley boy whenever we go there. All very well to notice the child, but not to talk to him for hours, about his pony and one thing and another. I wonder Captain Smedley doesn't object. Ridiculous to encourage the boy to show off like that.

Flat, winter fields slowly moving along the hedge; tangled grass, grey-green, and patches of dark ploughland; the roof of a house and a clump of bare trees in a hollow across the fields. An unending line of hedge: brown, stunted twigs and rank docks[6] splashed with mud; dull clop of the horse's hooves and the sideways and forwards pull of the victoria[7] alongside the unending hedge; the coachman's black cockade against a pale sky, and Harold's feet planted on the carpet and his hands on his knees as he stares across at the damp fields.

'Nice youngster, that boy of Smedley's. Jolly youngster.'

Oh, that's it, is it.

Jerk over a stone. The uneven clop of the horse as he recovers step and the onward sway of the victoria. Black cockade and the back of a green livery coat against the sky; unending line of hedge, bare and brown and thorny and endless, and the dank, long dock leaves stained with mud.

Well, it isn't my fault. No, it isn't. It's no use looking reproachful.

Or if you think it's my fault, why not say so?

Why can't he say so? Why has the subject never been mentioned between us? Why can't I say something about it myself? What is it that ties us like this, keeps us silent? So that though we are side by side here in the carriage, we're exchanging remarks on the state of the fields as if we'd met only an hour ago: strangers, waiting for a train. We might be fellow-guests, painstakingly passing the time for one another. What is it? Why can't we speak, either of us, about the things that concern us most nearly? What is it? It must be in him: I don't think it's in me.

Perhaps if it broke, life would be unbearable. Perhaps there would be too much to say: things that would make it painful for us to be obliged to see one another day after day. Perhaps if there ever comes a time when husbands and wives speak quite openly to one another, without reserve, marriage will become impossible. There

---

6 A perennial, herbaceous plant with large leaves and distinctive seedheads.

7 A low, light, four-wheeled, doorless coach with a forward-facing seat for two persons.

must be so many searing, wounding things that two people could say to one another after a number of years. If they were spoken it would be impossible to go on; the crust would never form over them again. A crust of smooth pleasantness and mutual, polite consideration: is it only that which makes marriage possible? Or isn't it so with other people, even now? Is it only we who need this protective crust? But in Harold's generation there must be a great number of people like him.

I don't know: mutual reproaches might be better. But it isn't my fault: either this or the other. And I don't want to reproach Harold. I'm glad things are as they are. Yes, I am. There's a certain — yes, a certain dignity, in silence. And I don't want a child. No, I'm glad we haven't got a child. And it's not likely now. I'm glad.

Unending hedge of brown twigs, thorny and bare, and damp docks drooping. Black cockade against the sky; a forward jolt and roll, and Harold's hands planted on his knees as he stares across at the brown fields.

'How about asking Margaret to send us Sonia for a bit? A good time since the youngster's been here. Set her up with a pony and let her ride to hounds with young Smedley. Jolly youngster.'

Yes I am: I'm glad. Though I don't know why I should be glad that Harold can't have what he wants. It's the way he hides it. If he ever showed he were feeling anything it might be different. But that resignation, and the unacknowledged resentment underneath: Harold, cheated of his rights: Harold, too considerate to protest.... It's not my fault. It's always been like that. It wasn't my fault, that night.

Candle-light on the polished frame of the mirror; cut glass bottles and silver brushes and the light glinting. Deep well of the mirror and a face lost and floating in the light of tall candles.

The door of Harold's dressing-room, closing.

He isn't coming yet. He's only just come up from the smoking-room. But he won't be long. He won't keep me up: Harold's too considerate.

I wish he weren't so considerate.

I wish he wouldn't come at all. Why does he? It doesn't bring us any closer together. We're never further apart.

We're closer, even, when we're riding together, when the downs are soft green in the morning and there are beads of mist on the grass; when the air is sharp and the horses canter and we slow down suddenly and turn on to the road and look at one another and know we've both enjoyed it.

But I wonder whether Harold does know. I don't think it occurs to him. I don't think he even knows the air is in his lungs and the mist beady on the grass: he only has a general feeling of well-being. But because I have too, we're closer then than we are at most times.

Polished wood slippery under the elbows, and knuckles firm against the jaw. Small face, pale in the candle-light, frowning between the dangling plaits.

I wish Harold wouldn't come. Why must he?

What's the use of thinking like that? Of course he'll come. He'll be here in one minute. He'll always come: for years and years. How long shall I live? Another fifty years, perhaps; and Harold's older, but he'll live longer than I. Forever, then. Have we really been married for only three years?

I couldn't possibly say to Harold that I wish he wouldn't come. He'd be hurt. Besides, it isn't that. I shouldn't mind so much if he really came; if I could really know Harold and get close to him; if we were two separate people who were close to one another. We can't be close because we're not two people. Harold's a person, but I'm not; or he feels I'm not. I've never been able to feel I was a real person, so I suppose Harold can't, either. I wonder why it is. I can't help feeling sometimes that I'm not really here at all, only playing at being somebody who's married Harold. As one used to do: now you're going to be Harold, and I'm your wife. What would Harold say if I told him I was nobody really? He'd laugh.

156

He wouldn't believe it. Of course I'm somebody: I'm his wife.

Round, small face, and plaits, and the nose wrinkled up.

Body. Why should it tie *me* to you? It isn't I.

Harold's door across the landing. Door opening slowly over the thick carpet. White face, startled, rising in the dark mirror.

'I'm sorry, did I startle you? Didn't you hear me knock?'

Harold, mildly surprised, solid, hands in pockets of the brown brocade dressing-gown, shadowy at the edge of the candle-light.

'Yes. No.'

What can I say? I don't know why I jumped up. What was I thinking? I couldn't explain. Certainly not to Harold.

'No, it was only... Nothing. I think perhaps I'm not very well.'

Harold, firm and solid in the circle of light, towering in the bright mirror. Golden lights on the brown brocade dressing-gown. Harold, bronzed and big, patting the shoulder with its dangling plait.

'What you want is a change. Run-down. Not feeling quite yourself, eh? Like to go away for a bit? No? Well, well, we'll see to-morrow. Get a good sleep now.'

The brush of a moustache and a firm pat on the shoulder and the door closing, softly, beyond a white face in the depths of the glass.

But I didn't mean that. I didn't mean to send Harold away. Why couldn't I explain?

Push of fists against chin; eyes questioning; end of a plait sliding on the polished wood.

Was it really so simple as that? But I didn't mean it. It's never happened before. I never thought of it.

I didn't think of it this time. It just happened. It may happen again. Not always, but it may happen.

It's a good thing it happened.

But why was it? Why is it?

157

Swish and drip of water; chill air; water, slapped, lapping up. Lap, lap. And slap and squish and drip.

Water splashing up against the rocks. Waves breaking, and the backward suck and lap.

Lap, lap. Flap lap of water on sand; long, flat sands and the long, low, flat waves rippling in: a long, wavering line of small waves flattened out along the flat, wet sands, and the chink and echo of china.

Cup rattling into saucer, and the splash of tea from the urn.

'Time we saw about reserving rooms for the summer. Perhaps you would be so good as to write to Brighton.'

Harold's face raised above the *Times*. Harold's face above the firmly stretched sheets of the *Times* and a sizzling dish of eggs and bacon.

Brighton? Must we?

Trim promenades and a well-behaved sea and a hotel dining-room with Harold's face above the *Times* and eggs and bacon.

'It's only April, dear.'

'May as well make sure of the rooms we had last year.'

The *Times* neatly folded beside his plate; Harold serving eggs and bacon from the sizzling dish: shining yellow yokes on firm saucers of white, and crisp, pink and white, crinkled bacon.

Why can't I say what I want to say? After all, there's no harm in suggesting. What is it about Harold that dries up one's words and makes them not worth speaking? It isn't that he means to dictate. It's just that firm assurance: the way he balances the egg firmly in the spoon without breaking it, and slides it on to the plate. No hurry. It never breaks. Naturally: it never occurs to him it might break.

The warm, sweet sting of coffee. Words in a rush: 'Why shouldn't we go somewhere else instead of Brighton? We might go somewhere else for a change.'

Spoon halted in mid-air: steam rolling back along the silver, like a mist at sea, leaving it smooth and shiny.

Harold quietly surprised, politely interested.

'And where would you suggest we should go?'

But he doesn't mean it. He knows we shall go there in the end.

Quietly judicious: 'Brighton may not be all it was in my father's time, perhaps. But we always *have* been there.'

Always? But there have only been two years. Does that mean always? That it will be always? But he used to go with his mother, of course.

With quiet decision: 'My parents always went to Brighton.'

'Oh yes, I know.'

Thick, sweet coffee.

Why can't I tell him? Why can't I say it? Why do I gulp like this, it must be audible across the table.

'I wish we could go to Cornwall. We used to go there when I was a child.'

Harold's mouth set judiciously over a mouthful of bacon. Firm sweep of the napkin over his moustache. Polite interest.

'And what did you find particularly attractive about Cornwall?'

I don't know. Yes I do. But I can't say it.

Harold, bending again to his plate; firm action of knife and fork efficiently handled. The dark walls behind Harold, and the dark portraits and the dark, heavy side-board with its silver sending up a light here and there, and a stretch of deep, dark carpet.

'I don't know. It's wild in a way.'

Dark, sweet coffee. Waves beating up against a wild coast, and a restless, haunting sea. Space, and gulls wheeling, and the suck of the sea very far below in green and purple inlets between the black headlands.

'I believe there is not a single comfortable hotel in Cornwall.'

'No? No, perhaps you're right.'

The servants' feet padding over the deep carpet and a discreet chink of forks at a side table.

Seagulls' feet, stepping noiselessly over the thick carpet: a smooth, white head and hooked bill — the red under-bill: like blood: as if they'd been tearing food — and the strong head flattened at the top, and an eye cocked, watching.

'I think you would find it most uncomfortable there.'

Wail of swooping gulls and the thud-thud of the sea in hidden caves.

'Yes, perhaps.'

Why can't I say it? Why can't I make him see what I mean? It's different: there's something different there. It makes you feel something that Brighton doesn't. It must be the same sea, but it makes you feel something. I don't think you could feel very much at Brighton.

Yellow egg oozing from a cut yoke on to Harold's plate, congealing on the smooth china. Plump dome of the yoke sunken, wrinkled and flat, to meet the white.

Why is it? Harold would listen politely, but I can't tell him anything. I can't tell him anything that matters. It's because he'd never be convinced. He'd listen politely, but he'd always have some excellent reason for not agreeing. It isn't even that: he'd agree, but we should go to Brighton all the same.

'Most uncomfortable place, Cornwall. I once had to spend a night at Truro.'

Harold's plate discreetly slid away; the pad of the servant's feet and the crinkling of the *Times* as Harold re-opens it and lifts a piece of toast from the rack, neatly; balancing the outspread page of the *Times* against the table edge.

Oh very well, if you won't understand.

But I haven't given him a chance. I haven't said anything.

But he wouldn't understand if I did.

What's the use. It doesn't matter. It isn't worth bothering about.

Dark, panelled walls and deep fire-place and the great, dark portraits in their heavy frames, dull, unshining.

I wish this room got more sun. If I had my way we should have breakfast in a smaller room. But Harold likes this. His father always breakfasted here.

It isn't worth bothering about. Why is it that sooner or later Harold always makes you feel like that about things? It doesn't matter: we may as well go to Brighton. Harold would dislike Cornwall and he'd spoil it for me. I may as well keep the memory of it. I have got that now. If Harold went there I shouldn't even have that.

I oughtn't to feel like that. I suppose it's my fault: I suppose I ought to want the same things as Harold.

'I'll write to-day, then, shall I? To the hotel?'

'It might be as well, if you have time.'

But you might see that I don't want it. You might *see*.

'And let me see, if we go away for June we might have that child of Margaret's here for a bit in July. Sonia, they call her. Let me see, she'd be — what — seven or eight by now. Now they've come to live at a reasonable distance you ought to make her acquaintance.'

Margaret's child: Harold's niece. But I can't be an aunt. I don't want to be an aunt. I'm not old enough. I can't do it properly. I don't know how an aunt ought to behave.

'I don't know whether I could manage....'

'Manage? You'll manage right enough. Child won't be any trouble. Jolly youngster, from what I remember of her. You ought to get along capitally together.'

It isn't fair. It comes of Harold's being older. I oughtn't to have married somebody older than myself. It isn't fair, having to be an aunt when I've hardly learnt to be a wife. And I don't think I've learnt that very well. I'm not much of a success as a wife. I don't see that I can ever be a success at anything.

Harold's wife. Harold's wife visiting among the tenantry.

I suppose I'm not so bad at this.

'Yes, m'lady.'

The woman bobbing; the dark cottage room, a black hole in the side of the village street. Stuffy, strangling smell of humanity and horse-hair; dusted chair-seat and the hideously flowered ornaments on the dresser.

'Yes, m'lady. Thanking you, m'lady.'

A coronation cup: Edward and Alexandra in twin gilt wreathes of laurel, very bright and new; china pig, a Present from Weston, and the thickly painted red roses on the side of a yellow vase.

How can they live in this atmosphere? Don't they smell it? Or do they like it?

'The children are all back at school again, thanking you, m'lady.'

They must see through me. They must know I'm a fraud. Do I look as if I were listening? Well, I am.

'Our Archie had his foot that bad.'

Oh yes, I'm listening. I'm sure he did.

'It must have been very trying for you, Mrs. Muggers.'

Why should she tell me this? Why should they have to tell me every detail of their lives? What is it to me? And what am I to them? Squire's wife, of course. They like to talk: things are better when they've told Squire's wife about them. It isn't only the beef-tea and blankets: somebody has to be interested. They feel they have a right to interest. Does she really not see through me? See that I'm not m'lady at all, only....

But I am. You see, I am, aren't I? I don't know how, but I am. When they have such small windows, why do they fill them with geraniums in pots? And cover with a lace curtain? It's like a cupboard in here: dark as a cupboard. But better than the street. The street's so light and empty.

It's worse than Market Chesborough. There are fewer people, but they all know you. It's horrible to be a marked figure; to have to notice everybody. It isn't only that it's a village: it was that at home, but it didn't matter if you were in a hurry or went the other way. It's the having a position to keep up.

Can I get past the vicarage before Mrs. Mayhew comes out? She'll want to know which villagers I've seen and what I think of Blodger's taking to drink and that dreadful family down on the common: they're bringing all the children up to be no better than poachers.

'Yes, I know, Mrs. Mayhew. Perhaps the Vicar could speak to Blodger. Yes, I'd noticed Jim Sparks had given up coming to church. Oh, he's taken up with a shop-girl out of Market Chesborough? Oh? Oh really? How dreadful.'

Long, dusty stretch of the road with its straggling cottages, and the turn past the inn. Safety around the corner.

Unless Miss Price has been down to Peacham's Farm to fetch her eggs. She goes at eleven as a rule. She ought to have passed the corner by now.

I suppose I shall get used to this. I suppose in any position one is given a year to adapt oneself. I don't think I've adapted myself so badly. I don't think I do so badly as the squire's wife, visiting among the tenantry. Not so badly, as the squire's wife. But how about Harold's?

I don't know what went wrong. I don't know how it went wrong. I don't know whether Harold knows that it did. So it doesn't matter very much, perhaps. But I should like to be a success as a wife, not only as m'lady. Because when you're only twenty-two and will never have a chance to be anything but what you are and you happen to be Harold's wife, you may as well make a success of it. And you can't make a success of marriage without loving your husband, can you?

I don't know why I don't love Harold. I did. Didn't I? I did, of course. I shouldn't have married him if I hadn't. Of course I did. But something went wrong. I don't know whether it was on our honeymoon. No, it was when we came back, wasn't it? It was so grey here, after Italy, and it seemed we were leaving something

163

behind with the sunshine. And I was so afraid: I wanted to hold it so that it shouldn't go.

It seemed as if Harold was quite different when we got back here. There was so much for him to attend to, and so much for me to learn. I ought to have understood that things would be different when we came back. Harold wasn't himself in Italy; it was an interval: a gap in his life. Then he came back to life. But because I hadn't been here before and been part of his life, I didn't know. I didn't realize that that was only a gap. And I wanted to bring back things that didn't belong here but belonged to the sunshine. Like the shells and seaweed you take back from the seaside, and they're coloured and alive and shining, and when you unpack them at home they're dead and dull and there's no place for them. It was like that. Now I've seen that, I expect I can make more of a success of being his wife. Only I never meant to be this kind of wife.

I never meant to be any kind of wife.

I suppose I'm a failure emotionally; that's why I couldn't make it last. Otherwise that might have been life, instead of only a gap.

I suppose I'm a failure, a failure. Yes, a failure.

But it's so grey, here. That grey park, and the trees like brown skeletons. That's England, of course, as I've always known it. I knew perfectly well England was like that. I never expected it to be different. But I hadn't imagined being married, here in England. I hadn't imagined coming back here, and looking at England from my own window in Harold's house. I wish Harold would come. I wish the maid hadn't left me alone. I wish I'd made the unpacking last longer. I wish Harold hadn't gone off at once to see to the stables, but waited until to-morrow.

That's absurd, of course. Of course he's got things to see to, when he's been away for so long.

I wish we hadn't come back, ever. We might still be looking at the sea and the mimosa and the sunshine. Why didn't I bring back some mimosa, this room is so big and dark.

It's such a large mirror, I look horribly small in it. I'm much too small for this huge room. It wasn't meant for me: Harold ought to have married somebody imposing. The dressing-table's so big that the bottles and things out of my dressing-case look lost on it. I wonder what was on it before.

It's rather horrid to think of all the people who've lived in this room. It must always have been the bride's room: the largest, like this, looking out over the park. Think of all Harold's ancestors, one after another, bringing their brides home to this room, and the brides looking at themselves in this big mirror. I wonder whether they all looked so small as I. They must have felt small, when they looked at that enormous bed. I suppose it used to have curtains, all round, but they've taken most of them away. Harold's mother did that, probably. All of them must have emptied their dressing-cases on to the table and thought how empty it still looked. Think of them arriving, long, long ago, in coaches; how cold they must have been; and then finding this room so big and unfriendly. And some of them must have died here. It's rather horrid.

'Harold, Harold, I'm so glad you've come!'

Harold, closing the door quietly, holding out a travelling rug he picked up in the hall.

'Where shall I put this?'

'Oh, I don't know. Anywhere.'

I don't know. How should I know? I don't know anything.

Harold, laying the rug on the settee at the foot of the bed. Quickly, surprised: 'What's the matter?'

Harold, so big and safe, and the rough tweed.

'We haven't left it all, have we? Everything's so big and dark. We haven't left it all: all the sunshine? Harold, you do love me, don't you? You do, you do. Harold, say you do. Harold, you do, you do love me?'

Gentle, shocked withdrawal. Harold, grave and puzzled: 'Of course, of course. Hadn't you better lie down for a bit? There are still a few things I ought to see to. Have a rest before dinner.'

Harold, pained and puzzled, tucking in the rug.

'Better rest. You've had a long day.'

I oughtn't to have said all that. It was stupid, giving way; just now when he has so much to do. Oh stupid, stupid. I oughtn't to have talked like that. He doesn't want it. It isn't suitable, here. Harold always knows what is suitable. Poor Harold, he's worried; he doesn't know what to do.

'Shall I have some tea sent to you, up here?'

The door closing softly.

Harold's so big: you wouldn't think he could be so gentle and considerate. But I oughtn't to have talked like that. It wasn't the thing to say. It doesn't belong here. It doesn't belong to this room, or the grey park. I'm not a bride anymore: I'm a wife. I ought to have gone down and poured tea in the drawing-room.

It was stupid. He drew away. He didn't mean to: he stopped himself. He was holding me all the time. But why did I say anything so stupid. He couldn't help drawing away when I behaved like that. It was the wrong time. It wasn't suitable.

Sun and sea: blue sea with white lights in the sun. Quaking, feathery tamarisk and mimosa; leaves in a dark flood poured down on to the white steps.

Harold's splendid, you know. He is, you know. Harold's splendid.

White balustrade of the terrace under the window, and the shivering, blue sea.

I'm in love with him. Yes I am. I am. I'm in love with Harold, did you know? Harold's so splendid.

I'm going to sit here by the window, where I can see him.

Bump of a wicker-chair over the polished floor.

It's absurd to say I ought to rest. It isn't hot in here. The sea's so lovely, I can't rest. I can't lose it; I want to look at it and take it in, all the time. I want to feel it. I want to feel the blueness of the sea and the whiteness of the terrace and being in love with Harold.

Harold, down below, on the terrace; foot up, on the pedestal of the balustrade; elbows on the white stone rail: Harold, smoking and looking out to sea. Harold in white flannels and a panama.

He's splendid. He's splendid. He is. I love him.

It's so lovely here, so lovely. I want to feel all the blueness and whiteness of it. So that it will stay. I didn't know the sun could be so much alive. It's a live thing, here; in England it's only a ghost. If only we could stay here. Why can't we stay.

But don't think about that.

We're here. I'm here. I'm here, in Italy. This is Italy, and I'm here. I've always wanted to be here in the sunshine. I want to take it all in. But there's too much of it. I want to feel it. It's so blue and so white.

But I do, I do. I do feel it. If I look at it long enough I feel part of it. If only one could go on looking. It would be wonderful to be alone here; alone with the sea.

No, I don't mean that. If Harold and I were alone, I mean. It would be wonderful if we were alone. You're so splendid, Harold.

Foot on the pedestal; strong shoulders; white panama against the blue sea.

'Harold.'

He can't hear, from there. There's nobody to hear; nobody near enough. And if they did hear they wouldn't know who I was. I want to say it aloud, into the air; to the sea and the mimosa; so that it becomes part of it all.

'Harold, I love you.'

How odd to hear one's own voice like that, all alone. It makes it so real. It's given, somehow, to the sea to keep. When I'm old, shall I come here and find it. It's queer how difficult it is to speak above a whisper, all alone with the sea.

'Harold, I love you. I do.'

Strong shoulders, bent, leaning. White shirt and blue sea. Peculiar strength of shoulders at rest, muscles slack under the thin shirt.

'You're so strong.'

I want to hear that again.

'You're so strong, Harold. So strong.'

All that strength at peace in the sunshine.

'I love you, I do. I love you, I love you.'

Yes I do. I do. Really I do. Only it's so dreadful.

The broad, dim hotel lounge and a sudden, stabbing light. Burning light beyond the open doors. Huge, staring, shadowless stretch of promenade and open, staring sea. And people.

People looking.

I must look so small beside Harold.

White, staring asphalt.

They must know we're newly married. The hotel people do. So do the others, they all look. A honey-moon couple. How dreadful, they can all see.

Staring. Light and space opening out, and fingers pointing.

No, of course they're not. They only look and smile and turn away. We must be horribly obvious. Harold, why did you come where there were so many people? How could you do this to me, Phil?

Rush of blood to the skin; and the horribly wide, white promenade, widening out. Walls falling back, and pointing fingers. People, glancing and looking away and smiling.

I mustn't blush. That makes it worse. How dreadful.

They're not looking really. Of course they're not. They're taking it for granted. I'm Harold's wife. Of course I am. But it's so dreadful, everybody knowing.

Well, I am. I don't care. I'm his wife.

Quick, shameful tingle of blood.

Nonsense. Ridiculous. I'm not going to think like that, it's silly. There's nothing to be ashamed of. I ought to be proud to be married to somebody like Harold. Of course I am, in a way. But that's different.

Well, so I am. I don't care what they think. Why should I care, after all? I am. I'm Harold's wife, and I want the whole world to know it. Yes I do. I'm Harold's wife, and Harold's splendid.

I love you, Harold. I love the sun and the sea and the band in the distance. I love being on the promenade among people: crowds and crowds of people. Walls opening out, and pointing. No, no, don't think, no. Yes I do: I wish there were even more people. I want to be among them. I want them all to know. I want to be among them and be part of them. I ought to feel I belong to them now. I do, don't I? I've never felt like that before about people, but I do belong to them now. And that's because of you, Harold.

Swift rush and tingle and the face burning.

Oh, what a dreadful thing to say!

But I want to say it. I do. I'm not going to be silly. I'm going to say it: it's because of you, Harold.

It's queer, they say brides feel shy, but I don't a bit, now. I'm not going to be silly. I don't mind a bit: it was silly to mind. I want to be among people. People, glancing and smiling and looking away. I want it, I do. I want them all to see us together and know I'm your wife. You're so splendid, Harold. I wonder what you'd say if I said all this to you. But just go on talking, so long as we can stay here among people: just be among them, and by the sea, and part of it all.

I've always disliked being among people; I've always felt different, as if I were made of glass and they could see through me. But it isn't like that anymore. It isn't, is it? Now that I'm your wife. Am I really your wife, Harold? I can hardly believe it. But I am. Of course I am, or it would be dreadful. But I mustn't think like that, it's silly. I'm Harold's wife. Harold's wife. I suppose that's why things are different: I haven't got to be myself anymore: only just that. And so I'm a person, like other people. You've made me into a person, Harold; I wasn't really a person before.

'Couldn't we take one of these cabs and drive out to the Old Town? I should like to see it, wouldn't you?'

Tall, tall, leaning houses with the windows flung wide; clothes flapping on lines from house to house, and high voices arguing, and heat and people. Mattress at a first-floor window and a woman in carpet slippers, with blouse undone, mopping a floor. Children in the gutters. There's no room in the houses. There are too many. They fall out into the street. A man stripped to the waist, arms folded, leaning against a doorpost. And a hot stench, musty and acrid.

These are people. This is life. It's horrible, it's indecent, it's bare. I don't care. I like it. Yes I do.

Sickness choked down.

'Oh, I like it, I like this. It's so full of people. I like the crowded, narrow streets and the people sitting at their doors. It's so full of life. Don't laugh at me! It is, really, isn't it.'

I like it. I like it. Yes I do. I'm part of it all. I am, I tell you. All this. I'm just as much part of it as that big woman over there at her door, stringing beans for her husband's supper. I haven't got to string beans, but I'm like that.

I wish I had; somehow it would make it better.

But I am like that. Oh, how dreadful.

No, but it isn't. How silly. This is real, and I'm part of it. It's wonderful to be part of it all. Not having that cramped, tight feeling anymore, of holding yourself against the world. Like having let go of something you were holding on to very hard. Because I have. I have let go. I don't mind anymore when people brush against me. It's a feeling, a feeling.... Yes, that's it: a feeling of being spread out among the people and into the sea and sunshine. Tall houses, and lazy, easygoing, happy people. I haven't got to be myself anymore. I like it. Yes I do.

'Harold, it's so lovely here. Couldn't we stay here always?'

It's lovely, it's lovely. Harold, Harold, I love you. Yes I do. I tell you I do, I do. It would be dreadful if I didn't. I love you.

170

But all these people. So many people.

All these people come to see that I love Harold. All come to hear me promise to love Harold as long as we live. How can I promise? And suppose I don't. I don't know. I suppose I do, or I shouldn't be here.

All the villagers crowding up between the graves. No room in the church. The church was too small. It's packed. They're all waiting in there, in the dark. All those people waiting for me. I must. There's no way back. They've closed in behind us. The carriages are waiting, I might tell them to drive.... Drive where? But the people have closed in over the path. They're following up. The villagers and a lot of Harold's tenants. They came in brakes. They're following up. They're going to see that it's done. The sacrifice. The victim mustn't escape. The victim in white, and the altar waiting.

No, what am I saying.

Faces peering, gaping, pressed together. Ranks behind pressing forward; a pressed, tottering line at the edge of the path. Children tumbling over the tombstones, to see.

Chill of the porch. Grey stone, very old. How many weddings has it seen? How many shivering, white brides? This is nothing. A moment lost in centuries. One step out of a million million on the worn stone.

Dark stone, and a sea of dark, quiet people. So I'm here. Nothing's happened. I'm here. Why am I in white: only I? Marked out. The victim.

Hush of carpet underfoot. The beginning. The path. Red, dusty carpet, uneven over the slabs. The worn floor. My feet won't wear it. There won't be a particle of stone the less when I've passed.

That's my path. Mine. I can't. Straight and narrow: straight, and the dark people like a high hedge. And the altar at the end, and somebody else in white. That's the clergyman. And Harold, waiting.

Rumble of the organ; flutter of gloves and books; wind over the sea. Ripple of faces discreetly turned: white flecks on the dark sea.

I can't do it! I can't!

Drag of a slipper on the worn carpet.

I can't go on.

Rumble of organ, and voices rising in a quaver: separate, quavering together. The sickly sweet scent of lilies. Harold in a dark suit. I wish he'd got his tweeds on.

I've got to get out, out. Get out.

Swelling together of voices into a jangled mass: a tumbling wave of quavers. Smooth cloth, thick under the hand. Feet on, on; slippers firm on the thin carpet, gripping through at the worn stone. They haven't noticed. They think I stopped to give them time to start singing. They didn't notice I stopped at all. I've got to be calm. It's a long way. Anything can happen before I get there. I've got to be calm. Be calm.

The altar, nearer, larger. The vicar's put on his white stole; he's all in white too. He only wears it at Christmas and Easter. So I'm like that. Which am I: born or risen?

Sickly sweet smell of lilies. Sickly faint. Suppose I fainted. I couldn't faint, I never have.

Toe against something hard: the steps. They've whitened the steps. They didn't put the carpet up the steps, it wouldn't reach, they had to start at the door. We don't go up the steps. Smooth cloth sliding from beneath the hand. They're beginning. No, we're beginning: I'm part of this. I'm this. They couldn't have it without me. So nothing's happened. I'm here.

Silence, and a voice. He's saying it well. He's taking trouble over this, I ought to be grateful. How quiet people are; what are they doing there behind me? I mustn't turn round.

I've got to be calm, calm. I've got to speak firmly. This has got to be done.

Sweet, sickly smell of lilies, stronger and stronger.

Did I say that? I will? I will what? I don't know. What will I? What will I?

That's the ring. Harold's taken my hand often before, but it didn't matter. This matters. I ought to feel it. I ought to feel something happen. Suppose it were Michael instead of Harold, should I feel anything then?

It's done now. I'm married to Harold.

Ridiculous, you couldn't marry somebody like Michael. Not somebody you've played with as a child. I never wanted to marry Michael. And Michael's married somebody else. Michael was just somebody you played with, and after that he was nothing but a dream. You can't marry a dream, can you?

It's done. They're going to have a sermon now. Well, that's done.

But I never meant it. I never meant it! I never meant!

This is real. This is something that's happened to me. This isn't a dream. Harold isn't a dream, he's real. Harold's reality, and I've married Harold. You can't marry a dream. You can't be in love with a dream. Harold's real. I've married Harold. I love Harold.

White and bare and quiet. Crawl of a fly, slow and painful, around the lamp-shade's china slope. Slow people moving.

"...satisfactory."

Satis... satis... satisfery. Satisfecery. What's satisfecery? Not satisfecery? But it is satisfecery. What's satisfecery. Who said.

'Most satisfactory. Most satisfactory from all points of view.'

Papa's hands briskly rubbed together; the swing back of the red plush portière as the door closes.

'You have had your talk then? It is settled?'

Gentle eagerness in Mamma's voice; faint, restrained impatience in the push of a slipper against the round, beaded footstool; hands, in suspended motion, hovering above the tatting.

So that's over. They're pleased. How exciting! It's exciting really!

Mamma's smile of gentle satisfaction under the smooth, grey hair brushed back and the flat moiré bow.

They're pleased. Harold's made a good impression on Papa.

Sunshine on the waxed floor, and a bee a-buzz against a window-pane. Smoky blue of lavender in a big bowl on the table beside Mamma's chair.

But Papa knew all about him before. He was quite ready to accept Harold, long before they had their talk in the study. He knew what Harold was going to say. They both knew it: they must have known it for ages. They wanted it, and they're glad.

But why should they? Why are they? Why am I?

They're glad: it isn't every country doctor's daughter who can marry into an estate like Harold's.

But I oughtn't to think things like that about them. They're not like that, a bit. They can't help being glad.

I don't know what's happened to me that I should think things like that. It's almost cynical. It's dreadful to be cynical. It isn't the way Harold would think. It's ever since Michael went that I've caught myself thinking things like that: the way Michael behaved. No, but Michael didn't, what do I mean.

Warm cheek, and Mamma's fond glance. They think I'm thinking about Harold. And the dusky smoke-blue of the lavender stiff in its china bowl.

But I mustn't think about Michael anymore. I shall never think of him anymore now. I didn't mean to think about him. I've forgotten all about him, really. Why, I can't even remember how he used to look when he came round the corner by the lavender bushes....

No, I can't. I won't. I'm not thinking about him at all, really.

I'm glad they're glad about Harold. They're glad. They're not thinking about his being Sir Harold Chesborough. They're glad because I'm going to be happy. Because, of course, I am happy now: now that I'm going to marry Harold.

Am I really going to? It sounds odd when you say it like that: to marry Harold. But that won't be for ages and ages. Anything can happen before that.

Of course it can. Anything.

Time rushing down, swift and dark: downward in a dark flood, on and on and swift and on, and the boom and suck of waters, unseen, and the swift, dark, fearful rush of time.

Not really. I can't really.

But what nonsense. I want to, of course I do. How foolish: what could happen? Besides, why should it? That's absurd. I didn't mean that. Of course I'm going to, but it's too far away to think about.

Mamma's hand gliding, quickly and more quickly, in and out over the tatting.

I'm glad they're glad.

I'm glad, glad. I'm glad, you know. Yes I am, I'm glad. What do I mean. I'm glad Harold's asked me. I'm glad I came here to-night.

Oh, I'm glad they're waltzing in there in the ball-room and the palms are so big and shady out here and Harold's kissing my hand. I used to wonder what it would feel like if somebody kissed my hand!

But how can he? It's ridiculous.

But I mustn't feel like that: it's silly.

I'm glad I came. I'm glad I didn't stay away just because I always feel so awkward up here at the Court. I wish I didn't always feel like the doctor's daughter when I'm up here at one of their grand parties. Though it isn't only that. It's Hilda, so bouncing and lively and always knowing how to behave. But how comical to think I'm sitting out here in a conservatory with Sir Harold Chesborough!

Big, dark palm-leaves against the white paint. Green painted tubs on the paved floor black and white in squares, and the funny, thick stems of the palms.

Like giant pineapples, some of them. And my feet and his on the checked floor: white satin slippers on a black square and black patent pumps on a white. Side by side. We couldn't have arranged it better, could we? Millicent, the doctor's daughter, sitting out in a conservatory at Sibsley Court, with Sir Harold Chesborough kissing her hand!

Oh dear, I oughtn't to be thinking like this, ought I? But it's so comical. It can't be real. Ought I to take away my hand or wait till he drops it? Or will he put it back on my knee? Among the white muslin frills. Like a bridal gown! No, that would be satin.

I really oughtn't to be thinking things like this. I ought to be feeling very serious, when I've just had an offer of marriage. But I haven't really, have I? He can't have meant it. I used to wonder, when I was small, what I should say if somebody proposed to me, and whether he'd go down on his knees as they do in books. Harold didn't go down on his knees, though. Perhaps people don't, now; or was it because I was only the doctor's daughter?

How foolish! Harold wouldn't think about that. Or else he wouldn't have asked me, would he?

But he didn't really ask me, did he? He can't have. It's so comical.

So I really am grown-up. I must be. But it's absurd. I don't know how to behave. But I must.

I wonder whether I said the right things. I have accepted him, haven't I? If Papa gives his consent, that is.

Of course Papa will. They must have known it was going to happen. I wonder whether I didn't know it too? Of course, I knew he was staying up here again, at the Court, or I shouldn't have come this evening. At least, I don't think so.

But I didn't know he was going to propose, honestly I didn't! Not until he suggested sitting out, in here. But I knew it the minute I saw the palms and their funny stems in tubs: now I wonder why?

I knew it the very moment I saw him coming in between the palms; coming across, with a smile, between the tables.

No, what am I saying. I don't mean that. There aren't any tables.

Yes there were, though: little tables.

No, how foolish. Isn't that odd: it's as if this had happened before, only it wasn't quite the same. Perhaps I dreamt it, but I don't remember. Besides, Sir Harold didn't come in; he was here all the time. We came in together, from the ball-room, when they began the polka; and it seemed very quiet in here, suddenly, and Sir Harold picked up my scarf which was slipping from my shoulders, and he said, 'You mustn't catch cold, these places are treacherous.'

Why did he say that? Why did he say treacherous?

And I said, 'I'm quite warm, thank you, Sir Harold.' And that was when he said I was to call him Harold. And I couldn't help blushing, though it must have looked terribly foolish.

Of course, I've often thought of him as Harold, but it seems so peculiar to say it aloud.

Oh dear, I shall never be able to behave like a grown-up.

I shall have to practise: Harold, I love you. You can't say, Sir Harold I love you, can you? It sounds silly. That's why you have to say Harold.

'But I wasn't laughing. Truly. It was only.... I don't know. Just thinking how happy I am.'

Oh, but I mustn't giggle. It's dreadful, really. Like a housemaid walking out! I simply mustn't. Oh dear, if only I could *feel* grown-up.

But why am I here? It's ridiculous. It doesn't mean anything.

Harold's face growing larger. So his eyes are grey. The small, fair moustache that moves when he smiles, and the palms waving. They aren't really waving. They're standing still, really.

And *I* love *you*, Harold: I ought to say that, oughtn't I? Because I do; I'm sure I do. And it seems unkind not to say anything when he says so much.

But I don't! I don't! Quick, stop, I don't.

Yes I do: of course I do.

The faintest murmur: 'I love you, Harold.'

'I never dreamt you could.'

But he must have. I must have let him see it last summer. That is, he must have thought I did. I oughtn't to have let him think so, ought I? But I believe I did. The day of the picnic....

Trees meeting overhead. The dark wood: a green, dark tunnel. Ferns with their brown, tightly rolled tips bent to the worn wood of the stile.

'The others must have gone ahead into the wood. Let me help you.'

Flap of skirts against the wooden rails. Foot entangled; strong tweed under the hand.

'Jump.'

Mud squelching underfoot. Tight, brown fronds of fern and a tinkle of water and a firm path of trodden moss.

Shall I let go of his arm now? He expects me to leave my hand there, doesn't he?

'Thank you. I wonder where they can have gone.'

I mustn't let go, yet. I mustn't seem to draw away. That's what happened with Michael.

How was it I couldn't take his arm or show I cared? He was hurt: that's why he went away. I don't know. I wanted to. Oh, I did.

Strong tweed under the hand. The arm beneath, strong, reassuring, and an answering pressure.

Oh, I didn't mean that!...

'We ought to look for the others, don't you think? We'd better look for them.'

I can't let go now, can I? There doesn't seem to be any reason. Now that I've held on for so long.

Leaves rustling up around the skirt-hem. Skirt clutched, at the back, with one hand.

And I'm still holding his arm. Ought I to let go?

'Which way can they have gone?'

'Suppose we sit here and let them find us.'

Softness of moss; dark, shiny celandine leaves, and Sir Harold's arm gently lowered.

'Oh, I don't know. Do you think so?'

Easier to sit.

The arm withdrawn. A bright yellow celandine, polished and
expressionless, smooth to the fingers.

I mustn't seem to mind being alone with him. He likes me, I
know he does. And I like him. It's foolish, I can never let people
know when I like them. He doesn't think I like him. I oughtn't to
have seemed so anxious to go on and find the others.

Smooth, yellow petals, cool to the fingers. Dark trees meeting overhead.

But he insisted on our waiting. Now Michael would have said,
Certainly; and we should have gone on without another word, and
he'd have felt hurt. But Sir Harold — Harold, it's a nice name, isn't
it? — he doesn't look hurt. He's looking amused. It's because I've
been playing for so long with this celandine. I like him. I wish I
could let him know I like him.

But why? I don't really. It's absurd, my sitting here. I don't
want to be. I wish I were right away somewhere.

No. No, don't think like that. Behave properly. How ought I to
behave? I ought to show Sir Harold I like him; but how?

But I don't really.

Yes, I do. It's ridiculous never being able to show people you
like them.

Bright, smooth celandine.

I like this. Why are things so much nicer than people? No,
that isn't fair. Sir Harold's nice, I like him.

Snap of a stem; tweed rough to the fingers, and a small, polished star very small in a large button-hole. Dark trees, and Sir
Harold looking amused somewhere....

Oh! Oh, but I haven't done it, have I? Oh dear, what ever shall
I do now! I won't look at him.

But I didn't mean it! I didn't!

Dark trees and yellow celandines and there's no sky showing.

That was too ridiculous. What ever made me do that? It was childish, ridiculous, horribly forward. Where's my dignity?

Moss yielding to the hand; chin up and a jump, and skirts dragging over the moss.

'I think we had better look for the others Sir Harold.'

Oh, foolish. That was too cold. That was too much the other way. How absurd to speak like that after putting a flower in his button-hole: as if it were he who had done something wrong! It's too late now. I've got to go on. He's following.

Cool wind on the cheeks, and eyes pricking.

Oh, but what a dreadful thing to have done. I shall never dare to look at him again.

A stumble, and a small voice: 'Oh. Yes. Thank you. The ground *is* rather rough.'

Tweed warm to the hand; an arm, strong under the tweed.

He's smiling, I can hear it in his voice. So he's not angry. But I won't look. Oh, how I wish I hadn't done it. And how I wish I didn't.... How can you look dignified when you blush?

Oh, it's still in his button-hole....

Oh, he must think me silly!

Silly. I don't know why I always feel so silly. I don't see why I should feel silly. I don't see why. I don't see. But I always feel so silly, up here at Sibsley Court.

They must think I look silly, sitting here by the tennis courts, trying to look interested. They know I'm not. Hilda knows I'm not. She knows I dislike tennis, and playing things. But she can't be horrid now as she was when we were small; she has to ask me up here because she can't leave me out, because of Papa. But they think the same things as they used to, she and Dick, though they can't say them so plainly. They think it's silly I can't play better.

It's silly to keep on looking round like this. Of course he isn't staying here, or he'd have come out by now. It's silly to think he'll come back here anymore. Michael won't come back now, now that he's married and gone abroad. I'm glad he went abroad. I don't want to see him, or his wife. No, I *don't* want to see her. I don't want to see him either.

Though I shouldn't mind, if he were here. It's silly to mind. I shouldn't mind in the least if he came out of the house this very minute, swinging his racket as he used to.

Oh. Oh, isn't that... there....

Coming round the corner by the rhododendron bushes....

No, of course not. Of course it isn't. I can't think why I'm thinking about him like this. Of course he isn't here. I shouldn't have come if I'd thought he was. Of course I shouldn't. It's only because I'm up here that I'm thinking about him like this. I wish I hadn't come.

Smooth, empty lawns and the tennis courts with their white nets, and swift figures moving about. Men in white flannels, and the women's white, cashmere blouses and sailor hats, and their wide, dark skirts swaying over the grass: dark, bell-shaped patches on the smooth, bright greenness of the lawn.

I wish everybody hadn't moved away from this end of the court. Ought I to go to those chairs over there or stay where I am? But if I go there and sit, there are two chairs, and then if he came out....

Don't be ridiculous, he's abroad somewhere. I don't know what's the matter with me to-day. I don't believe I've thought about him once, for quite two or three days, either. That shows he doesn't matter anymore. It's ridiculous.

Grass blades bending beneath the full, dragging skirts: tug-tug at the hem.

I'd better sit over here. It'll look really awkward if they don't ask me to join in the next set. I must look so peculiar, standing all alone. I don't know how it happened. Lady Sibsley called to Sir Harold Chesborough, and he excused himself, and I didn't know whether to move or stay there. I ought to move smoothly, nonchalantly, towards the chairs, swinging the racket lightly. As if I'd just thought of coming over.

Swish of skirts against the swung wood.

I've got to behave like a grown-up.

Well, I am one: why do I keep feeling I'm not, and having to pretend?

But I'm not, I'm not. Why should I have to be? It isn't fair.

And then sink into the chair: as if I'd just seen it and thought I might as well.

I don't care about his being married. Why should I care? If he wanted to marry I suppose he was free to do so.

I wish Sir Harold Chesborough would ask me to play again. How is it, I don't feel so awkward with him as with the others.

Swoop of a white figure; ping of a ball; a clap. Figures moving up to the net, coming down towards the chairs.

So they've finished the set. What will happen now? Look nonchalant. The rhododendrons are coming out, over on the drive. Now suppose he suddenly came around them; round the corner....

'Oh, yes, thank you. I was resting for a moment. Yes, I should like to play again.'

Did I sound nonchalant enough?

Swing of racket against skirts and tug of grass-blades at the hem.

I wish Michael could see me playing with Sir Harold Chesborough,

Sting of ball against racket, and the faint rebound; streak of the ball along the smooth turf on the far side of the net.

How ever did I do that?

'Well played, partner!'

Oh, I wish he'd come, just for a minute. Just to see. I wish he would.

I wish he would come, just once.

182

Just once. It wouldn't hurt you Phil, just for a minute. If you'd only come just for a minute. I wish he'd come. I wish he would.

Clip of scissors and plop of sweet-pea pods into a basket.

Why doesn't he come, ever? Why doesn't he bring his wife to stay at the Court? I wish he'd come. Not to stay for long, but just so that I could see him.

Furry, green pods nodding on thin stems, and the click of the big gardening scissors. Mauve and blue and white winged flowers perched like still butterflies on their clumps of green.

I should like to see his wife just once. It would make it more real. I shouldn't have to keep on thinking about him.

Fat, smooth hearts of cabbages ashine in the sunlight; apple-trees, dark-leaved, and a white butterfly moving among the still flowers with their folded wings. Warm, brownish red of old brick: the high wall with its neat, crucified plum-trees and their dangling, red fruit.

I wish I hadn't got to keep on thinking about him. It's silly. It's no use.

Plop of pods, green and furry, into the stiff, boat-shaped basket.

I suppose it's fate. This garden is my fate.

Warm, red bricks of the house between patches of creeper; low eaves; a comfortable stir from beyond the open kitchen window, and the distant glow of a fire. Square and low and safe. Nothing could possibly happen here, ever. Quite safe. And the high, warm wall with its trees crucified, and their heavy, dangling fruit.

It's quite safe here. I suppose I ought to be glad.

But I'm not. Why am I here? I don't belong here. Why am I at all?

Everything's safe and comfortable. Nothing could really happen in this house.

Only it's happened.

Because one can think: that's the trouble, you see. One oughtn't to be able to think and worry, it's wrong, it doesn't suit the house. But the house doesn't care. It goes on being square and safe. And there's nothing to worry about: why do I worry? It's foolish. I don't worry exactly. But I wish I could see her.

I wish I could see his wife.

I wish he'd come back, just once, so that I could see them both. He must be quite different by this time.

I suppose it's all fate. She was his fate. I wish I could see his fate, just once. It would make him more real: I should understand him better. What's the use: *I* wasn't his fate, or things wouldn't have happened as they did.

Noiseless fall of pods, green and furry, on to a green, furry heap. Boat-shaped basket heavy on the arm.

It must have been fate. It wasn't my fault: I'm sure it wasn't. I don't see what happened exactly.

I don't see what happened. I don't see why this happened. He just went, that last time. Nothing particular happened. And then....

Papa closing the door. The fall of the heavy, red curtain as it swings to, across the closed door. Papa coming to the fire, rubbing his hands.

'So you have returned, dear? And how did you find things, up at the Court?'

Mamma, looking up from her tatting. Scarcely a pause of those quick, slim fingers. The sweep back of the smooth, greying hair under the flat bow.

Papa's professional voice, discreet from habit: 'Nothing. Nothing very seriously amiss.' Then the conversational, family tone, and the dry rub together of hands. 'I heard a piece of news that may interest you. That young Donovan, he's got married. Gone to some appointment abroad.'

Michael! But he can't have. But....

Mamma, and her placid smile. Mamma's swift fingers on the tatting. Papa's back, and the fire-place on either side, with the looped, plush curtains and their dangling bobbles.

They're just the same. All of them. They haven't changed. Nothing's different. Only that Michael....

But why? Why?

So it's happened. That's how it happened. Yes I know, but what *happened?*

But he hasn't gone? Not gone right away, abroad? But why?

Michael, you haven't really? You are coming back, aren't you? But you must.

But I don't want you to go. I never thought you'd go. You've got to stay, to go on coming, as you always have. But you must. You must stay, I want you to. But why didn't you know? How was it you didn't know? Because you did want it, too, didn't you?

Papa's voice booming up steadily from under the floor. Mamma's, now and then, quietly questioning.

They're talking about it still. If I'd stayed downstairs I might have heard more.

No, they've forgotten about it. They're talking about something else. It didn't mean anything to them. They didn't notice how quickly I said good night. They've forgotten already. They didn't know it mattered.

But why is it? Why?

Snap of the blind going up; grate of the window-sash; the dark garden. A sheet of chill air. Why did I shiver, I'm not cold.

The dark, quiet garden. Wide, clipped hedge of privet[8] beneath the window: pale yellow where the light falls on it, and the rest dark. Dark lawn beyond the hedge, and the high wall only a little darker than the sky.

But not really gone? Not right away?

But I didn't want that. I never thought he could go. Not away like that. And marrying.

---

8 A shrub that is related to the olive, has small white flowers, and is widely used for hedges.

185

Why did he? How could he? No, I don't mean that: why shouldn't he. Only it never seemed that he could.

But you must stay. I want you to. You must.

Cool, dark air; moisture dripping somewhere from unseen leaves in the darkness.

It was my fault: I never let him know. I knew he liked me, and somehow the more I knew he did the more I had to draw away. Every time. I couldn't help it. And all the time I liked him. But I felt myself grow stiff and speak stiffly. And all the time I knew he liked me. But I didn't think that was the last time I should see him.

I didn't think at all: not about that. It seemed as if he must always go on coming here. But it can't be the last time. He can't have really gone. You can't really have gone.

Michael, I didn't know it would matter so much. I didn't, or I shouldn't have been distant like that. At least, I don't think so. Or was it when I really did know it that I was worst?

No I didn't, really know. I didn't, I didn't. Not until Papa came in and said that: just now. Michael you can't have. And you must have thought I didn't like you at all.

Cold air; hedge quiet and yellow in the light from the window, and the dark lawn.

But Michael, don't you *know?* You must know. Where are you? You must be somewhere. You must know.

You must be somewhere. Where are you?

The dark, still garden.

But I didn't know myself, even, until now. So you can't have.

But I did. Yes, I did. I must have known all the time. That's why I behaved like that. It was: it was always when he was nicest and I felt most singing inside that I heard my voice stiffen. I felt myself stiffen, and couldn't help it.

Darkness, and cold, drifting clouds.

But you can't have, you can't. You can't have gone really. Not quite gone. You'll come back, won't you, some day?

Huge, muttering clouds. Darkness banked up, and clouds lapping the darkness.

But he can't. It's impossible. It must be a mistake. He can't have gone. It isn't possible.

Phil! Phil! Come back to me, Phil. I don't mind about anything. Only just come back. I don't mind about your going. I won't ask why you went. I won't ask anything of you. Nothing matters, only come.

You can't have gone like that, Phil. You can't have just walked out and left me. If you'd said anything, Phil, I shouldn't have minded so much. If you'd only just sent me a little note.

It was the going like that that was so terrible. Letting me ring up like that. But why did you, Phil? What had I done to you? I didn't do anything, did I? You can't go. You can't walk out on me like that. You've got to come back. You've got to come back to me, Phil, why don't you come. But why was it; I don't see. I suppose I asked too much. I oughtn't to have wanted so much. I ought to have known you couldn't give any more. Not to me.

Darkness, and a pale, gleaming hedge.

But I didn't ask you for anything. I didn't want anything, Michael, honestly I didn't. Only just to be with you. I only just wanted you to be here and everything to go on being as it had always been. I believe that was why I used to stiffen: whenever I saw things might change and be different. I didn't want any new relationship, or anything like that, even though we had grown up. Only just for you to go on coming here as you always had.

Spray flung up, dark and cold, against the cold glass: clouds afret at the cliffs of the dark.

I ought to have been content with the little you could give me, Phil. I oughtn't ever to have wanted anything but friendship; it wasn't fair to you. I was wrong, I believe. It wasn't fair. It put you in a false position, and then there was no way out but the one you took. It was my fault: I ought to have known things couldn't go on. It was wildly impossible. We were living in a dream — I was — and it couldn't last. A dream, a dream, it was nothing but a dream. But it wasn't that, was it, Phil? Say it wasn't. But it wasn't fair to you: to expect you to live in an old woman's dream.

Pale privet and the dark, damp lawn and scudding clouds.

But I didn't, Michael. I didn't want anything at all: really I didn't.

Or was that the trouble: that I didn't want enough? You must have needed to give more, and I only asked you to be there and let me look at you. It wasn't enough. So you found somebody else, who wanted the things you could give her. She doesn't love you as I do, but she wants ordinary, human things: grown up things: marriage and a house and children. Oh Michael, couldn't we have been like that? Perhaps we might, if I'd known. Only I didn't know. I never thought of wanting it. You see it would have been.... I don't know, but all that is a kind of degradation. It was perfect as it was; I don't think that could have added to it. It would have spoilt things, they wouldn't have been so perfect. All that's only body; but it got in the way. Why should it get in the way?

Why is it? Why should it spoil things?

I oughtn't to have had those feelings. They were wrong. And you knew I didn't want anything — earthly — like that, so the only thing you could do was to go away. You knew I only wanted just to keep you here, in a dream. I expect it was only a dream, really. And you had to escape from my dream. It wasn't fair. It was foolish of me. You couldn't be tied to a silly, childish dream.

But if I'd known, I should have been different. Really. I should have made myself want those things. I could have, if I'd tried. I could do anything for you, Michael, if you wanted it. There's something horrible about marriage, but it wouldn't have been horrible with you. At least, I don't think so. Nothing at all could be horrible if you wanted it. Nothing, nothing. I'd do anything at all if you'd only stay. Michael, don't go. Come back, come back.

Darkness driven up in banks and shaken. Darkness shaken; spray in great whorls veering, and the boom and suck of darkness.

Come back, Phil. Only come back. I won't ask anything from you, if you'll only come back. Only come, and let me see you. Just come. Only come back. Only come.

I oughtn't ever to have wanted more than that. Just to see you. Right from the beginning. I ought to have known that anything more was impossible. It couldn't last: not at my age. I don't know what possessed me to let things be as they were. I used not to be like that, when I was a girl. I'm not that kind of woman. I don't know what you must have thought of me. You must have thought I ought to know better: I was old enough to be your mother. I don't know how it was, Phil: I don't know how it happened. You must have thought I saw the way things were drifting, those first days at Brighton.

Phil, come back, don't think too badly of me Phil. I don't know why it was: it was the sea and the summer: I hadn't noticed the summer so much for years and years. It was the being there on my own by the sea, and then your being there. I don't know what it was.

Phil, I never meant it really. I knew I was too old for you; I ought to have gone away. I oughtn't to have stayed there. It was that evening we went out together when the moon was on the sea. I oughtn't to have gone; I ought to have known.

I did know, Phil; I did know. I knew something like that would happen and I could have prevented it, but I didn't want to.

It wasn't fair to you, Phil, I didn't want to. I wanted to feel young again, but I'd never felt like that when I was young. I wanted to feel you loved me as if I were twenty years younger than I was, but I shouldn't have behaved like that if I'd been twenty years younger, or else it wouldn't have mattered.

If I'd been younger and had a beautiful body it wouldn't have mattered. Body, that's all that matters; but I'd never bothered about it until now.

But why should it be? Why is it?

Don't judge me too hardly, Phil. Come back, I won't ask anything from you. I don't want anything, only to see you, just let me see you once. Phil, you are here, aren't you; no, I don't mean that; only come, Phil, I won't ask you anything. Phil, come back, I want to tell you. Phil.

Urgency and struggling and the tongue heavy as lead.

"Uh... Uh...."

Heavy as lead and struggling and the clouds beating up against the glass and Phil hovering and drifting away.

"Uh... ahah... uh."

Why do you do that, what is it, why are you pricking my arm? Do it again, Phil, it hurts, I like it. If you'll only come.

Phil, I won't ask anything from you. Tear me to pieces, I don't mind, only come.

Tear me to pieces, Phil, I wish you would, I don't want to be anything if you don't come anymore. Phil, Phil, I don't want anything but that. I don't want anything but that, I swear I don't: only kill me. Phil, it's so wonderful to be killed by you, only kill me. I don't, I don't: I don't want anything but that.

Michael, why have you gone? Why have you gone so far away?

Ice, grey and lustreless, laid flat over the fields.

So cold. I wish I hadn't come out here. I wish he hadn't gone.

Michael, shooting and gliding in strong curves, away out on the ice.

He's splendid.

And the others quite small in the distance, beyond the bleak, thorny clumps where the hedge ought to be.

Michael, all alone, out on this grey sheet of ice.

Why have you gone so far?

Not like that. I don't mean like that. I know you've stayed with me really, to-day, though you're flying out there in the patterns I can never manage. Or you'd have gone to join the others at the far end. But you wouldn't leave me here, stumbling along by the edge. Grass struggling up in green prickles through the ice, and grit on the grey surface. You mean to stay with me. But you've changed so. I can't talk to you.

I wish I could skate well, and fly out there and sweep in patterns with you. But that wouldn't make any difference really.

'Come on, your teeth are chattering. Let's get the skates off and have a sharp walk.'

So he's come back. He's grinning. Of course, it's the feeble way I was trying. He was like a bird out there on the ice: something not quite earthly: something that can take on different shapes, fluid, like a spirit. He's like that. And he left it to come and walk with me.

Skates kicked off; firm ground underfoot: grass solid and hard as iron.

'But you don't really want to walk. You want to stay here and skate.'

'No I don't. Had enough. Let's get on and walk, you're freezing.'

The same way: lordly, commanding. Only I used to be closer to him. Wasn't I?

He's queer and silent. He hasn't said anything for five minutes, since we began to walk. Neither have I. I suppose he only left the ice because he was sorry for me, and now he's sorry he did. No, that isn't Michael.

Ground hard as iron, and grass in stiff, drooping tufts. As if they had grown limp and drooped, and then were frozen stiff like that. A pinched look. Tufts hard to the foot, stubbing the toe.

'Here, hold on. Let me help you till we get out of this.'

Michael's hard, thin hand, firm and vibrant through the sleeve. A stumble and quick recovery; that swift, tiny jerk away.

'I can manage, thanks.'

Why did I? I wanted him to help me. I like the feel of his hand: firm and bony and alive. Why did I sound cold like that? It said itself, I didn't say it. I won't let it happen again. I'll be nice to him.

'Shall we go round by the copse? You like that way, don't you?'

'It's hardly worthwhile.'

Now he's offended. Now I've hurt him again, and I didn't mean to. Michael, why are you so far away? What's the matter?

A stifled yawn; watch slid into pocket.

'Suppose we get back and see if there's any tea going.'

Now he's bored. Oh, very well.

'Yes, if you like.'

But why?

Stubby, uneven ground and the cold, grey gleam of ice in the distance and the chimneys of the Court across the fields.

'I'm not coming to the Court. I'm going home.'

'Oh? Right you are.'

But we can't go on like this. It's dreadful. And he hasn't told me anything. I don't even know where he's going when he goes away.

'What are you going to do, when you've left Cambridge?'

'I don't know. Colonies, I expect. Look for a job, or something.'

'Oh.'

Stubbly, cold fields and the gleam of ice and the windows of the Court through the trees.

But you can't do that. You can't go right away: you wouldn't be able to come here. You can't do that.

'I... I think I will come to the Court, after all and go home afterwards.'

'Right.'

Open hearth; logs blazing and a gleam of fire-light on the silver urn. Lady Sibsley, fussily kind, behind the tea-tray.

'So here you are. The others came in a few minutes ago.'

Dick, with his hair over his eyes, grinning at his mother, his huge boots ashuffle on the carpet. Hilda, red and jolly, in her wide skating skirt, bouncing on the teacakes.

'That's better. I say, you were cold, weren't you?'

And Michael's grin.

So he's the same. It wasn't anything really. I only imagined it. He's the same, really.

But it was horrible out there. It was a bit like that before, back in the autumn, but not nearly so bad. When I wanted to tell him about Cornwall, and the words wouldn't come.

Michael and his gun. Michael, preoccupied with his gun. Damp path and yellowing trees. Hart's-tongue fern, long and smooth and very green, against the bank where the wood stops at the edge of the fields.

Michael preoccupied. Quite still. I mustn't talk. A distant shout and a swir of wings and a close, loud shot.

He hit. He's splendid. Michael's splendid.

Why is it splendid to kill something?

It isn't that. It's Michael. It's something about Michael when he does it. It isn't like somebody killing something, it's just Michael.

'Where did you go this summer?'

Michael, back to earth; doing something to his gun. Politely interested, but not very.

'Cornwall; the same place.'

Fern damp against the hand. It's no good talking; he'll shoot again in a minute. Words in a rush: 'I wish you'd come there, it's fine.'

'What, good weather?'

Absent-minded, taking aim, waiting.

I mustn't make a noise.

'No, not very. The sea, I meant.'

'Oh.'

He isn't interested, really. He'd listen if I said something interesting. What's the use: I could never make him see what I mean about it's being fine. Besides, I don't know. It was just silly. I don't know why it matters so much that he should see it.

Great, black rocks and waves breaking in foam. Rushing back of surf and a rising boom and a crash and backward rush of water.

It's so big. So tremendous.

Mutter and boom and crash and upward rush and the white spray thrown back: white flecks on the grey, oncoming wave. And the mutter and boom.

On and on It's so tremendous. It's cruel and splendid.

Crash and rush upward over the black rock; thrown back and champing; the downward suck and hollow against the rocks, and the backward wave small fretful and the oncoming, muttering surge, and the boom and crash and upward dash and the foam thrown back.

Oh, it's tremendous. So tremendous. It'll wear the rocks away. It'll wear away this cliff I'm standing on. It's like time, wearing everything away. And life.

Boom and crash and suck and boom.

It's like life; it's horrible; it's cruel. When I'm old I shall come back here and all these rocks will have gone. Gone, completely, forever. But there'll still be rocks, and the sea will still be wearing, wearing.

Crash and outward dash and suck and mutter and boom.

It's wearing away the world. It'll take thousands and thousands of years, but then there'll be nothing but sea. One huge, cruel sea everywhere. And then there won't be any more rocks, nothing more to wear away, so it'll be calm at last. Calm and smooth and cruel, like a big animal after food.

Oh, it's horrible. I don't know why it's so horrible. I wish Michael were here, he'd know. He'd know what it was.

Suck and mutter and boom and crash and the hollow suck and mutter and boom.

It's so big and aching. You'd go mad if you had to watch it always. It's so hopeless. Something somewhere that's too big to understand. Something hopeless and terrible, like life. It's so terrible and hopeless and splendid and tremendous.

Why is it? Why am I? Why is everything?

Boom and surge and suck and mutter and roar.

It's like Michael. There's something splendid about it. Splendid and cruel.

Michael isn't cruel.

But it's like Michael all the same. Big and splendid and careless. When he's impatient with something: breaking it. Big and strong; it can't wait to look at little things like the mussels clinging to the rocks. It's big and impatient, and if they stopped holding on for one moment it would suck them down.

There's something patient about it, too. Like Michael when he wants something very much. Like Michael now, when he's taking aim. Only when he was small he'd be patient for a long time with anything, and then suddenly get impatient and throw it away.

Swir of wings and a sudden, loud shot.

Why can't I say that kind of thing to him anymore? I used to be able to tell him about things.

Michael grinning, relaxed, doing something to his gun.

'How was that?'

'Fine. Splendid.'

Michael's grin.

'What were you saying just now, about Cornwall? What's so good about it?'

Smooth, cool hart's-tongue, long and thin, drawn through the clenched hand.

'Oh, I don't know. It's rather nice.'

But it used not to be like this. It wasn't like this before, when he used to come in the holidays. It's since we're grown-up that I can't talk to him properly. But why? Why should it spoil things? It wasn't like this before.

Sweet, prickly smell of hay. Soft sweet-smelling hay-cock[9]

---

9   A cone-shaped pile of hay left in the field to dry.

yielding to the back, a prickle here and there through the muslin blouse. The smoke of Michael's cigarette in a tiny, blue thread across the pale, cropped field and the big, dark gold cocks of hay.

'I'm going to row, when I'm up at Cambridge.'

Michael's plans. Michael so splendid, planning it all. Michael with the forbidden cigarette, splendid and smoking.

'When I'm up at Cambridge....'

Michael, smoking and splendid, his long legs drawn up, heels dug into the loose wisps of hay.

'When I go up next term....'

Quietness and heat and the warm prickle of hay against the neck. The distant rumble of a farm cart in the lane across the field, and the bob of a shapeless hat along the hedge, between the hay-cocks.

'That's Perkins bringing in the cider apples. Race you to the barn?'

Michael up and stamping on the cigarette. Michael grinning, eyes bright, hair in a tangle with bits of hay sticking in it.

Rough, stubbly ground and the hay-cocks low and fat, row after row, and the breath quick and hot, and a stumble. My skirt. I'd forgotten.

Michael quick, back again, sobered.

'Oh I say, sorry.' And a grin. 'I forgot you were a grown-up young lady.'

Cheeks burning and a quick shrug. I'm not. I won't be. Hay-cocks stretching away, row after row, right across, back to the barn.

'I'm not a grown-up young lady.'

'Yes, you are.' And the grin. 'Come on then, let's walk.'

Hot cheeks and stubbly ground, prickly to the feet, and stubble catching at a skirt hem; an impatient tug away.

Michael saying nothing. He's cross now. What's the good of being cross.

Dark, cool barn and the squish and drip of juice into the vat under the wet wooden press. The men's grin and their wet, dirty hands working the press.

'Like some, Miss?'

Brownish, sticky juice and the dripping wood.

'Doesn't it look horrid.'

'Jolly good.'

Michael, chaffing with the men; Michael, himself again. The slow, sickening squish and drip of the squeezed apples: shapeless, discoloured pulp oozing out between the wooden blocks.

How horrid. Why couldn't they leave them as they were, round and red and looking nice. Though they're sour really. It's horrid. It's like me. What they do to me: trying to make me into a grown-up young lady. I don't want to be a young lady. I won't.

I won't, I won't, I won't be grown-up.

Kitchen garden outside the window, and a narrow strip of mirror in the door of the wardrobe. Tight, stifling pressure of a bodice pulled in, tighter and tighter, and squashed, struggling breasts.

I won't be grown-up. I'm not. I won't have it. I won't let it show. If I pull tight enough it'll stop growing, it won't show.

Breath coming quickly and a sickening hold: helpless push and growth of flesh against the stout, unyielding calico.

I won't, I won't.

Michael with a straw in his mouth.

'Can you see how it works? Come over here.'

Slow, sickening squish of the oozing pulp from between the wooden blocks.

But he doesn't take hold of me and drag me over as he would have before. It spoils things. It isn't fair. It's ever since my hair was up.

Michael's stop and stare in the lane; a dawning grin.

'When did you put your hair up?'

'Oh, haven't you seen it?' Hand to the head. Weight at the top and dragging pins. 'I forgot. Last Christmas. It's silly. I didn't want to.'

A long stare.

'Looks all right. Come on, then,'

Michael, half a pace ahead, stumping down the lane, fishing basket ajolt on his strong, narrow shoulders.

It's all right. He's accepted it. It doesn't matter. It doesn't make any difference, of course it doesn't.

Michael's rod in its leather case, smooth to the hand and heavy. Don't bump it on the ground, he'll be cross. Michael's back; Michael's rod: the smooth, shiny leather. I'm carrying Michael's rod. Michael wouldn't let either of the others carry it, so there. He knows I don't bump it.

Michael, turning suddenly. 'Here, give me that rod.'

'What? Why?'

'You can't carry things now you've got your hair up.' Michael's voice, rough and cross. 'Give it here.'

'No, I won't. I always carry it. Why shouldn't I?'

Michael snatching it. Smooth, shiny leather wrenched out of the grasp.

'A man can't let a woman carry his rod for him.' Pitying contempt.

Face hot and eyes prickly. I mustn't cry, Michael would laugh.

'I'm not a woman. You're horrid.'

'Yes, you are.'

He'll say Cry-baby, in a minute.

But I'm not. It's horrid. I'm not.

Scrape of carpet under a bare foot; a hand out, steady: smooth wall of the wardrobe. The stratching of woollen combinations dragged off; cold air, and a bump back against the icy brass of the bed-foot. Gate-like pattern of brass rails in the narrow wardrobe mirror and a figure on one foot, clinging, clutching at the dragged-off wool. But I'm not like that, am I? That isn't me?

Painful blood in a rush to the face, body stooping to gather the heaped wool. Cold sting of brass on white, shrinking flesh.

It's beastly. It's like grown-ups.

Quick. Warm, sheltering flannel night-gown: straight, wide flannel tube in the strip of mirror, and a fading flush.

But not really? I'm not really like grown-ups, am I? What's it like, really?

Flannel tube slowly drawing nearer; wide eyes in the glass; a button popped from its hole, and two small soft mounds quivering under cold fingers. But why is it like that? It wasn't like that before. Warm and soft and small, shrinking from the chill of curious fingers; and the rasping edge of flannel tightly drawn back. Why is it?

Hot blood, suddenly, to the cheeks; flannel roughly dragged across and button done up. It's body, it's nasty, I don't want to look at it.

Gritty, crunchy lane and Michael turning away, roughly, stumping on, half a pace ahead.

'I'm not a woman. I'm not.'

'Well, come on, anyhow. You'll waste half the morning.'

Now he's cross. It isn't my fault. He wasn't like this before.

Pendulum swing of a plait, and legs swinging; swaying motion of the branch and grass warm and green, only a little way below.

It wouldn't matter if I dropped. But I shan't drop from here, even though Michael's swinging the tree. I don't mind being on the first branch: it's a nice, free feeling being off the ground, and Michael doesn't tease me to go higher. It's the others: I hate climbing with them. Michael doesn't mind going higher and leaving me here. He's shaking the tree, but it isn't to make me fall off. He likes the feel of it when it swings.

'Here, catch.'

Hard, green ball of apple in the hand. Apple sour and hard to the teeth, warm with sun. The swing of a boot against the tree trunk just overhead. A shout from the garden, across the quiet, leafy orchard.

There. The others. They aren't coming, are they? Oh, don't let them come.

A shout and scramble and the tree shaken. Hold on; don't let her shake you off. Hilda wants you to fall off and look a fool.

'Here they are, the slackers!'

Dick, bursting through the heavy branches.

'What are you sitting here for? Aren't you coming?'

And Michael, his mouth full of apple: 'Come on up.'

But he doesn't want them. He doesn't. He'd rather we were here by ourselves.

Hilda's scorn. Hilda's face red with shaking the tree. But I won't fall off. I won't. Hilda, pushing against the sturdy trunk: 'Well, if *that's* all you can do! I say, Millicent can't climb any higher than that!'

Michael, lordly, from the upper boughs: 'Shut up. Get out, you two, if you aren't coming up.'

'No thanks.'

Hilda's loose, brown hair tossing, and Dick, puzzled and hot, gaping up along the trunk.

'Why don't you come down?'

'Oh, *come* on.' Hilda stalking off, head tossing.

Dick following at a run; their steps chasing away out of sight, under the trees.

She didn't want to go, though. She wouldn't have gone if Michael hadn't told her to. They'd have stayed and dared me to climb. Getting hot and falling back, and the scratchy grazing of the trunk, and bark crumbling under the hands. Hilda'd get up to the top in a minute if she wanted to. But Michael doesn't like her any better for it, so there.

The scratch of a boot against the trunk and a leg sliding down. Michael, lowering himself to another branch just overhead.

'There's a fellow at school who can get up a tree like this and swing on to another, like a monkey.'

Michael's splendid, splendid. He could do anything if he wanted to.

Hard, green crunch of apple, and sun through the leaves and Michael's boot kicking against the brown, crumbly bark. Silence and a long, thoughtful crunch.

'There's another fellow who can put his legs round his neck and then turn somersaults, like a circus.'

Michael's splendid, splendid. There isn't anything he couldn't do. But he doesn't mind sitting on a lower branch so we can talk.

Warm, chewed apple, and legs swinging. But it wouldn't hurt if I fell.

'Where you going for the holidays?'

'Me?' Tough, warm apple, hard as it goes down. 'Expect we'll go to the sea. We did last year.'

'Decent?'

'Um.'

Swinging legs and a crunch, and green, sunny silence.

Great big waves splashing up over the rocks, making a lot of noise. Banging up against the rock, and that breaks them, and then they splash up high, all white, right up against the sky, and then another one comes.

They're like great big dragons, all green and fat, with curly tails, and when the rock throws them back it's like when they stand up on their hind legs and curl their backs and paw the air. Big and fierce and angry with the rock. And that's when they breathe out white steam: big clouds of smoke right up into the sky.

Great big, fierce dragons, all green and scaly and breathing smoke, and Michael on the rock with his spear, all in shiny armour, prodding them, like that, so that they curl back and hiss. I say, Michael's like a knight, isn't he?

I say, Michael ought to be in shiny armour and have a spear and fight dragons, he's like that. I say, isn't he?

I say, I couldn't tell him, could I. But knights always have a lady or a damsel-in-distress or something, and they're very beautiful and tied up with big ropes to the rock, and then the dragons come and stamp up against the rock and breathe out fire, and they're all angry and fierce, and then Michael comes with his spear and pokes them, and then they curl up their tails and hiss and then they die, and then another one comes. And Michael stamps about with his spear, and he says Come on, I'm going to kill you, you aren't going to get at Millicent. But the ladies always have to be beautiful and worthy.

I say, you'd have to be dreadfully worthy to be Michael's lady.

Rubber sand-shoes sticky and twisting in the hard crevice of the rocks.

I say, I couldn't say that to him, could I? About his being a knight and all that?

Big, curly dragons, green and scaly and terrific. And seaweed, brown and slippery,

I say, it doesn't matter if he doesn't know it. I can be worthy just the same. I'm going to be dreadfully worthy and not let him know, because that's noble. And then one day when he finds out he'll kneel down and say Millicent you're my lady. Like they do. Michael's spear clanking on the rocks. And he'll say.... No he won't, he wouldn't be so soppy.

I don't care. He's big and splendid, just like a knight.

'Millicent, what are you doing, mooning about here?'

'Nothing. I'm not.'

Knobbly rocks, hard and slippery.

I don't care, he is. He's big and splendid. He's a knight. He isn't big and rough and beastly like Dick and Hilda.

They're beastly. I hate them.

Smack of bat against ball out there in the sunshine and the thud of the ground as they run and the bat dragged over the grass. Ground shaking under the tummy, when Hilda runs, and the free, loose feeling of legs waving upwards from the knee. They're going to leave me alone.

But they won't. They never do.

Friendly bits of grass with a hard stem down the middle. It

isn't like that when it's just something you have to run on. Hilda doesn't know it's like that: she always wants to run or play at something. Bits of grass sticking up straight, like swords, along the white shiny edges of the book.

'Here, you slacker, come on and field. Why shouldn't she field? Millicent never does anything.'

5hiny blades of grass, and Hilda's big, rough feet. Hilda's brown leather toe kicking at the book.

'Leave me alone. I want to read.'

'Oh, she wants to read, she wants to read. Millicent wants to read.'

Book flying into the air, coming down, face downwards on the grass; white, shiny pages crumpled underneath.

'I hate you! You beast! I hate you!'

Hilda's leg hard to the toe, through the brown, ribbed stocking.

'Oh I say, you little beast.'

Hilda's bony hand digging in, and the maddening, helpless tug of hair from the roots. Hilda's arm, warm and tough to the teeth.

'You... you....'

'Here I say, she's biting. Come on, stop her.'

Panting, and the rough scrape of stockinged legs interlocked.

'I say, Millicent can't fight without biting.'

'Shut up, you two.'

Michael. But I don't care.

'She bites and scratches. Cat. Cat.' Hilda, waiting to spring.

Michael picking up the book. What's he going to do? Throw it at Hilda? Do throw it at Hilda.

'Cat. Cat.'

I'll fight her. I don't care.

Dick bounding up, shaggy, like a big dog: 'Come on, let's see them fight it out. Let's see how the girls can fight.'

'Cat. Cat.'

'I hate you.'

'Shut up. Girls can't fight, anyhow.'

Panting, and the grass flat all round; limp when it's kicked up. Yes I would, I'd have fought her. I'd have beaten her, too. But she won't fight now Michael's told her not to. She's afraid. Yah, yah. I'm not afraid.

'Clear out, all of you. I'm going to read.'

Michael with the shiny white book in his hand, with the pages bent; the thin tree shaking as he sits and leans against it.

'Oh I say, aren't you going to play anymore?'

Dick's cross now. What'll they do now?

Hilda's hair tossing. 'Oh, come on, let's do something by ourselves.'

Michael not looking at any of them. Opening the white book.

'Can I stay?'

'If you like.'

Earth solid and warm under the tummy. Have they really gone? Why do they always want to do something, I hate doing things. Long, stiff blades of grass where they haven't walked. Michael isn't cross, he's only pretending. Why didn't he go with them?

'What were you fighting for?'

Hard, smooth earth between the grasses.

'I hate her.'

'Why don't you want to play cricket?'

Earth thick and heavy in the nails.

'I don't know. I hate it.' Earth clogged and heavy and hurting. 'D'you like reading?'

'Yes, don't you?'

'Yes.'

Sun on the white book. Michael's hair over his eyes, his heels digging at the grass. Shouts, away over the lawn. They've gone into the kitchen-garden: they'll catch it. Stringy, wet pull of grass between the teeth. 'D'you believe in the Bible?'

'Rather not. Do you?'

'I don't know.'

'Pooh, nobody does. Only mothers and people like that.'

'Why not?'

'Pooh, nobody does.'

Michael's heel pushing into the grass. Strong, firmly planted legs with the knickerbockers buttoned round tightly under the knee over the black stockings; his dark, thin face with the straight hair falling over it, and a long, stiff grass wagging up and down between his teeth as he reads. What a lot he knows. I wish I knew such a lot. I wish I knew everything, like Michael.

'I don't really, either. Believe in it, I mean.' Grass sticky and limp between the teeth. Free wave of legs upwards from the knee. 'Rather not.'

Grass, wet and stringy, and a stale, bitter taste on the tongue.

The bitter, dry taste of lead where the wood is chewed away, and the damp, mashy wood, chewed and drawn between the teeth, and a tickly tuft at the end that won't bite off, and the slippery, unbitten varnish further down.

'Put your pencil down, Millicent. You don't need it while you read.'

'Yes, Miss Cresset.'

Chewed, shiny yellow pencil with tooth-marks in the varnish, all alone on the big, shiny table with the closed exercise books.

'Now read from page twenty to page twenty-two, where I told you.'

'Yes, Miss Cresset.'

The principal exports of Australia are....

Clouds coming up over the pink geraniums in the window-box. Big, black clouds. If it rains this afternoon they'll play indoors. It's nasty when they play indoors at the Court. Michael isn't so nice and the others are always there. Big clouds half-way up the window. 'Is it going to rain this afternoon?'

'I don't know. Go on with your reading.'

It mustn't rain, I hate it. I don't mind when it rains here, it means not going for a walk. I hate it when it rains at the Court.

Many-sided pencil, soft and chewy at the end, and the sharp edges further down. Edge between two teeth, and bite. Crack, and the break of the teeth into the new, smooth varnish and the rough side where the gold writing is. Rough to the tongue.

'Put that pencil down.'

'Yes, Miss Cresset.'

The vegetation of Australia is....

'Michael's going to go all round the world when he's grown-up.'

'Go on with your reading.'

'Have you been all round the world, Miss Cresset?'

'No. Go on with your lesson. Don't talk.'

'Do you want to go all round the world?'

'No. Now that's enough.'

How can you be so old as Miss Cresset and not even *want* to go all round the world? Why do Miss Cresset's glasses pinch her nose? Papa's don't.

When Michael goes all round the world I shall go too. He said I could. He'll let me go if I carry his bat and things.

Michael striding along with his hands in his pockets, whistling. Europe, all small and funny down below: big, black towns, and rivers wind-y and blue. A black knickerbockered leg reaching over the blue piece of sea between Europe and Africa, and then the other, and castles, and deserts full of sand, and then on, and one foot on Africa and one on Asia, over the Red Sea, and deserts and big forests, and then on, and the bat not heavy really, with the black, stringy bit at the end scraping your hand; and a jump, down into the sea and up again, and Michael going on and on, and palm-trees and things.

'Miss Cresset, do kangaroos run very fast?'

'They can jump for great distances.'

'Could you catch them if you ran after them?'

'No. Don't be silly.'

'I bet Michael could catch them. Michael can catch anything.'

'Attend to your lesson, Millicent. It would be better if you thought less about Michael and more about your books.'

Why would it? Why ought I? It's always like that.

'You don't want to think about Michael now, here by the sea. Come along, now.'

'Yes, I do.'

'And don't answer back.'

Tug on the hand; bored, wooden clatter of spade over the rocks, and big splashes into the pools where there are lots of things if you lie down flat and look in.

'Don't want to go on the sands. Want to look in the pools.'

If Michael was here he'd look. He'd know how to look. He'd dig things out and look at them.

'Why isn't Michael here?'

'Because he doesn't live here. Don't be tiresome.'

'But we don't live here, either.'

'No, but that's different.'

'Why is it different?'

'Come along, now.'

'But Michael doesn't live at the Court, Dick and Hilda do. And he comes there. Will he be there when we get home?'

'I don't know.'

'Don't want to go on the sands. Want to look in the pools. They're funny and 'sterious. I want Michael to look in the pools.'

'Come along. You ought to be able to play by yourself, a big girl like you.'

Don't want to play. Want to look in the pools. Playing's nasty. It's nasty going to the Court to play, 'cept when Michael's there.

Lady Sibsley shaking hands, and a hot feeling, and Dick grinning and Hilda with the funny laugh in her nose.

'There, there. Run along and play, children.'

'Come on, we're going to play cricket. Millicent can field.'

'I don't want to play cricket.'

Bang and shout, and the ball bouncing over the ground. Hot and prickly. I'll never catch it. Let me catch it. Do, God, let me catch it just once. Bounding and bending and the ball bouncing off somewhere else. Hot and prickly and running and the ball going on and feet heavy and a big hammer in your ears. And Dick's contemptuous, 'Oh come on,' and Hilda's laugh.

'I don't want to play cricket.'

'She doesn't want to play cricket. She can't play cricket, that's why. Millicent's a muff. She can't play anything, can she, Dick?'

Another boy, taller than Dick and thin, with hair hanging over his eyes, walking on and on and not taking any notice.

'Who's that?'

'Michael.'

'Who's Michael?'

'That's him, silly. He's come for the holidays with Dick. We're going to show him how you can play cricket.'

Face hot and eyes prickly. 'I don't want....'

'Cry baby cry! Michael, look at the cry-baby!'

Thin face and eyes quiet, not like them. That's Michael. He's bigger than Dick, too. Ever so big and strong.

'Oh, leave the kid alone.'

Oo! That's Michael!

Then: 'Here, kid, you can carry my bat.'

Grass and the big field, and Hilda pointing. I won't. I don't care. I won't run.

And legs heavy as lead. They won't move.

I don't care, I won't. Michael, don't let them come.

And the safe, dark tent of the sheets. It's like a tent. I'm in my tent. I don't care, they can't come. Michael don't let them.

Quiet, safe night-nursery; little shine of the nightlight in the basin on the wash-stand, and the dark, warm tent down below in the bed. Snuggle down. Warm and dark and safe. I don't care, they can't come, I'm in my tent. They can't come here, ever.

Flop-flop of Miss Cresset's big feet in the lane along by the church. Miss Cresset in her black jacket buttoned up the front with a lot of buttons, and her funny flat hat and funny big sleeves.

'Tell me a story.'

Squish-squish. My feet make more squishes than Miss Cresset's. Miss Cresset's silly.

'You're old enough now to tell them to yourself.'

But that's different.

'You'll have to know what eight eights are before you have any more stories told to you.'

'I know! 'Eyes screwed up tight. 'Eight ones are eight, eight twos are....

Eight eights are fifty-six!'

'Wrong.'

Flap-flap, and squish-squish-squish.

I don't care. They're silly stories. Little Red Riding-hood and things. Pooh, I know that.

Big, high banks, right up as far as you can see, until the sky. All green; with grasses and black ivy and long, shiny ferns sticking out and bits of cobwebs joining them up.

Flap-flap; squish-squish-squish.

Round, shiny, flat, bright green leaves, fat and juicy looking. I like them. What are they.

'What's this?'

'I don't know. I think it must be what is called pennywort.'

'Why?'

'Because it's flat and round like a penny, I expect.'

'It isn't. It's fat and squashy.'

Round and smooth and cold and fat and bright green.

'I'm almost sure it must be pennywort.'

'Well it isn't: it isn't nice.'

Flat and fat and squeezy.

Pennywort. Penny. Brown and flat and dirty. Pennies and Saturday morning and the nursery and dusting. Helping Nanny to dust; Mamma coming in: Saturday morning and pennies.

'That's my wages, I'm dusting.'

'That's it. Rub hard.'

Mamma hurrying out: 'I'm busy.'

'I'm busy.' Rubbing: 'But it won't shine!'

'Then use some elbow-grease.'

'What's that?'

'You rub and you'll see.'

Rubbing, and the shine coming up; arm aching, and the shine. Bright yellow door-knob, with a splash of light. And brown, jingling pennies.

It isn't like pennies. It isn't nice.

'Come along, you'll make your shoes muddy. Walk in the middle of the road. Shall I tell you about Humpty-Dumpty?'

'That'll do.'

Pooh, she doesn't know any nice stories. Not like Nanny.

Nanny, big and round and comfy, with the ribby white stuff all over and the black belt, ribby too, round her middle where it isn't so fat, and the big silver buckle with stags on it that her last lady gave her. Nanny, knowing stories and looking at things and knowing what things are, and being comfy in the nursery with her cup of tea, and the big fire behind the high, black guard.

Why have you got that funny thing on your head, Nanny?

But Nanny doesn't have a funny white thing on her head. Why's Nanny got that?

Why have you got that funny white thing on your head, Nanny?

Why's Miss Cresset here too? Miss Cresset's got a funny little hat. Why's Miss Cresset here with Nanny? Nanny, why's Miss Cresset there?

Big, red fire jumping in the nursery grate. Jumping up the black chimney behind the tall, black bars of the guard.

But Nanny, what have they done with the guard? Miss Cresset's taken away the guard. Nanny, why do you let Miss Cresset take away the guard?

"It's Sonia. Don't you know me?"

Sonia? What's sonia? Take it away. Don't let them come. Nanny, don't let them come.

The big, red and blue hearth-rug outside the black bars, and the fire jumping inside, jumping up around the black kettle.

'Nanny, what's sonia?'

'Somebody's name.'

'Oh.'

Rug, rough to your fingers: hard, scrapy wool, nasty feeling, and the smooth, red velvet arm of Nanny's chair.

'Then who's Sonia?'

'I don't know. Why?'

'But she was here. Why was she here?'

'Nobody's been here. You imagined it.'

'No I didn't. She was here just now.'

'Well, bring your chair and come along to the table.'

Nanny lifting the kettle over the bars; the big, fat, brown teapot hissing when the water goes in.

'Why does the tea-pot hiss, Nanny?'

'What a lot of questions. Here, have your milk.'

'Thank you, Nanny.'

White, thick warmness and slippery, thick mug. Thick, rounded edge slipping from between the teeth, warm and sticky. Plate, with yellow ducklings, on the white cloth; thick bread-and-butter with the smooth, brownish-yellow honey in a flat sheet falling over at the edge in uneven little drips on to the smooth, white china. Nanny, white and warm and round, above the big brown tea-pot, with apron straps going up over her round front and disappearing behind the shoulders. Nanny's hand holding the white cup-with-a-saucer.

'When shall I have a cup-with-a-saucer?'

'When you're old enough.'

'When will that be?'

'We shall see.'

Warm comfy nursery with the long curtains drawn against the cold out-of-doors; big fire jumping and popping behind the bars, and the warm, sticky trickle of honey, and Nanny nice and comfy in the big, red chair with the thick arms.

'It's nice when there's nobody here.'

'Why, there never is anybody here, is there? You're a funny little thing. Don't you want to have other little girls and boys to play with?'

'There's only Dick and Hilda.'

Honey sticking round the teeth as the bite goes in.

Dick and Hilda, big and noisy; not knowing what to play at, and Dick and Hilda laughing together in a corner.

'Well, don't you want to have them?'

'No.'

Drip of honey caught on the tongue: soft and sweet, with bits of grit in the smoothness. Nanny's dark, fuzzy head bent over the cup, with the combs showing on top, one on each side of the parting, behind the puffed-up pieces; and Nanny's brownish-red cheeks with little lines on them, dented in by the edge of the cup.

'I like it when there's only us. In here.'

'You are a funny one, the way you like to be indoors. One would think you'd want to be out in the garden all day.'

Why? It's nasty in the garden. Dick finding worms, and Hilda wanting to play ball, and nasty cold grass, and it hurts when you run. It's nasty except when there's nobody there.

'Well, you can walk around alone if you want to. But don't touch anything, mind.'

Miles and miles of cabbages and potatoes and things, and the straight, yellow paths going on and on and fruit trees hanging on wires on both sides of the path, and the warm, red wall with more trees on it right away at the end. Now I'm going to think.

Up one path and down another and round and round and a big lupin you can't see round at a corner. Suppose I got lost here. Shiny cabbages yellow in the sunshine. Everything green and yellow and all alone. That's a white butterfly, they live in the cabbages. And yellow, crunchy gravel. Now if I go up here and round the next corner and round the next without looking, where shall I get? And then I'm going to think.

Big, white box with a glass top lying up-against the wall. That's a frame. That's where you put things to grow. And green, shiny things in it. That's Christmas roses, they don't have flowers like other things do, only at Christmas, but they aren't roses really. Now I'm going to think.

I'm going to be seven to-morrow. It's very important, being seven.

Square, white, wooden box with a wooden cross flat on the glass top, and bits of white on the glass at the edges, where it ran over.

It's very important, being seven. It's the beginning of growing-up when you're seven. The day after to-morrow I'm going to start lessons. Not to-morrow, because it's my birthday. Then I shall be seven and start lessons, and that's a... a.... That's a milestone, like the road to Toddingham. Toddingham 7. Only it's seven backwards. It's like when you're coming out of Toddingham.

Dark clumps of leaves under the glass, and a big, flat leaf here and there pressed flat against the top, with veins showing on it. That's where it grew too high.

I'm going to be seven to-morrow. It's very serious, being seven.

The night-nursery getting dark, and the creak of bootlaces as they come undone and bump of boots on to the floor.

'Well, what did you do all alone there in the garden?'

'I was thinking.'

'Ho, that's a good one!'

'A good what?'

'Never you mind.'

'Nanny, shall I be taller when I'm seven?'

'What do you want to be taller for?'

'I don't know. You have to be taller when you're seven.'

Seven. I'm seven.

'Is it to-day?'

'Yes.'

It's my birthday. I'm seven. It's different from other days.

Night-nursery and sunshine and the top of an apple-tree outside the window. Sheets pushed back and a foot out. Foot out, on to a long, white road: a long, long road going away, with tall straight trees on both sides; tall, thin, straight trees, and a white, empty road on and on, away and away and tall trees. I'm seven. Away and away in front, and tall, straight trees. And the night-nursery and sun on the floor, and the bed, and the window with the kitchen-garden outside.

'Nanny, there was a road, when I got up. In the night-nursery. A road with funny big trees on both sides.'

'Fiddlesticks.'

'Yes, there was. A big long road, and I was on it, when I got up. Going right away, from the bed. Wasn't it funny?'

'You're a queer one, aren't you.'

I'm a queer one. What's a queer one. It's when you think, you're a queer one. Is it queer to think? I like thinking, it's funny.

The nursery fire with big flames jumping up around the black kettle.

'That's Hell-fire.'

'No, it isn't.'

'But Hell's a big fire, and this is a big fire.'

'Yes, but this fire's in its place.'

Red flames jumping up behind the black bars of the fender.

This is fire and it's in its place. Hell's fire, and it isn't in its place. This fire can't get out because the bars are in front. So it isn't Hell, it's only fire.

That was a big think!

The long road, and Nanny's hand pulling and the grass green and the sky all blue. I'm going to think, all by myself.

Head back and hair tickly in the neck and woollen cap weighing heavy on the shoulders.

It's blue up there. It's the sky. You can't ever get up there, except that Heaven's on the other side; but then you're dead so you don't know what it's like.

Now I'm thinking!

Stiff, funny feeling in the neck as if chin was too heavy and Nanny's hand pulling.

'Come along. Walk properly.'

'But I'm thinking!'

Arm jerked.

'Walk properly, now, and don't talk nonsense. You ought to be ashamed, dragging about in the road, at your age. What will people think?'

'Don't care what they think.'

'Then it's time you learnt to care. Don't-care was hanged.'

Nanny's cross.

Hot drops at the corner of the eye. But I'm not going to cry. I don't care.

'A big girl like you.'

Nanny cross. Feet going on. Nanny's feet, clump-clump: cross.

Nanny stopping to puff at the top of the hill: 'Well, it's a lovely day, I'll say that. There isn't a cloud.'

So Nanny's stopped being cross.

'No, there hasn't been a single one, has there? Yes there was!' When Nanny was cross. That's thinking! 'Yes, there was, just now. One tiny, weeny little cloud.'

'Humph.'

Nanny looking suspiciously. But she doesn't know if that's what I mean. She doesn't know, quite. But she can't say You're a queer one, because I didn't say it.

'Well, come along.'

Sudden turn in the road; gates; house up over the field, round the corner of the drive. Wister House Cradstow Nr. Toddingham: that's where I live.

'Why's it called Cradstow Nr. Toddingham?'

'Because Toddingham's a town.'

'Isn't Cradstow a town?'

'No. Only a village.'

'But it's got houses in it.'

Pink brick walls of the dolls' house, with green lattice on the front like Wister House; and the squeak of the hinges as half the front swings back from its hook. Drawing-room and one bedroom come open, into the nursery, and the pink bricks and green lattice over the rest; and the hall and dressing-room behind the brown front door and porch, under the gable. That's Wister House Cradstow Nr. Toddingham. Squeak: all the front open; people sitting up stiffly in tight chairs with their legs out straight, and lobster and duck on crinkly cardboard dishes just a tiny bit too big for the dinner-table. They can't sit at the table properly, poor things, because their legs stick out and get in the way.

I wish there was a kitchen. You can't have the kitchen in the hall, can you.

Like God: taking the front off people's houses and making them do what you want.

Now this one's going to bed, her clothes are too dirty and she won't sit up properly. 'Now, you.'

'Why don't you give the poor things names?'

'These don't have names. Only the proper big ones in the drawer.'

Now these two are going to sit in the drawing-room, because they're married so it's their house. When people are married they have to have houses.

'Nanny, when people marry do they always live happily ever after?'

'You'll find that out fast enough!'

But you never do find things out. It's always like that when you want to know things.

The sky blue and blue, as if it went on forever and little bits of cloud so small you could pick them up, only you can't get there.

'Is it Heaven where the clouds are?'

'No.'

Then Heaven's further on. Where you go when you're good.

'But if you only go to Heaven when you're good, where do you go when you're naughty?'

'Little girls who are naughty go to Hell.'

'Where's that?'

'Down under the earth, where it's full of fire.'

Fire. The fire in the nursery, being red and making crackly noises and jumping up round the kettle and making it sing.

'Fire's nice.'

'Hell-fire isn't. It's a big fire, and it burns up little girls who aren't good.'

A great big fire, red, and jumping up all round.

'Does it go up all round you, like round the kettle?'

'Yes, I expect so.'

'But it can't burn me, because I'm good. So will I go to Heaven?'

'We'll see about that.'

Great big dark clouds, and the sun's on the other side, you can see it through a hole.

'Why do I live down here and not up where the clouds are?'

'Because this is the earth and you're a human.'

'What's that?'

'Somebody who lives on the earth.'

'Then I don't want to be it, it's nasty. Do people live somewhere else, besides when they're dead?'

'I don't know. Nobody knows. How you do bother one.'

Earth, nasty and flat, and prickly grass and people; and the sun all alone up above the clouds.

'How did I get here?'

'I'll tell you what it is, you want to know too much. Stand up, now, and walk properly.'

White frost like sugar on the corners of the nursery window, and the big, bare nut-tree outside. It's cold, it hasn't got any warm nursery to get into. And the lawn and the field and the roofs of cottages down on the road below the field. Why is it all dark? It's because it's winter.

Out beyond the cottage roofs, something wide and grey like the sea, and little black bits here and there. That's where the trees are, through the water.

'Nanny, the floods are out, all over the fields.'

'Yes, I know. They'll be skating soon, if it gets much colder.'

Snip-snip of Nanny's needle, behind in the warm nursery. I won't turn round. It's all dark out there, and 'sterious and nice.

'Why don't the floods come here?'

'Because it's too high. The floods are miles away, if you tried to get there.'

'Further than the Court?'

'A long way.'

All big and lonely like the sea when it isn't nice. A long, long way. You couldn't ever walk there.

Water, flat and quiet and lonely, spreading away and away over the wide, flat valley; and the blue hills beyond, low and even and empty and quiet, and no people there at all: only the monument at the top on one side of the window, all alone, so tiny you can hardly see it. Much, much smaller than a needle. That's because it's a long way away. Shall I go as far as that when I'm grown-up?

'What are you thinking about?'

'About being grown-up.'

What will it be like, being grown-up?

It won't be like anything. When I'm grown-up I shan't be me. Or shall I be me, only people will think it's a grown-up lady? How shall I know when I'm grown-up? Shall I just say one day, Nanny, I'm grown-up, and she'll say, You do talk rubbish, and I'll say it isn't, I am.

You have to grow-up, everybody does. But am I somebody, or shall I always be me and not grow-up? I don't want to be grown-up. You have to do lots of lessons and things unless you're very, very old like Nanny. I couldn't ever be a proper grown-up. I don't want to be a grown-up.

'Nanny, am I a real person?'

'Of course. Don't talk such nonsense.'

'What's nonsense?'

'Not sense.'

'Oh.'

I'm not going to do lessons, when I grow up.

'Can I be a grown-up without doing lessons?'

'Not if you can't read and write.'

'But I can write now!'

Paper, all smudgy, and the thick, heavy pencil hard to push. And writing: ∿∿∿ ∿∿ ∿∿ .

'I'm writing. Look!'

'You're not. That isn't proper writing.'

'Yes, it is.'

'You can't be grown-up till you can write properly.'

'Don't want to be grown-up.'

Long, long blue hills, quiet and asleep. They don't want to grow up either. So far, far, far away. I wish, I wish.

'Why is it not-sense to say am I a real person?'

The click of Nanny's teeth as she bites off the cotton.

'You want to know too much.'

Chairs and tables all in a heap and piano on top and dust choky in a cloud. I'm going to clean out the dolls' house. This house is disgwaceful.

Now this will be the dining-room and this will be the drawing-room. This chair has got a leg gone, it can go against the table like that, and nobody sits on it.

Nanny and Annie behind by the fire. Annie's brought up the tea. Voices buzzy and fuzzy. Why is it Annie and not Nanny? Annie's the housemaid and Nanny's Nanny. Now this is the spare-bedroom.

'I believe you. She won't ever be no higher than *this*.'

The tall, black guard with the big bars and the fire jumping inside. Voices buzzing and fuzzing. Me. That's me. But I will: Nanny is!

'Why won't I ever be taller than that?'

Heads turned. 'What?' Nanny's laugh. But she's cross.

Annie grinning. 'Little pitchers have long ears.'

'What's little pitchers?'

'Never you mind. You go on with your dolls' house.'

What has long ears? Rabbits. Little rabbits have long ears. And this is the other bedroom.

'Queer little piece of it.'

Voices buzzing a long way off: "Won't last through the night."

What's a piece-of-it? What won't last? Was that Nanny or was it Annie? Who said....

Annie's voice: 'Well, so long.'

It wasn't Annie. And this is the nursery, over the hall.

'Now come along and have your milk.'

Nanny's face, cross, with the lines down from the mouth, above the fat, brown tea-pot. Scrape of chair on the rough rug, and bubbles on milk.

'Nanny, what's a little-piece-of-it?'

'Piece of what?'

Piece. Piece of something. Piece of It.

'Then what's It? And who said....'

'Oh never you mind. Little girls should be seen and not heard.'

Scrape of chair over the rug. Chair-leg warm from the fire.

Little chair, hard and safe. Feet on the shiny, green floor beyond the hearth-rug. Rain pattering on the window across the nursery and drip-drip on to the brown earth in the window-box.

'Why don't you play with the dolls' house?'

'Don't want to play.'

'You're a funny one.'

Snip-snip of Nanny's needle. Nanny's feet on the rug in front of the big chair, and Nanny's big, white skirts all round. Wouldn't it be funny if my feet were as big as Nanny's.

Hand spread out on the green and white check pinafore.

Why does it grow like that? Why don't people end in hoofs like horses, or just end with an arm, or not have arms at all? Why aren't they square or round or something. Feet and hands are funny.

Fist clenched; white marks on the knuckles. Fingers spread out, crawling. Like a big spider crawling over the check. All crawly and nasty. Hands are nasty. Why do I have to have them.

'Nanny, why am I inside this?'

'Inside what?'

Hand stretched out and crawling along the rug.

'Arms and legs and things. Why am I inside it? It's nasty.'

'You aren't inside it. It's you.'

'No, it isn't. It's nasty.'

Nanny's frown at the needle held up to the light. Her mouth

pinched up and the lines running down. 'Why don't you play at something instead of sitting there?'

'Don't want to.'

Don't want to play. Arms and legs having to move about: crawly and heavy.

Running. Hilda running, and her legs going fast, all by themselves. Running: legs heavy and heavier and heavier, and Hilda laughing, and it hurts inside. Playing's nasty. Hilda running as if she hadn't got any legs, like in dreams. Just going on and no body. Running with the others: you go on and on and your legs won't, they drag and drag. And they laugh. Don't want to play. Want to stay here. Nanny, don't let them. Don't let them come.

'Don't let her come, Nanny.'

Nanny and Cook. Cook all big and black, Nanny all white and not so big. Cook big and angry: 'Complaining about the nursery bacon! Let me tell you....'

Nanny, red in the face: 'Not fit for the pigs!'

'Just let me hear you say....'

Nanny going to the door and Cook going backwards. 'Get out of my nursery.'

Cook red in the face and Nanny red in the face and Cook turned round, and Nanny's hands on Cook's big, black shoulders, and Nanny, fat and white, pushing, and Cook, fat and black, going out in front of Nanny, and big voices and red faces.

That's right, Nanny, turn her out. Don't let them come.

Cook's voice, big and angry, outside: 'Might give a body a civil answer.' And the door slamming.

Give a body a civil answer. How can you give an answer to a body when you're inside it?

Nanny, red and puffing, patting her hair: 'Such impudence.'

'How can you give a body a civil answer?'

Nanny, hot and cross, coming back to the big chair and picking up her sewing. 'Never heard such impudence. Coming up here.'

'But how...?'

Body. That's body: hands and things with bones inside, and you're inside again. Skin and stuff, and bones, and then you.

Body's funny.

Nanny's face funny and red through the steam, and the swish of water and the hard, scrubby rub of flannel, and that's body: all that white thing.

'Nanny, what are these things for?'

Two of them, in front, hard and round like buttons.

'Never you mind.'

'But what are they *for?*'

'You'll find that out all in good time. Stand still, now.'

And the squishy, hot sponge.

Annie, and the squishy sponge and the scrubby flannel. Nanny's day-out. Annie, with her white cap all limp and flat, with its long strings: 'That's the steam, Miss Millicent. Because I've got to bathe you.'

'Why?'

'Because you've got to have your bath, of course.'

'Annie, what are these things for? Like buttons?'

'Well I never. You'll know fast enough, when you're a grown-up young lady.'

'Why can't I know now? I don't want to be a grown-up young lady.'

'The idea! Stand still, Miss Millicent, do.'

Grown-up young ladies are like the fashion-books.

Shiny paper that the paint won't stay on properly; colour running over the edges on to where the writing is. Ladies with tiny waists and big long skirts down to the floor, and hats like plates put crooked on their heads, and feather boas. I couldn't ever be like that. Ladies with very red faces and green boas and purple skirts. And, 'Nanny, can I make the top a different colour from the skirt?'

'Yes, if you want to.'

I couldn't ever be like that, so I can't be a grown-up, can I? If I was like that it would only be pretending, it wouldn't be me truly.

'Nanny, why must I be a lady? Why can't I be a man like Papa, with big whiskers?'

'Don't be so silly. Because you're a little girl and not a little boy, of course.'

Yellow top and purple bottom and green boa and.... Why's the hat so black I can't make it anything else. It's nasty.

'Then if you're a little boy you're a man when you're grown-up, and if you're a little girl you're a lady?'

'Yes, of course.'

'Then why am I a little girl and not a little boy?'

'Because you are.'

'But what's the difference?'

'Never you mind.'

'But I want to *know*.'

'Annie, what's the difference between a little girl and a little boy?'

Scrubby flannel and steam and Annie's cap all floppy down on her head.

'Well I never, you mustn't ask questions like that.'

'Why not?'

'Because it's nasty.'

'Why is it nasty?'

'Because it is.'

Hard, scrubby flannel and prickly soap in the eyes.

'But what *is* the difference?'

'Never you mind. You'll find out all right when you're grown-up, Miss Curiosity.'

'Why am I Miss Curiosity?'

'You want to know too much.'

'But Curiosity killed the cat.'

'That's right. Then don't you go asking nasty questions about things you didn't ought to know.'

Something nasty that you find out when you're grown-up. I'm not going to be grown-up. I won't.

Wide, flat fields a long, long way away and going on and on forever, and the long, long straight blue hills.

'Why are the hills blue?'

'Because it's going to rain.'

Raining on and on and on, on the long long hills, a long long way away.

But if you've got to be grown-up why are you small first? If you've got to be grown-up why aren't you grown-up to start with, and if you're a little girl why don't you stay a little girl, and why are you?

'Nanny, why am I here?'

'Where?'

'Here.'

Blue hills and far-ness and being small and me.

'Where's here?'

Where. Where. But I know: 'Wister House Cradstow Nr. Toddingham!'

'Because your Papa lives here, of course.'

'But why is Papa my Papa?'

'Because he is. You wouldn't be you, if somebody else was your Papa.'

'Then why am I me and not somebody else?'

'Gracious me, what a lot of questions. Curiosity killed the cat. I'll tell you what, come and sit down and sew your dolly's dress.'

Pink stuff, all crumply, that won't hold. Prickly feeling in the tummy, and needle that won't stand still, and cotton won't go in. Squiggly prickles down the back of your legs.

'Nanny, I *can't* thread this needle!' Foot stamping.

'Then you must try. Little girls ought to be able to thread needles. If at first you can't succeed, try try try again. Hold it up to the window.'

225

Damp, chewy end of cotton, and the needle standing up with the little bit of sky in it, and cotton flopping against it and going off again into the other sky all round. Squiggly, jerky prickles in the back of the neck. I *can't*, what's the good of trying. Don't want to be a little girl. Don't want to be a grown-up either, grown-ups are silly. They don't know anything. Don't ask so many questions: that's when they don't know things. Don't be silly, you'll know that when you grow up, you'll find that out soon enough, plenty of time for that when you're older, little pitchers have long ears, little girls should be seen and not heard curiosity killed the cat.

'Nanny, why did Curiosity kill the cat?'

'Don't ask such silly questions.'

'Mamma, why am I me?'

'Oh, what a lot of questions!'

Fat, shiny behind of the pony and jog-jog-jog of the pony-cart and jiggle-jiggle of the harness, and the shiny yellow sides of the cart, and the reins going all the way from Papa's hands over the bar at the front and joining on to the pony. Mamma sitting beside, facing Papa, with the funny veil over her face, why don't I have a veil, and leaning forwards from the middle over her little muff, and the prickly rug slipping from bare knees, and jog-jog.

'You're you because you're not somebody else, of course!'

'If I weren't me, should I be somebody else?'

'I expect so.'

Mamma looking at Papa and laughing, and Papa with his mouth shut tight, between the whiskers, and the smile shut inside, watching the jog-jog of the pony's behind.

'Let's see now, what was that book you were reading?' And the reins going jiggle-jiggle.

'Oh, what Nanny was reading!' The hard, shiny seat when you bump on it, and the rug slipping, and cold knees, and pulling it up, heavy, from the well of the cart. 'Yes, I know! It was all about a

GERTRUDE TREVELYAN

knight and he had a great big horse and he was very brave, more braver than anybody else and there was a lady and she was shut up in a dungeon in a big castle and the knight came along and killed the dragon with his sword, like that. Only I forgot, there was a dragon and he was going to eat the princess, because she was a princess, and he was nasty and there was smoke coming out when he roared, all black, and so they said he could eat the princess so he wouldn't eat them....'

'Who did, the knight?'

'Oh Papa, you know he was brave. He was very brave and all in armour, no the other people said it who were in the castle, and he came along and killed the dragon and they married and lived happily ever after.'

'What, the dragon? That would be an original ending.'

'Oh Papa, you know he was killed. What's a 'riginal ending? No, the lady and the knight did. Why do ladies and gentlemen always marry and live happily ever after? Can't two ladies or two gentlemen marry and live happily ever after?'

'No, of course not.' Mamma, pulling up the rug. 'Look, we're nearly at home now.'

'But why can't two ladies or two gentlemen live happily ever after?'

'Well, they might, but that wouldn't be marrying. Now, that's enough questions.'

'Then it isn't marrying if they aren't different?'

'That's it. Look, there's the beginning of the field.'

'But why are they different?'

Papa, watching the jog-jog of the pony's behind.

Mamma, looking for her umbrella at the bottom of the cart, under her big skirts. 'Now, that's enough. You'll know it all, all in good time. Look, here we are.'

Jog-jiggle-jiggle, jog-jiggle-jiggle, up over the drive, and the turn to the front-door, and climbing down, a long, long way, and the swing-back of the cart when you jump from the step, and the hall-door open, and Papa walking up and down slapping his hands together to make them warm.

The breakfast-table by the nursery window and the door opening and Papa coming in, rubbing his hands.

'How are we this morning? Good-day, Nurse. Don't get up.'

Nanny sitting again and helping the bacon, and the sunshine from the window up against the table making the buckle shine on her black belt.

Lifted up at the end of Papa's arms, and the sunshine down on the lawn under the window, and porridge plate a long way down below with the cream trickling over the smooth porridge.

'I'm Brer Rabbit to-day.'

'That's it, is it?'

Papa gone, and the chair pulled in again to the end of the table, and the big spoon, and valleys in the porridge for the cream to run into off the big mountains.

'I'm Brer Rabbit to-day, and to-morrow I'm going to be Uncle Tom's Cabin.'

'Don't play with your porridge now, eat it up.'

Nanny, and the big tea-pot, and hard, round, white bits like shillings on the fat left in the bacon dish.

'You mustn't talk to me, I'm Brer Rabbit and I'm pertending to be dead.'

'Now come along. Stop your nonsense and eat up your porridge.'

Spoon making a hard knock on the table. 'But I *am*.'

'No you aren't, you're Millicent.'

'I'm Brer Rabbit.'

Big pond in the porridge, and little boats. I'm Millicent. No I'm not, I won't be, it isn't nice. I'm Brer Rabbit. And a river to the edge. That's the hills that go all round the world on the other side of the floods.

'Why am I Millicent?'

'Because you are.'

'I won't be. It's nasty.'

'Well you are. So if you don't like it you can lump it.'

'Won't lump it.'

'Well, never you mind, eat up. Little girls should be seen and not heard.'

All the floods drying up and the picture coming at the bottom of the plate. Blue sky outside the window, and the scrapy tape when Nanny unties the bib.

Why is the sky blue?

Prickly, hard grass that's brown, and yellow bits that come up when you pull.

'Why's the grass brown and prickly?'

'It's where they've cut the hay.'

Why is the sky blue and why can't you walk on it when you lie on your back?

'What's up there if you went on and on?'

'Heaven.'

Heaven: blue sky and angels with heads and wings flying about, and God on a big chair, all gold, and all on a white, shiny card with a gold edge to it.

Heaven, that's where you go when you're good. 'But I am good. Can't I go there?'

'You're not good enough yet.'

'Why can't you see Heaven?'

'It's too far.'

Hard thump on the ground, and stubbly hay. That's *here*.

Blueness and blueness and emptiness, and Heaven so far you can't see it. Why are we at the bottom and everything on top?

'Have I always been here?'

'No, not always.'

'Then where was I before I was *here?*'

'Up there in Heaven.'

Then it was a long way to fall. More than falling off the chair in the nursery and hurting.

Wispy hay and limp, white daisies with yellow middles.

'Can we go and pick flowers?'

Over the stile and bump and wet mud on a knee. 'There, you ought to have waited.' And the bumpy field: that's where the moles are, but they never come out. And the trees beginning, and the ground all blue, and little bells hanging, and wet, juicy stalks going snap. 'There, take care, the juice is going on your coat.' And juicy, long leaves that come up when you pull, with funny white ends. Why are bluebells blue and the sky's blue and it isn't the same blue? 'Because one's bluebells and the other's sky.'

Long, heavy bluebells with long, hanging stalks and funny white ends. 'They won't hold.' And bluebells all over the ground and arms aching, and lots and lots more bluebells.

'Well, leave some for another day.'

'But I want to pick them all.'

'Well, you can't. Come along, that's enough.'

I'm the old man that was carrying wood and it got heavier and heavier and heavier.

'Give them to me, you're dropping them.'

'No.'

And the jerk away, and bluebells dropping.

And it got heavier and heavier and heavier, and he went on and on and on. Great big bundles of wood all brown and heavy.

And every time he dropped it he had to pick it up, and he went on and on, and then he came to a cottage in the middle of a big wood and then he put it all down.

'Now look what you're doing. Now you just pick those up.'

'Shan't.'

'Yes, you will.'

Scrapy earth in the nails and long, limp bluebells heavy and dropping and upside-down. 'You take them.'

Funny, snappy stems and little yellow bells in a bunch. Oo.
'Don't pick flowers and throw them about.'

Snap, snap, snap. Lots and lots. And grass tickling your legs,
and tickly red stuff very tall, and snap, snap, and there's another
one over there, and big hills of earth you tumble over, and cold
grass on your hands, and come along don't go so far. And pick
them up, hot stems, hold them tight, and there's another, coldness and snap and yellow, yellow.

Hot, hairy stems and little white, tight heads with yellow
eyes. 'There, see the pretty daisies.' And daisies dropping. Daisies
dropped, why did they drop, want daisies. Daisies gone, out over
the side of the pram. 'Now look what she's done.' And somebody's
back picking them up. Daisies back on the brown, woolly cover,
and pick up, yellow eyes with long stems, and throw, and daisies
gone and somebody picking up.

Efelant gone, efelant on ground outside the cot, with his legs
in the air. 'Efelent! Efelent gone!' And bump, bump, and cot shaking, and Nanny's white back bending over and efelant back in cot.
Grey efelant with red thing on his back, red and thin and soft that
flaps, put on top, and efelant hard and grey and warm. Efelant
not hard and hurting like cot-rails; and fire a long way off over
the floor in a big, black cage, and me in a cage too. Fire and me in
big cages. And Mamma by the fire, stood up tall, and Nanny and
talking and grey efelant and pull the red thing it won't come off.

Me. It's about me.

Me. Pink, curly fingers that wriggle and shut up tight: that's
me. Pink and bitey. Fingers crawling along the bars, and hold
on to efelant and climb him up. Pink fingers holding on hard.
Up and up, on to the flat rail at the top, and fingers open. Bump.
Efelant gone.

Mamma and Nanny and big voices, brr, brr, brr.

Me. There's more me.

Mamma and Nanny not looking.

Up and out and me. Pink, curly toes twiggle wiggle. That's me. Why is me.

Nanny coming, big and white. Curly, pink toes. Nanny tugging at the blanket and pink fingers holding on. Round, pink, funny hands holding. That's me.

Nanny, tall and thin with a stiff, high collar and a big white thing on her head. That isn't Nanny. Go away. It isn't Nanny. Where's Nanny? Nanny!

Go away, it isn't Nanny! Nasty Nanny!

Hand holding on tight: that's me. Fingers, tight and holding. Go away! Nasty, nasty!

Nanny!

Fingers holding on tight so that it hurts. Grey, long fingers and thin, grey hand white at the knuckles, desperately clutching at the sheet.

Go away!

Table with a white cloth and enamelled basin, and a stretch of white wall and a white wicker-chair and a small fire in a sunken grate and somebody — Mamma? — with high heels and a short, wide coat hanging loose from her neck, and a little hat.

Mamma!

No.

No. Not. Who is it. Who. Ought to know who it is. It's... it's....
A dark, high, high well, tall and black; and climbing, up and up. It's....

Mamma and Nanny and Annie and Miss Cresset and....

No, that's not it.

And the light, white room, a long, long way away, up at the top. Hilda and Dick and Michael.

No.

The dark sides of the well, slippery, and darkness. Darkness; and the light room very small, away up there, and somebody. Who is it. Where am I. What is it.

And up and up and up and up.

Blank, white, white room. White. Blank and white.

Harold and Sonia and Mrs. Mayhew and Miss Platt. Harold's dead. Harold. No, that's not it.

Up and up and up and through and out.

Phil! Phil! Where are you? Phil! Phil, don't go. You haven't gone, have you. Phil!

What is it. Where am I. Why don't you say something. Why do you stand, I tell you; don't stand. Go and bring him. Why don't you bring him. No, he's gone.

Phil. Phil. Phil.

Light and hurt and the sheet straightened out and a hand soothing.

Phil, I knew you'd come. Phil.

Phil's arm. Strength, and peace, and the warm cloth.

Quite still.

Stay there, quite still, just like that.

Warm cloth against the cheek, and a strong beat, and safe, safe. Safe on Phil's shoulder.

Why did you go away? Why?

But it doesn't matter now. Stay like that. Just like that.

Red and green and yellow lights of the Circus, changing and sweeping and flashing on and on overhead above the dark buildings and the quiet, grey pavement. The broad, silvery street curving away like a wide ribbon, and the great, silent lights dancing and flashing and changing and darting high up on the sides of a grey well, and nobody at all. Just Us.

Grey, curved street and grey pavement and grey buildings and a pale grey sky, quite empty. And the smooth, warm cloth, and Phil's arm, and Phil looking down.

Just like that. Yes, yes. Not me anymore.

Soft, grey clouds drifting, and silence, and the thud of a heart.

And softness, like a wing enfolding. Softness and peace and

the empty, silver curve up from the Circus, and warm, drifting clouds, and the thud under the firm cloth, and peace.

But there was something, Phil. Something I wanted to tell you. Why it was. What went wrong. With Us. Now that it isn't, anymore.

Strong beat, and peace, and the quiet, smooth, empty street.

Listen, Phil, it was something. Something.

Grey, drifting clouds.

Quick, quick. Something. What was it. Darkness, and a pale, gleaming hedge. What do I mean. Some-thing. No, what was it? It was in my mind, just now. All at once. Something about.

No, what was it?

Grey, swirling clouds. Little puffs of cloud flecking the tall, quiet buildings; waves pounding, dully, far off.

Don't let me go, Phil. Don't go. Stay, just like that. Don't let them come, you won't, will you. It was something. Yes, that was it: something.

No. Not that. No.

And the pounding waves.

Haste, haste. Quick, what was it?

Crumpled sleeve rough to the hand.

I know, it was questions. Something about questions. Don't ask so many questions. Don't ask so many questions, Phil. No, you don't, do you. No, it wasn't that. What was it? I must tell you. No, don't go, Phil, stay. Stay like that, always, always.

You'll know all in good time. That was it. No, it wasn't that. No, that was Michael. No, I don't mean that. What do I mean? What was it? I mean. No, I don't mean that. Something else. What was it?

Grey, scudding clouds, and the swift, fierce beat of the tide. Quick, quick, he mustn't go, quick.

Phil, I've got to tell you, I must tell you. Phil, don't go, I've got to tell you, to tell, to tell. Phil, where are you, it's only that.... Phil, where are you, Phil!

234

Light flashing in, and space. And the boom and suck of darkness — darkness receding — far out beyond the glass.

Phil. Phil.

Emptiness and space and an ache through space. Blank, shadowless light, and reaching. And the cold, blank glass.

Phil. Phil. Phil.

White space, and boundless, endless reaching: a blinding ache.

And Nanny taking the light away. A big screen in front of the light: grey-white screen with a yellow splash where the light is, on the other side. So they've put a screen.

The screen around the nursery door, with pictures all over and mixey colours all mixed up, bright and bright, and Mamma coming round the screen and Nanny in the big chair by the fire and the fire bright on the pink wall of the dolls' house.

And fire on the ceiling and somebody at a big table and a rumbling noise. Rum rum rum, rum rum rum rum. Stop. Rum rum rum. Stop. Rum rum rum, rum rum rum, rum rum rummmmmmmmmrnmm. And a handle going round, and a head, and somebody big and white. Somebody big and white and a handle going round and rum rum rum rum, that's Nanny.

Nanny and Nanny's lap cold and slippery, and fire on the ceiling, and the soft rubber sides of the bath, and warm and wet. And hard and shiny and red and round and a yellow beak and sitting on the water, bob-bob: Quack-quack.

And pink fire on the ceiling, and somebody, and cold and hard and long and white-inside, and bump-bump of the white inside the bottle, and white getting less, and warm and soft going down inside, and dribble-dribble, and somebody taking it away, and chin dried, and warm and soft and nothing.

And wetness and cold and mouth open, ae, ae; and picked up and dryness and warmth and the big baa-lamb on the wall over the fire-place, and the fire going rock-rock, and warm and swinging.

Woolly ball, big and soft and ends to pull, and bright, bright.

Big and soft and ends in mouth, tickly and hot and wet, ae, ae, and somebody, and tickling gone.

Rock-rock, and veil on face, and suck, and wet in mouth, and blue ceiling with white dots, and bump-bump, and greenness and big people, and suck and wet and bump and blue.

And white ceiling, and pink-on-white; and cold and damp and ae, ae, and up; and dry and warm and down and pink-on-white; and empty, want want; and suck and warm and full and nothing.

And empty and want and full and nothing.

And cold and wet and want and warm and nothing.

And want and full and nothing, and want and warm and nothing.

And want and want and want and want.

Alone and alone and alone. Huge aloneness. Alone and alone and the huge world unknown and hostile. Huge and hurting, and the menace of big movements and the future pressing down. Time and hurt and having to be and things lurking in time. Enormous emptiness; and light, pressing. Why. Why.

Pressure of air and the hurt of breathing: hurtful, hard compulsion; and the open world opening out, shelterless, on and on, into time.

Hurt and dark chaos and the hard slap of light on lids and buffeting of air.

Tearing and hurt and helpless clenching and the kind, dark world slipping back: slipping back, back, away forever: a steady, relentless drawing back: blind, ineffectual clutching and the onrush of light. Walls opening out, falling away; the harsh, rasping edge of light. Light and hurt and huge aloneness.

Back, back: sheltering darkness and safe, yielding warmth. Warm and strong and safe and quiet. Merciful nothing and long peace and the beat of dark waters. Strong, perpetual beat of the dark. Sleep and quiet stirring and a still, steady beat: peace, peace, strong and still. Dark surge of waters, pounding, far off; away, rocked away, on a strong, lapping tide. Dark and safe, strong and still. Peace, peace. Dark and hidden and timeless and muffled, and still and deep.

Tearing of a sheet of darkness: noise dazzling; light and space agape and the rushing out of time. Phil, Phil. I can't. Phil. Light and blinding space, blank and boundless and without shadow: stark, unending light.

Afterword

by Stanislava Dikova

As It Was in the Beginning is hard to follow. Gertrude Trevelyan presents the memories, hopes, dreams, and fears of an entire human life as its end nears in a breathless stream of consciousness narration delivered by the dying subject herself in reverse-chronological order from the confines of her nursing home bed and her own mind. She seeks to encapsulate the life she depicts fully and return it back to the beginning, to where it all started, as if dissatisfied with the form it has taken, while celebrating its defiant resistance on every page. Trevelyan's novel is built on negations, contradictions, and juxtapositions of such calibre that it produces a narrator whose personhood is perpetually called into question and a narrative that seemingly regresses instead of progressing. Both subject and form constantly oscillate between self-constitution and self-nullification, presenting a curious conundrum that defies facilitation and insists on remaining defyingly unsolved.

Published in 1934, Trevelyan's third novel presented a challenge to its contemporary readers and critics and provoked a mixed reception upon its original release. This was not unusual at the time, especially for experimental modernist novels, and most especially for those written by women. Reviews of Virginia Woolf's fiction often followed a similar pattern. The *Aberdeen Journal* admires the creative skill, noting that Trevelyan's ability 'To translate into unemotional print the disjointed memories of a nursing home patient re-living the past before death's kiss is a technical feat of daring.'[1] The anonymous reviewer at the *Saturday Review* notes that Trevelyan had avoided the otherwise strong likelihood of a narrative about a dying middle-aged lady becoming extremely 'wearisome': 'That Miss Trevelyan manages to keep one's interest sustained in a story thus unfolded backwards,' they write, 'is proof of her great capacity as a writer.'[2] Richard King in *The Tatler and Bystander* strikes the middle ground, calling the novel 'painful, but enthralling'.[3]

Others do not take to the experiments with form too kindly. Vernon Fane despairs of the text's attributed technical innovation: 'There is a dearth of verbs; an abundance of full stops; a fumbling at word patterns. Technical fiddlesticks! Miss Trevelyan is suffering from an overdose of Gertrude Stein.'[4] Eleanor Carroll Chilton is even more scathing, opining that 'The publishers hail this book as an "experiment" — but in reality it is a pretentious excursion into triviality, and reads like an unkind parody on some of Miss May Sinclair's early work.'[5]

---

1   Anonymous, 'Books from Day to Day,' *Aberdeen Journal*, no. 24776 (Aberdeen, Scotland, Wednesday, 30 May 1934), p.2.

2   Anonymous, 'Some Novels for the Library List,' in *Saturday Review of politics, literature, sciences and art*, v. 157, no.4104 (London, 23 June 1934), pp.738-739.

3   Richard King, 'With Silent Friends: As Island of the Blest, Perhaps?,' *The Tatler and Bystander*, v. 132, no. 1720 (London; 13 June 1934), p.484.

4   Vernon Fane, 'The Book World: In Early June,' in *The Sphere*, v. 137, no. 1793 (London, 2 June 1934), p.360.

5   Eleanor Carroll Chilton, 'A Goodly Heritage and Others,' *The English Review* (London, July 1934), p.115.

The flippancy of Chilton's comment above notwithstanding, the comparison with Sinclair is certainly apt, especially in connection to the concern with encapsulating women's lives in their entirety demonstrated by both writers. Sinclair's *The Life and Death of Harriet Frean* (1922) is a similar cradle-to-grave narrative, delivered in chronological order, while making use of fragmentation and other experimental techniques to provide access to Harriet's mind. The focus on the 'I' in Trevelyan's text, however, is more striking in its persistence especially when coupled with the denial of personhood, so often reasserted by Millicent. The obvious tensions in construction, emphasised through experiments with form and character, are connected to Trevelyan's broader project of fully integrating women into modern fiction. Providing access to a woman's mind requires navigating through the literary models of a tradition that has historically occluded such direct acts of representation in order to generate a clear space, where a new history can begin to emerge. As is the case with *As It Was the Beginning*, this process utilises creative invention as an instrument to challenge dominant structures and positions of power, including those associated with language and genre conventions.

In this sense, it is not surprising that most reviewers make at least a passing comment on the novel's experimentation with form. Modernist texts more broadly often mobilise artistic innovation to bring about a new, more fruitful relationship between readers and texts through a process of estrangement or defamiliarization. The terms come from a tradition of literary criticism associated with the Russian formalists. In his 1919 essay 'Art, as Device', Viktor Shklovsky contends that one of the key functions of art is to reawaken human consciousness, dulled by processes of repetition and automatization brought on by the advance of modernity. 'All our skills retreat into the unconscious-automatic domain,' he notes; 'you will agree with this if you remember the feeling you had when holding a quill for the first time or speaking a foreign language for the first time and compare it to the feeling you have when doing it for the ten thousandth time.'[6] To counteract the resulting staleness of feeling, thought and expression, Shklovsky recommends practicing incongruity and celebrating connections that are unlikely, novel, and surprising. This kind of experimentation, the theory goes, will jolt readers into wakefulness again and force them to pay renewed attention.

Trevelyan's writing responds to this call from the start. Her first novel *Appius and Virginia* (1932) offers the bizarre story of a spinster who decides to adopt an orangutan and raise him as a child to question the boundaries of the human and the construction of social personhood. In *As It Was in the Beginning*, her plot is less shocking, but the form works to reverse expectations and provoke its readers into confronting their understanding of human life. Through this confrontation, the novel develops an alternative mode of life-writing for recording, documenting, considering and inventing women's lives that is both resistant to the constraints embedded in patriarchal narrative models and generative of new forms of agency.

As It Was in the Beginning confronts the traditionally established sense of personhood and makes a case that it produces an oppressive, restrictive, and utterly confining human experience. 'They're all anxious,' Millicent thinks looking at a crowd of people on the street, 'and they're all people. What do I mean. People. They're all people. They're people just because they're anxious and dissatisfied, I expect that's it.'[7] But is that it? The anxiety and dissatisfaction she notices in others seem to follow her too, and yet she denies her own personhood repeatedly throughout the narrative. So, what makes her different? What makes her a non-person?

---

6   Viktor Shklovsky, 'Art, as Device,' trans. Alexandra Berlina, *Poetics Today* 36, no. 3 (September 2015), p.161.

7   G. E. Trevelyan, *As It Was in the Beginning*, p.140.

Lost among the crowd hurrying along with parcels and weighted down by daily cares, she considers herself separate and free to cross the road, or buy something frivolous, because she does not have anyone to reprimand and judge her. Admittedly, this is a limited understanding of freedom, a sense of being untethered through the removal of an obstacle to movement, rather than an experience of positive freedom rooted in the ability to act and choose.[8]

The sense of entrapment and corresponding glimpses of freedom Millicent identifies are connected to her obligations to others and the social roles she is expected to fulfil as a woman, wife, Lady Chesborough, daughter, mother — a set of demands imposed on her externally over which she has had no control. This extends to her relationship with her own body, which she experiences as foreign and constraining from a very early age, a feeling which does not leave her until the end. 'Nanny, why am I inside this?', she asks.

> 'Inside what?'
> Hand stretched out and crawling along the rug.
> 'Arms and legs and things. Why am I inside it? It's nasty.'
> 'You aren't inside it. It's you.'
> 'No, it isn't. It's nasty.'[9]

Millicent feels her embodied self is disassociated from her internal self, as if the two constitute different entities altogether. What is more, she feels trapped within a body she does not consider representative of herself and does not want to claim as her own.

---

8   Ian Carter, 'Negative and Positive Freedom,' *Stanford Encyclopedia of Philosophy*, last revision 19 November 2021. https://plato.stanford.edu/entries/liberty-positive-negative/. Accessed 10 December 2023.

9   *As It Was in the Beginning*, p.221.

No ownership is attached to the hand — it is a separate entity, crawling along the rug. In her final days, this juxtaposition persists. When she feels her body handled by her nurse in the care home, she is grateful that she does not feel more exposed:

> One would think in these places one's body wasn't one's own. What business have you got. It's lucky, I've never felt much personal interest in my body: don't care whether it's mine or not. Never could feel it was myself: lucky isn't it. I don't feel *I'm* exposed to you, in the least. Always thought of it as something I happened to be inside of by accident. Phil used to laugh at me about that.[10]

And, yet, as we read over these lines, with their multiple possessive and personal pronouns, a sense of artificiality and pose makes itself felt. The accentuated negation of connection with another body, or another person — 'I don't feel *I'm* exposed to you' — also convincingly conveys that numbing sense of horror that is associated with the possibility of such exposure. The fear of the inevitable impending censure that accompanies the experience of womanhood is conveyed strikingly by that one touch, the italicised '*I'm*', contracted.

Trevelyan's selection of protagonist — an ageing, dying woman, a woman, furthermore, who has not been able to bear children — also stands in defiance of patriarchal norms which only recognise women as mothers, objects of desire, angels in the house and similar roles defined by their utility. Millicent considers her life, mostly confined to her obligations has a wife, to have had little purpose. 'I never meant to be any kind of wife,' she tells herself. 'I suppose I'm a failure emotionally; that's why I couldn't make it last. Otherwise that might have been life, instead of only a

---

10   *As It Was in the Beginning*, p.51.

gap. I suppose I'm a failure, a failure. Yes, a failure.'[11] Her defiance rings out firmly in the rejected assumption of intentionality — she never 'meant' to take this role — as if the denial of intention can remedy the absence of choice. Still the assertion of failure follows, affirming itself with a final yes.

Millicent sees her marriage to Harold both as the step that saves her from having to be herself and the commitment that suppresses her identity. Her statement, 'You've made me into a person, Harold; I wasn't really a person before',[12] is clearly contradicted by 'I can't help feeling sometimes that I'm not really here at all, only playing at being somebody who's married Harold.'[13] This pattern of refusal to commit to a version of herself produces an almost sensory sense of confusion, which is palpable throughout her story. The refusal to provide a coherent narrative is symptomatic of modernism's wider culture of disruption, of disjointing and breaking apart states of being and practices of the self that have come to be regarded as habitual to open up spaces for those which exist outside the norm. Trevelyan's novel, however, complicates this experimental routine by insisting on the return to the enclosure and to the material lives of those unable to reach beyond its barriers, where women are forced to grapple with the political conditions of their own oppression.

Millicent's portrayal as a woman existing on the margins of personhood is symptomatic of Trevelyan's persistent preoccupation with the distance between women and political activity. Like Millicent, Jane in *William's Wife* and Frances in *Theme with Variations* find it difficult to relate to politics. Millicent considers the matter in the following way:

---

11   *As It Was in the Beginning*, p.164.

12   Ibid, p.169.

13   Ibid, p.156.

I wonder why I haven't any political opinions, everyone else seems to have. I can never see that it matters: what I think can't make any difference to the country, and it doesn't interest me. I suppose it ought to interest me, but I never seem to have time nowadays to think about anything. It makes far more difference to me after all whether Phil likes my hair when it's done than it does whether we reduce unemployment or have communist government.'[14]

Millicent's position should not be entirely surprising. It emerges from a political culture which routinely silences, excludes, and diminishes women by denying them existence as political agents, to the point in which being sexually appreciated by a man becomes the only possible form of recognition. Even political novels concerned with radical reform such as Lewis Grassic Gibbon's *Grey Granite*, published in the same year as *As It Was in the Beginning*, and John Sommerfield's *May Day*, published only two years later, caricature women either as fearful reactionaries whose concern with the immediate provision for their families blocks the promise of collective emancipation, or else, as over-sexualised objects of desire whose main function within the narrative is to reward the efforts of male characters.[15] Still, Millicent's off-hand dismissal of her usefulness to the country, another symptom of the pervading powerlessness she experiences, also conveys a sense of irritation. The way she formulates the problem of her political position is framed as a lack, another type of failure to have what seems to come easily to everybody else. Politics here is performative. It functions as an accessory, an artificial token of validation, and produces 'opinions', not actions and certainly not change.

14   *As It Was in the Beginning*, p.93.

15   See Nick Hubble, *The Proletarian Answer to the Modernist Question* (Edinburgh: Edinburgh University Press, 2007).

Early twentieth-century feminist thinkers grappled with these questions as emancipation struggles unfolded across the globe. In Britain, women's contribution to the war effort and accompanying suffragette struggle resulted in securing voting rights for some in 1918 and an equal franchise in 1928.[16] Access to the professions was granted in 1919 with heavy stipulations around marriage.[17] Woolf, writing after these landmark victories for women's political and legal integration, found their effects limited as the wider system of patriarchal governance remained unchallenged. She formalised her thoughts across two of her most widely-read feminist polemics *A Room of One's Own* (1929) and *Three Guineas* (1938). Both essays aimed to empower women by re-casting their historic exclusion from the institutional and social constructs of patriarchal governance as a type of intellectual freedom that underpins the cultivation of independent thought.[18] Women's separation from the usual governing structures, from the education system, to the judiciary and the clergy, Woolf argues, has protected them from indoctrination in 'unreal loyalties' and their accompanying commitments.[19] Paradoxically perhaps, according to Woolf, the resulting distance from the governing system of patriarchal domination can bring women the freedom to imagine a new political construct for a more equitable, democratic, and just world. *As It Was in the Beginning* strides towards such independence of thought and against the intellectual docility which allows fiction to settle for established models of representation, instead of making and remaking, diagnosing and reinventing, imagining and hoping.

---

16   The Representation of the People Act (1918) and The Equal Franchise Act (1928).

17   The Sex Disqualification (Removal) Act (1919).

18   This argument has received support as well as ample criticism, particularly in relation to its treatment of class. See Clara Jones, Virginia Woolf: *Ambivalent Activist* (Edinburgh: Edinburgh University Press, 2015).

19   Virginia Woolf, *Three Guineas*, (London: Hogarth Press, 1938), p.160.

Gertrude Trevelyan's experimental work deserves its rightful place within the tradition of radical modernist women writers whose contributions to the literary and intellectual histories of interwar Britain have remained obscured for decades. 'Recovering' these voices and bringing them to new audiences is a much-needed act of feminist revival, which generates new knowledge and brings new perspectives on vital historical and contemporary problems. The representation and categorisation of bodies, the politics of intimacy, of reproduction, of inequality, of life and death are all forcefully interrogated in Trevelyan's fiction as this powerful novel exemplifies. Her attention never flickers and is unfailingly focused on the efforts of a dying woman to tell her own story. This, we must remember, *remains* a radical act of creation.

Gertrude Eileen Trevelyan was born in Bath in 1903. She came to fame as the first woman to win the Newdigate Prize for best undergraduate poem at Oxford in 1927. Starting with *Appius and Virginia* in 1932, she published eight novels, her last being *Trance by Appointment* in 1939. Her novels *Two Thousand Million Man-Power* and *William's Wife* have been reissued in the Recovered Books series from Boiler House Press.

Kim Adrian is the author of two books of creative criticism (*Dear Knausgaard* and *Sock*), and a memoir, *The Twenty-Seventh Letter of the Alphabet*, which was a Next Generation Indie Book Awards Finalist.

Dr Stanislava Dikova is a postdoctoral researcher and a Visiting Fellow at the University of Essex. Her articles and reviews to date have been published in the *LSE Review of Books*, *The Modernist Review*, and *Feminist Modernist Studies*.

As It Was in the Beginning
By Gertrude Eileen Trevelyan

First published in this edition by Boiler House Press, 2024
Part of the UEA Publishing Project
As It Was in the Beginning copyright © Gertrude Eileen
Trevelyan, 1934
Introduction copyright © Kim Adrian, 2024
Afterword copyright © Stanislava Dikova, 2024

Proofreading by Lindsay Hause

Photography of Gertrude Trevelyan by license from the National
Portrait Gallery

Cover Design and Typesetting by Louise Aspinall
Cover Photo by Jan Koetsier via Pexels
Typeset in Arnhem Pro

ISBN: 978-1-915812-12-4

Printed in the USA
CPSIA information can be obtained
at www.ICGtesting.com
CBHW071934160324
5453CB00010B/73

9 781915 812124